HAPPY EVER AFTERLIFE

MELISSA WHITNEY

ABOUT THE BOOK

She doesn't believe in ghosts—or love. He's out to prove her wrong on both counts.

Nora Scott has no patience for the paranormal—or relationships. As a no-nonsense field producer for the Destination Network's hit ghost-hunting show, she's only sticking around long enough to climb the ladder to her real dream: producing a top-tier travel series. But when her latest assignment involves the notoriously haunted Putman House, things take an unexpected turn.

August Chandler has spent his life chasing spirits and spotlighting the supernatural. As the heartthrob host of Haunted Hideaway, he's got fame, fans, and a relentless passion for uncovering the truth. Turns out the skeptic behind the camera, Nora, is the only thing he wants more than proof of the afterlife.

When Putman House reveals its tragic secret—a ghostly couple locked in a century-old feud—Nora and August trade ghost-hunting for matchmaking. But as sparks fly in the eerie halls of the inn, Nora starts to accept that love isn't such a scary story after all.

Can a skeptic and a believer find their own happy ending? Or will the ghosts of their pasts haunt their future?

Happy Ever Afterlife is perfect for fans of opposites-attract romances, black cat-golden retriever dynamics, and the paranormal with a side of sizzling chemistry!

AI RESTRICTIONS

DEDICATION

To those left behind to pick up the pieces. Loss is like a never-ending cold January night, but memories keep us warm and remind us that the sun will rise. The dead are never truly gone as long as they are loved and remembered.

I love you, Dustin (Dusty). Without you this book would not be, and in so many ways I may not be who I am. Thank you for all the love and joy you gave.

A NOTE FROM THE AUTHOR/CONTENT WARNINGS

Dear Reader,

Thank you for choosing *Happy Ever Afterlife*. There are so many books, and I am deeply honored that you've chosen to read mine. This story began on a brisk February weekend in 2023, at the Southern California Writers' Conference with one of my favorite people, Dustin Thompson. I had an idea for this book and shared it with him. Through his deep belly laughs and sassy East-Texas lilt he said, "Write that immediately!"

Fast forward to May 2023, I started writing this book. By June, I was halfway through the first draft and my pearl-clutching Dustin was teasing me about the sexy parts. Dustin never got to read the finished draft. He died unexpectedly that June. My heart still breaks at the loss and soars with the memories of his big life. Dustin was a beloved son, brother, and friend. He was a powerful voice for Veterans and the LGBTQIA+ community. He was an amazing writer. He was an enthusiastic healthcare leader. He was an amazing husband to his Ben. He was so much. I was lucky, no matter how brief, to call him friend.

Crafting a book about loss in the midst of grieving the person that encouraged you to write this story is a unique experience. So much of my grief wove itself into this story. While *Happy Ever Afterlife* is a sexy, fun, and sweet romance with a guaranteed happy ending it does deal with grief. You don't become a ghost without losing a lot. As thoughtful as I've tried to be with this story, please know that it's important to me for you to take care of yourself while reading. If some parts are too difficult, do what you need to do to protect your mental health.

That being said, let me help you make the best decision for yourself on whether you should proceed with this book. This book contains on-page depictions of consensual sex, use of vulgar/foul language, casual consumption of alcohol, discussion of death of a child, grandparent, parents, sibling, and others (none on page), mention of an execution (not on page), mention of a murder (not on page), discussion of transphobia (not on page), discussion of a car accident (not on page), depiction of a panic attack, mention of ableism (not on page), mention of cancer (not on page), mention of drowning (not on page), and a golden retriever MMC you will crush hard on (you've been warned about August).

As well, this book weaves together both fictionalized and real places. With the real places I do take some liberties and did add some fictionalized details for the sake of the story. I did do my best to accurately depict both paranormal investigation and TV production. During the drafting process, I interviewed/consulted with producers and paranormal investigators to do justice to these worlds. Again, I took some dramatic license as an author for the sake of the story, so I'll apologize in advance for anything that isn't perfect.

This is a work of fiction, so any resemblance to real places, people, or events is pure coincidence.

Again, please take care of yourself as you read. While I

hope you do read and enjoy Happy *Ever Afterlife,* I would prefer you take care of yourself more. There's only one of you after all.

Happy Reading!

Melissa

CHAPTER 1

It's not a Ghost!

The click-clack of Nora's ruby red stilettos against the lobby's terracotta floor sang in her ears. Most days on set she rocked sneakers, which lacked the delicious tap of her heels, but stilettos were nonsensical on busy shoots with sprawling cords and equipment, and Nora didn't do the nonsensical. Even as a kid, when not calling her baby girl, Grandpa Scott had called her No-Nonsense Nora.

Today, rather than walking onto the set for whatever show she was hired to associate produce, she strutted through a glass building in Burbank. Yeah, she strutted. Sometimes a lady needed to strut, and today was one of those days. On the thirteenth floor of this rather unremarkable building were the production offices for the Destination Network, a channel Nora had dreamed of producing shows for since childhood. With a click of the remote, the Destination Network transported her to far-off places and secret hideaways.

I'm finally achieving our dream, Grandpa—to bring the world to everyone. She smiled as she checked herself out in the mirrored elevator doors. Her caramel-colored strands were pulled back in a sleek low pony. The new black skinny jeans she'd bought for today's interview hugged her curves. With her silky black camisole and a fitted red blazer that matched her shoes, Nora's outfit straddled sexy confidence and "don't fuck with me" boss-queen energy.

Waiting for the elevator, she pulled her cell phone from her oversized leather tote and messaged Mae Williams, her ride-or-die best friend.

Nora: I'm about to head up for my interview. Not going to lie, I'm 90% confident with 10% anxious imposter syndrome.

Mae: And 100% badass future field producer. You got this! *Cheerleader Emoji.* **Let's meet at Grandma Hoang's for celebratory chardonnay and chocolate cake after your interview!**

Nora: What if I don't get the job?

Mae: First, don't put your Midwestern "I Don't Deserve Nice Things" bad energy out there.

A small snort escaped Nora. Leave it to Mae to call her out.

Mae: Second, same plan only conciliatory chardonnay and cake.

Nora: Love ya! *Kissy Face Emoji.*

Mae: Love ya more! *Purple Heart Emoji.*

Mouth tugged up, she slipped her phone back into her bag. There were few people Nora held close. For so long, it had been just she and Grandpa Scott. Then it was just her until Mae came along like a rainbow in the middle of a storm, refusing to allow Nora to remain safe in her solo bubble.

If only we had teleporters. Sighing, she tapped her stiletto's toe against the floor waiting for the elevator. The eagerness that jittered inside her had less to do with wanting to get on the elevator and more to do with just getting the experience over with. The stairs were her preferred mode of travel, but Jimmy Choos were built for style, not comfort. Thirteen floors would leave her feet aching and produce a sweaty glow that may not solidify the impression Nora was going for.

"Nice shoes."

She turned and found herself looking into a pair of brown eyes that reminded her of creamy hot chocolate. A lazy lopsided grin kicked across a strong jawline accentuated by a sprinkling of dark stubble. His brown hair appeared as if freshly mussed in a heated makeout session.

"Thank you," she said, averting her eyes and trying not to stare. She was there for a job interview, not to checkout random attractive men.

The elevator dinged and the doors swung open. An absurd number of people in suits filed out like circus clowns from a Volkswagen. Nora stepped to the side, but she was still bumped by the wave of departing people. Some apologized. Others knocked by as if she had a lot of nerve being in their way.

As the current of people thinned, she slipped onto the elevator. She pressed the button for the thirteenth floor, tucked herself into the corner and braced for the oncoming crush of passengers. Big buildings like this always had too many people crammed into elevators like canned sardines.

It's okay. It will only be a few minutes. With a deep breath, she snapped the thin rubber band on her wrist, resting below her watch. Each quick snap against her skin pulled her focus away from the anxious thoughts swirling inside her.

The handsome man with the chocolatey eyes stepped onto the elevator, and turned to the panel of buttons, where *thirteen* was already lit up. "Lucky thirteen." A twinkle danced in his features as he claimed the corner opposite her.

Nora's gaze flicked between the only selected floor and the man. He leaned against the metal rail, an easiness radiating off him. An untucked black button-up shirt stretched across his broad chest, his sleeves were rolled to his elbows, and his hands pushed into the pockets of his dark blue jeans.

"Nice sneakers," Nora said, her attention drawn to his black Converse.

"I also have a pair in red." He winked.

The flirtatious nature of his voice caused a tiny flip in her abdomen. Very tiny. The butterflies in Nora's belly had long lain dormant. They were so inactive that Nora worried they'd relocated to someone else's body. In fact, Peter had told her she was dead inside. Such sweet words from the man that two days ago was her boyfriend. No, that didn't seem like the appropriate title. Perhaps the man that she occasionally hooked up with and seldom had dinner with was more fitting. Whatever he was, he was no more.

"What are the red shoes for, Dorothy? Are they magic? Can you click your heels three times, say 'There's no place like home,' and get out of a terrible meeting?" he teased.

The corners of her mouth lifted into a small smile. "My name isn't Dorothy."

The elevator doors closed. Nora scanned the enclosed space. Her pulse kicked up, but not at being alone with the handsome stranger. *Just a few minutes and the door will open again,* she internally assured herself with another quick snap of the rubber band.

"Alright, not-Dorothy, what *is* your name?"

"Nora."

"August." He reached his hand out to her.

Nora took it, her nerves settling with his touch.

"Do you rock red shoes every day, or are they for something special?"

She looked at the points of her shoes and back to him. "Job interview."

"Nice." Tiny crinkles kissed the edges of his eyes. "You make me wish I had worn my red Converse for *my* interview."

"Are you here for the *Haunted Hideaway* interview?"

"Yep," he said, mischief sparked in his expression.

It was foolish to think she'd be the only one interviewing for the field producer position. She knew that but still had hoped not to run into any of the other candidates for the new show centered on the paranormal adventures of the Chandler brothers. Derrick, an American history professor, and his younger brother Gus, a documentary filmmaker, would travel the country in a RV investigating alleged haunted locations. Gus's films about supposedly haunted locations had been featured on the Destination Network during their "Scare-tober" when all the shows that Nora adored about far off places, historical sites, and the best place to get a cupcake in the US were replaced by a string of paranormal shows to capitalize on the Halloween season. The brothers would be the executive producers and hosts of the show.

Working on shows with grainy night vision footage of people that fancied themselves scientists yet would have trouble describing the scientific theory taught to fifth graders wasn't why Nora studied TV production at the University of Missouri. But thanks to a professor who had a connection, her first job out of school was as a production assistant on a ghost hunting show.

That first job led to another, and then another, and another. All paranormal shows. If the show hunted for ghosts, Bigfoot, or the Loch Ness Monster, she'd worked on it. The last one had gotten her a free trip to Scotland, which she wasn't complaining about. It was the first time she'd been out of the US. These shows weren't her passion, but they paid the bills.

"Are you here for the interview?" August jutted his chin toward her.

"Yes." Her focus was locked on the illuminated floor numbers above the panel of buttons.

"That's wonderful!"

Nora's jaw tightened at his happy-go-lucky tone. Was he just *that* confident that he'd get the job, or was it something about her? Had he assessed that she wasn't a threat?

Fuck that! I'm a badass. Channeling Mae's words from earlier, she straightened her spine.

The number twelve flashed on the screen, and she tapped her foot, ready to depart. As the elevator jolted to a stop, Nora sucked in a deep breath, preparing to step off the moment the doors opened. With her head raised, shoes stomping, she'd leave him in her badass-diva dust.

Yes, queen! The self-assurance surging within her caused a momentary wiggle of her hips. Self-doubt may try to creep in, but she had this. The last ten years prepared her for this opportunity. This was hers to lose. *And I won't lose it!* She took a step forward.

"Oh, I think we're stuck," he said.

"What?" She blinked at the blank screen, the elevator not moving. "Nope. That's not right." Heart racing, she jammed her finger against the *thirteen*. Nothing. She tapped again. Nothing. She slammed other buttons. Nothing.

Her gaze darted around the elevator. It had seemed larger than this when they were moving, but now the walls crept in on her. Her breath grew shallow. Sweat peppered her hairline, under her arms, and at the small of her back.

Snapping the rubber band on her wrist, she closed her

eyes and tried to envision being in an open field. If only she'd taken the stairs with their many doors for quick escape at each floor. *Stairwells never get stuck.*

"Well, at least this building isn't haunted," he said, his voice steady.

Nora's eyes shot open. "Excuse me?" Her response breathless as if jogging the last leg of a race.

He slipped his phone out of his back pocket. "No signal."

Nora took her phone out of her bag, a tight line anchored on her face at the confirmation of what he'd just said. *No signal.* Sliding her useless mobile back into her bag, she addressed him, "What did you mean by that?"

"The building isn't haunted, so we know it's just mechanical and not a mischievous ghost, so it should be fixed quickly. If ghosts were involved, we'd probably be stuck here for a while. They do like their tricks." The tiniest dimple on his left cheek accompanied his boyish grin.

You are not into dimples. You are not into dimples. "Ghosts aren't real," she scoffed, her breath settling.

"Ghosts *are* real."

She turned her entire body toward him, placing her hands on her hips in a stance she imagined a fed-up mother would take with a disobedient child. "Ghosts are the result of an overactive imagination."

"An overactive imagination can be very beneficial," he said, playfulness braided with his voice's low timbre. "If ghosts are the product of an overactive imagination, why are you here interviewing for a paranormal investigation show?"

"One doesn't have to believe in ghosts to tell a compelling story."

"You don't believe in the show's premise to prove ghosts exist?" he said, his tone reminiscent of a child finding out Santa Claus wasn't real.

Is he serious? She scoffed.

"A skeptic." Challenge glinted in his eyes, as if they were playing a game. "Why don't you believe?"

"Why *do* you believe?"

As far as Nora was concerned, she didn't need to justify her belief. The only ghosts that existed were the metaphorical kind that one dealt with in therapy, which reminded her that she needed to reschedule her appointment with Dr. Unaka.

"There's so much evidence. That's what *Haunted Hideaway* will be investigating. I mean paranormal science is filled with…" He stopped speaking at the deafening roll of her eyes.

"It's entertainment, not science."

August nodded, not in agreement but seeming to consider her argument. "So, what would make *Haunted Hideaway* more sciencey?"

"Sciencey?" She guffawed.

"Yeah." He straightened to his full height with a determined expression anchored on his face. "Sciencey."

"That's not a word." Nora bit her lip, trying to stop her smile from getting bigger.

"How do words become words? Someone says them, someone else uses them, and before you know it, they're in the dictionary."

She bit harder on her lip. A charming sweetness wafted from this man.

Running her fingers along the scratched surface of her watch, she considered his question. "Here's how you make it more sciencey." She made air quotes, eliciting a silent chuckle from August. "One, interview actual scientists and experts that aren't all paranormal believers. Two, stay at the location for a week versus a single night. Three, run legitimate experiments." Nora counted off each suggestion on her fingers.

"Interesting."

Their gazes mingled. Nora's right hand pressed against her stomach, attempting to control those rogue butterflies. How dare they flutter at his warm stare!

"I like it," he said, his lips curled up into an impressed smile.

"Thanks." *Good god, did I just wiggle my hips again?*

Fiddling with the button of her blazer, she looked at the elevator screen. She'd almost forgotten they were stuck. Had he noticed her anxiety? Had he intentionally distracted her with his talk of ghosts? Just as she opened her mouth to ask, the elevator shook to life.

"Looks like we're moving," he said, stepping to the middle.

Nora stepped beside him. "Yup."

The aroma of bergamot and sandalwood drifted from him. Its sweet scent was reminiscent of a summer stroll through the woods. Relaxed. Calm. Refreshed. Each sensation sighed through her with his proximity.

The elevator dinged, and the doors eased open. For a beat, they stood, inches apart, their matching stares fixed forward to the lobby on the other side of the threshold.

"Good luck on the interview," he said.

She bristled at the word "luck." Like ghosts, luck wasn't something Nora believed in.

"You're the one that will need the luck." Head high, she stepped over the threshold.

His laugh lingered behind her as she made her way across the vestibule to the long hall leading to the Destination Network's offices. She checked in and took a seat in a cushy leather chair. Besides the receptionist tapping on a computer, she was the only one there. She wasn't sure where August had disappeared to and tried to ignore how many times her eyes flicked to the door, totally not looking for him.

"Ms. Scott." A tall, lean man stood in the open door to the right of the reception desk. Like her, he was a little over-dressed in his tan chinos and a green plaid button-up, a pen poked out from the shirt's right chest pocket.

What was up with this building and its stock of attractive men?

Nora rose, smiling.

"Sorry for keeping you waiting," he apologized, adjusting his black-rimmed glasses.

She crossed the small waiting area. "That's okay."

"I'm Derrick Chandler, one of the executive producers, show creators, and hosts," he chuckled with self-deprecation, reaching to take her outstretched hand.

She liked him instantly. Grandpa Scott told her to always listen to her gut and her gut liked Derrick. Though, after the gymnastics her stomach had done on the elevator, she wondered if maybe she should rethink grandpa's life philosophy.

Derrick led her down a long narrow hallway lined with framed photos of different Destination Network shows. Mid-afternoon sunshine streamed through a glass door at the end of the hall.

Derrick held the door open, motioning for Nora to walk into the sunlit conference room. "Glad to have you joining the team," he said, his angled face crinkled in a warm smile.

"Oh yes, I am..." Her brow dipped. "Wait...joining the team?"

Derrick slipped the pen from his chest pocket, clicking it. "My brother loved your pitch."

She blinked. *My pitch?*

Before she could clarify, the door opened and the man from the elevator strode in.

"I believe you've already met Gus." Derrick motioned to the man, who was mid-bite of a pink sprinkle donut.

"You said your name was August." She wagged her finger at him.

He swallowed. "It is." His tongue poked out of his mouth, licking crumbs from the corners of his full lips.

"Gus is short for August," Derrick explained. "The only one that calls him August is our mother when he's in trouble, which is a lot."

August shrugged, taking another bite of his donut.

Both men took seats at the table. She sat across from Aug—no…*Gus*.

She bit the inside of her mouth, giving her gnawed-at lip much needed respite. She'd gotten the job. *I got the job!* This repeated in her head like a new favorite song. Nora Scott would be a field producer. The next rung in her career ladder had been reached. *Bring on the chardonnay and cake!*

"Gus walked me through your pitch to him regarding *Haunted Hideaway*. It's unique and will help us separate ourselves from the other similar shows out there." Derrick smiled.

"Your resume and references are also very impressive. You'd be able to hit the ground running, which a new show like ours needs," August—*Gus*—added.

Why was referring to him as Gus so difficult? Perhaps it was the fact that the only Gus she knew was the mouse from *Cinderella*. And this man was no mouse. The fabric stretching over his biceps as his folded arms leaned on the conference table's surface punctuated his very un-mouse-like physique.

She crossed her arms, listening to Derrick go on about the production schedule and if it would fit with her availability. Her focus drifted between Derrick and the gentle flex of August's muscular body swiveling in the chair. By the time the meeting wrapped, and August escorted her to the elevator, she wasn't entirely sure what had happened.

"I'm excited to work with you," he said, pressing the button for the elevator.

"You should have told me who you were," she said, her tone a little curt.

His brow creased. "But I did. I told you my name was August, and it is. I told you I was here for the interview, and I was."

Her finger pointed and mouth opened and then shut. *Fuck beans, he's right.* He'd not lied.

With a loud ding, the elevator opened. Nora stepped on and turned to face him. He remained on the lobby side of the threshold, hands pushed into the pockets of his jeans and a crooked smile on his face.

"Goodbye, August," she said, deciding he would remain August to her and not Gus.

"I can't wait to convert you to a believer in ghosts."

"You'll be waiting a long time."

"Good thing I have a *very* overactive imagination to help me pass the time." He winked as the elevator doors shut.

CHAPTER 2

Two Years (No Ghosts) Later
Her Only Moron

"Die a slow death," Nora grumbled at her cellphone as its alarm's chirp yanked her awake.

Unwinding from the hotel sheets, she rolled out of bed. It wasn't a graceful roll of a Disney Princess but the lumbering of a newly reanimated zombie. One in desperate need of an extra-large cup of English Breakfast Tea.

Tea must wait, though. Before she could drink the sweet elixir of a strongly brewed cup in her *Kelly Clarkson for President* travel mug, exercise was in order. Exchanging sleep-rumpled pajamas for workout clothes, she headed to the hotel gym.

A gentle hum filled the gym as she turned on the lights. The room was both stale as if the windows had never been opened and cold like the sleepy Northern Arizona city outside. With a yawn, she hopped onto the treadmill. She tried every button but could not make it turn on.

With a perturbed breath, she stepped off the dead machine and jumped onto the elliptical next to it. Clicking the buttons, her firm line deepened to a frown.

Her displeased expression appeared almost permanent until the realization came that it was one of those "you must exercise first in order to exercise" machines. Who knew what the actual term was. Four a.m. was not the time to learn words. She popped her earbuds in and cranked the volume of her curated diva playlist. Kelly Clarkson filled her ears as her muscles eased awake with the start of her workout.

Twenty minutes later, her sweat-kissed body radiated with energy. The rhythm of Nora's day was in full effect. The groan of the alarm, followed by the grumble of the workout, and topped off with the "Ah!" after the first sip of tea. Each morning the same: lather, rinse, and repeat.

"Nor!" A cheerful voice boomed, drowning out her music.

It would be a losing battle to compete for supremacy with what she knew would be his forthcoming endless chatter, so she clicked her music off. "Don't call me Nor," she huffed.

"Would you prefer Ms. Scott?" he drawled, sauntering toward her.

She rolled her eyes.

Slipping his hands into his mesh workout shorts' pockets, his brown eyes glinted with playfulness. "Nora, then."

A creased formed at the center of her brow. "August."

The entire reason she woke up at four a.m. when she could have slept until five was to avoid August Chandler's far too chipper early morning disposition. His ever-present cheerfulness was only rivaled by a pack of Care Bears hyped up on an illegal substance.

"Getting your sweat on?" His brows quirked.

"No, I'm baking a cake."

After her second eyeroll of the morning, she moved her gaze forward to the mirrored wall in front of her. Why did hotel gyms have these mirrored walls? Nobody needed to see themselves working out. If it was for motivation, it did *not* work. The only motivation she had right now was to leave.

"I forgot you're not a morning person." His teasing grin telegraphed that he did *not* forget she wasn't a morning person and just seemed to delight in engaging with her.

With a shrug he moved to the treadmill beside her. Thanks to the mirror, his every movement was on display. His tongue darting out with the lick of his lips. The flex of his bicep as he rubbed the back of his head. Those thick strands of his always had that sexy bedhead look. So many men spent hours perfecting that look but he just rolled out of bed with it. The last two seasons of overnight shoots confirmed that fact.

For a moment, Nora wondered what it would be like to weave her fingers into his hair. That inappropriate thought, interrupted by the flash of stomach thanks to his shirt riding up as he stretched. A trail of dark hair skated down the center of his stomach's cut ridges.

Nora shut her eyes. It wasn't appropriate to look at his abs and wonder what it would be like to kiss down that dusting of hair that led lower. First, they worked together. Second, he was August Chandler. Men like him did not date women like her. He gave golden retriever energy. She gave… well, *not* golden retriever energy. Third, he was her boss. As executive producers, he and his brother Derrick hired and fired the production crew, including her.

Nora's eyes opened at the distinct sound of sneakers slapping against the treadmill belt. "That doesn't work," she warned.

Grinning, he tapped a few buttons, and the treadmill moaned to life. "Guess I have the magic touch." It wasn't just his right eye that winked at her but his entire body. August seemed to express every emotion with his entire self, and his range of emotions went from happy, to happier, to even more happy. In the two years they'd worked together, she'd not once seen a glimpse of a frown or annoyed crease of his brow.

Her face pinched. "Maybe it just needed to warm up."

"Or maybe there is just a little magic in the world. Just a little luck, Nora."

"There's no such thing as luck."

"But there is," he countered, his smirk baiting her.

"There is *not*." God, she took the bait. Again.

Arguing was her default mode with him ever since the first day they'd met. *No, ghosts didn't exist! No, an IPA wasn't the chardonnay of beer! No, sneakers weren't appropriate to wear with a tuxedo! No, a peanut butter and honey sandwich wasn't superior to a classic PB&J!*

"I'll prove it." A daring confidence filled his expression.

Despite his now glistening face on full display in the mirror in front of her, she turned her narrowed eyes to him. "Prove it then."

"I *luckily* set my alarm for four a.m. instead of five a.m., which brought me down here an hour early for my workout, and now I get to spend time with my favorite field producer."

"I'm sure you tell the other two field producers that *they* are your favorites when you work with them."

He placed his hand on his heart. "Wounded. To think you think I am above playing favorites."

She laughed. "You're a moron."

"Lucky for you, I'm *your* moron," he said, waggling his eyebrows at her.

Fighting the smile on her treasonous lips, Nora turned her gaze back to the mirror but still took in their side-by-side images. Her hair pulled tight in a low ponytail, a firm line anchored to her face, and her questionably too-short pink running shorts revealing long but far too pale legs.

It's not that Nora didn't smile. It just wasn't her factory setting. It made people paint her as the stereotypical Ice Queen. The villainess in every Hallmark movie, who gets defeated by the plucky bookstore owner and their precocious child sidekick. Nora wasn't the sweetheart, but she also wasn't the "not" sweetheart. Despite what others thought, ice didn't run in her veins.

On the other hand, August appeared the handsome male lead of a romcom, waiting for a whirlwind of happy chaos to steal his heart. The girl who was the complete opposite of her.

It amazed her that there was always a sun-kissed glow about August. With all the late-night shoots, days spent interviewing people indoors, and traveling to new locations, it never made sense that he had the look of someone just back from a week at an all-inclusive tropical resort.

Maybe luck does exist...for some people, at least. The corners of her lips ticked down.

"Are you okay?" August's attention fixed on her in the mirror.

She shook her head, not because she wasn't alright, but in frustration that her face betrayed her emotions, and he'd noticed. Why was he looking at her? Those mirrors needed to go.

"I'm fine," she whispered.

His eyes remained tethered to hers in the mirror's reflection.

"I'm really okay," she insisted, her voice as soft as a blanket.

An unexpected urge to assure him that she was okay took over. That this was just her normal "annoyed-at-August" face and nothing more. Even though there was something more. Those something mores were reserved for herself, Dr. Unaka, and sometimes Mae.

"Alright," he paused, gnawing his lip as if holding back what he wanted to say. "I think this one will be it."

"This one will be what?" she cooed with a bat of her lashes. This game they played before each shoot was a little ritualistic, but the flex at the corners of her mouth indicated her enjoyment.

"The location that finally gets you to believe in ghosts." His right brow arched, matching hers.

"Nope." She bit back that blooming smile.

Since being hired as one of three field producers for *Haunted Hideaway*, August had made it his mission to convert her skeptical heart into a believer. "I'll prove to you that there are ghosts, and you'll buy me a drink," he'd said the morning of their first day of filming. Two years later, she still hadn't bought him a drink.

She'd never admit it to anyone but herself – or to Mae after one too many glasses of wine—but she found some enjoyment working on the Destination Network's highest rated show. With two seasons under her belt working with the brothers, she got the appeal. Unlike other ghost hunting shows, they braided actual history, tourist spotlights for the location, and brotherly antics with the popcorn entertainment of the paranormal.

Even if it wasn't her dream job, *Haunted Hideaway* allowed Nora to become a field producer. She'd thought it would last six episodes. She was wrong. This week started the filming of the third season. One would think its popularity would have led to countless job offers, but it had not. Unless it was for a rival ghost show.

She stepped off the elliptical and grabbed a towel. "Can't wait for that big glass of chardonnay or, perhaps, an espresso martini that you'll be buying me at the end of the shoot," she teased, wiping the machine down and then tossed it into the dirty towel slot before turning toward the door.

"Nor," he called, as she reached the door.

An annoyed breath huffed out of her at his insistence to call her that.

"It's going to happen. I'm going to convince you. Ghosts are real and so is magic." His cocky declaration was somehow earnestly sincere.

"You're a moron," she laughed, opening the door.

"Lucky for you, I'm *your* moron."

CHAPTER 3

Nineteenth Century Sex Workers

English Breakfast Tea in hand, Nora strode across the busy lobby. Fellow guests and members of their ragtag production crew sat around the clusters of square tables in the hotel's breakfast nook. They were a crew of seven including Nora, her associate producer Dusty, two camera operators, a sound/boom operator, a director of photography, and a production assistant. August and Derrick would stay at the shooting location, while the crew commuted from the hotel. Nora would be on site for the majority of the shoot, only heading back to the hotel for power naps and showers.

Dusty, who had been working with Nora since season one, said this was because she was a "control freak." She'd not pretend he wasn't right. After all, true "control freaks" had enough control to own who they were.

The brothers living at their location was one of the things that separated their show from the rest of the paranormal

TV landscape. It made the show authentic. At the end of the day, the show was about the brothers' relationship.

It also didn't hurt the ratings that both men were equally sexy and charming. Derrick had the "hot nerdy teacher" thing going on. The almost bashful sexiness caused anyone penis-leaning to daydream of the good Dr. Chandler keeping them after school for some *extra* tutoring. August was a mix of brawny yet charmingly sweet masculinity.

"Morning," Derrick said, appearing in front of her with a plate of runny scrambled eggs.

"Derrick." She raised her tea to her nose, allowing its aroma to wash away the knowledge of those eggs from her nostrils. Nora ate meat like the former Missouri farmgirl she was, but something about runny eggs curdled her stomach and brought back memories of the baby chicks on her grandpa's farm.

"Are you going to join us for breakfast?" he asked, pushing his glasses up the bridge of his nose.

Peering around Derrick, she took in the pointed stares from Benji, one of their camera operators, Dusty, Raj, their sound person, and Lucy, their production assistant, over the rims of their raised coffee mugs. August sat dead center of their table, his focus fixed on her. The upward curve of his mouth dared her to join them.

Nora never did. It wasn't that she was unapproachable. She just kept the crew at a distance. In the ten years of working in TV production, she'd learned that the "families" or "friendships" formed on set were like the seasons. They burned bright for a few months but scattered away with the coming of the next project. There was no reason to get attached. This aspect of TV's project-based work comforted her. Temporary relationships meant nobody was left behind, because there was never an expectation for anyone to stay.

"I'm going to run to the location to check on a few things before we set up for the day," she said.

From across the lobby a silent laugh lit August's face as he shook his head at her. Each shake seemed to chide her with a "Come on Nora" and tease with an unsurprised "Of course."

Derrick's lips slanted into a crooked smile. "I feel like a slacker with you around. Here I am leisurely eating eggs, while you're working."

"After reading your notes on the script for the narration over the historical montage, I would say you are anything but a slacker," she assured, her attention still fixed on August who smirked at her over his white ceramic mug from across the room.

"That means a lot, Nora." Derrick tugged on his ear with his free hand. "I find it fascinating that this location high-lights the economic disparity caused by the limited employ-ment opportunities for women in the late nineteenth century mining communities..."

Nora's gaze remained linked with August's. The playful expression etched to his features seemed to tease her for getting sucked into a "Dr. Chandler" lecture. As hot for teacher as most people were about Derrick, his unbridled geeking out about all things history and the research he'd put into each location would cool down even the lustiest individ-ual. August called it the "Dr. Chandler Vortex" when Derrick slipped deep into his nerdy ways and sucked up whoever was within his orbit.

As Derrick went on talking about gendered work in the nineteenth century, August's already bright smile erupted like a starburst. Nora bit her lower lip, trying to tamp down a matching smile. She wouldn't give August the satisfaction of thinking he knew what went on in her head.

Want me to rescue you? August mouthed.

Nora shook her head. *Damn it!* She squeezed her eyes

tight. The headshake had just confirmed that he had read her mind.

"So, you don't think that's an angle we should take?" Derrick's question pulled Nora's attention back to him.

"Umm?"

"About interviewing that professor from Arizona State that did her dissertation on the economics of gender in mining communities."

"We already have all the interviews scheduled and releases signed."

His hopeful expression deflated. It was like taking a stuffed toy away from a puppy.

"Let's talk about it after we complete this morning's interviews and see if we can make some adjustments," she offered with a soft smile.

Even if they didn't use the footage for the episode, it would make great online content. It also would make Derrick happy.

"Great!" He beamed.

As executive producer, Derrick trumped Nora, but he never did. Neither did August. If she said no, they would plead their cases but never override her. Both had a deep deference to her expertise. It was something she respected about them. They weren't like any executive producers she'd worked with in the past.

"I should probably go eat these before they get cold." He raised the plate of eggs.

Nora stepped back. The only thing grosser than drippy eggs were cold ones. "Good idea. I'll see you at the location by nine," she said.

"We'll bring you more tea," he offered.

Nora nodded. It was the production assistant's job to get the snacks, lunch, and beverages for the crew, but ever since their second episode shooting together, Derrick always brought her a fresh cup of tea when he arrived on location. She was sure he was having someone else actually get it, but it was appreciated, nonetheless.

"See you soon," he said, heading back to his table.

Her gaze dropped back to August. *Thank you,* he mouthed.

Nora blinked. Not knowing what else to do, she just smiled. Then she turned and headed out the door.

The icy March air pricked her face as she walked across the parking lot. The crunch of hard snow beneath her boots sang in her ears until the ping of her phone interrupted the late winter song. A smile spread with the message notification on her phone.

Mae: My fellow goddess, I have arrived!

Nora enlarged the attached picture of Mae, a cocktail in hand, big smile beaming, and her asymmetrical purple bob popping against the pale blue coastal Brazilian sky.

While Nora wasn't a fan of on-set relationships, Mae was relentless. They'd met nine years ago, when Nora was a production assistant on a commercial and Mae was the camera operator. After splitting the last orange on the buffet table, Mae insisted they would be orange sisters for life. Nora was fired when Wes, the producer, lost his shit because there weren't any oranges when he went for his mid-afternoon snack. Mae found Nora crying in the parking lot. It was the last time she was fired, the last time she cried at work, and the first and only *real* friend she made on the job. She could be friendly with colleagues, but she'd never allowed any of them to know her. Not like with Mae. Though her best friend's vibrant warmth had this power to melt most of Nora's defenses. Most, but not all.

Nora snapped a picture of the snow dusted parking lot and sent it to Mae.

Nora: Clearly, so have I.

Mae: *Laughing Emoji.* **You could always join me.** *Winky Face Emoji.*

The idea was appealing. Just shove off the shackles of responsibility and fly unencumbered in the breeze…

Nora: I've got to run to set.

Mae: Nice job NOT answering my question.

Nora: *Eyeroll emoji.* **Remember to send your daily check-ins, please.**

Mae: Yes, Mom!

Ten minutes later, Nora walked into the Blackhorse Inn. The still-operational nineteenth century hotel would be their home for the next seven days.

A man in a brown cowboy hat, rumpled white shirt, and brown suede vest tipped his hat in greeting. "Ma'am," he drawled. It was as if he'd stepped out of a scene from one of Grandpa Scott's favorite westerns.

"Morning." Goose pimples blossomed along her skin.

With an easy smile, he strode across the lobby and disappeared into the darkened bar.

She smoothed down her ponytail and continued across the lobby to the front desk, where the creak of the worn wooden floor announced her arrival. The receptionist looked up from her computer, a bored expression covering her face.

"Morning, I'm Nora Scott." She held out her hand.

"You're the Destination Network lady!" She took Nora's hand in a firm shake. "I'm Jolie, the inn's manager."

The Destination Network Lady? That's a new one. A small laugh escaped Nora. "Sure."

A certain level of recognition came with being part of one of the Destination Network's top-rated shows, although most people didn't know who Nora was. People knew August and Derrick because they were the stars. She was behind the scenes, aiming the audience toward the brightness that was the Chandler brothers. It was how she liked it.

Jolie leaned on the counter. "Is Gus as cute in person as on TV?"

This was just one of the strings of typical questions asked about the show, including: *Is—insert brother's name—as cute in person? Does—insert brother's name—have a significant other? Have you all really found ghosts?* and *Can you introduce me to—insert brother's name?* It never failed.

"He seems sweet. Is he as sweet as he seems?" she went on, pulling out paperwork from below the counter. "Will Gus need just *one* key or two?"

Nora bit the inside of her cheek, trying to stifle an incredulous laugh.

Jolie's subtle way to suss out if August was single and if he'd have someone staying with him was skillful. To Nora's knowledge neither brother was in a relationship. Since first meeting them, neither brother had appeared attached. There hadn't even been rumors of them dating anyone. The demanding filming schedule and relentless travel made relationships outside of short-term hookups or a very understanding partner difficult.

Nora understood this. Her last relationship fizzled out a few days before taking this job and there'd been *no* room in her schedule to pursue another one. At least, that's what she told Mae and Dr. Unaka each time they asked about romantic relationships.

"Just a reminder there's not supposed to be any guests or staff during filming," Nora said, thinking of the Pedro Pascal look-alike cowboy in the bar. As much as possible they worked with locations to ensure only the crew was on set. It was easier for filming purposes and maintaining the integrity of Derrick and August's experiments.

"Yep. I'm the only one here. Housekeeping will come in

the mornings at the times you outlined, but otherwise it's just me."

Nora's left eyebrow lifted. "There was a man when I arrived. Not sure if he's an employee or guest. He's in the bar."

Face scrunched, Jolie tipped her head toward the bar. "There's nobody there."

What? Brow creased, Nora twisted toward the bar area. Aside from the three bistro tables and rows of alcohol bottles lining the mirrored shelf above the dark walnut bar, the small alcove was empty.

Ghosts are real. For just a moment August's voice whispered in her ear. It would be so easy to fall into his magical thinking, but she knew better. Logical explanations could always be found. Likely the rogue cowboy was someone who wandered in to get a look at the historic and allegedly haunted hotel.

It happened all the time. After news was out in small cities like this one, there'd always be folks poking around. During their investigation of Fort Niagara, a group of frat guys showed up dressed like Revolutionary War-era soldiers in an attempt to masquerade as ghosts. Their Nikes gave them away as pranksters and not actual phantom soldiers.

Probably another prankster. "He must have left." She shrugged, shuffling the paperwork on the counter.

"We've got you set up on the second-floor conference room." Jolie handed her room keys and a packet of information about the hotel. "The elevator is around the corner."

"Are there stairs?" she asked, slipping the packet into her production binder.

"Oh, you're one of those 'take the stairs' people," Jolie quipped.

"Yup." Nora's firm grin tightened.

Nora found the stairs and then proceeded to the conference room on the second floor that they'd use for their command center. Stepping fully into the room, she clicked on the lights and her pulse ticked up. A yellow glow from the above florescent lights illuminated the small windowless room. Flicking the rubber band on her wrist, she leaned against the table at the center of the room. Her stare locked on the open door reminding herself of its existence…of the ability to escape if needed.

Pulse settling, she exhaled and rolled into her pre-shoot routine. Nora always arrived early at each location. She'd wander through the space inhaling its scent, taking in its aesthetics, and allowing its overall energy to dwell within her. Communing with the location tapped into her ability to capture its essence and guide its translation onto the screen.

"Is the room speaking to you?" August appeared in the entry way, a large to-go coffee cup in his hand and playfulness dancing in his expression.

She looked at her watch. "You're early. Shouldn't you be at the hotel taking selfies for your social media or being adored by prepubescent fanboys and lovesick college coeds?"

"Jealous?" His right brow cocked.

She rolled her eyes. "Hardly."

"Oh, I think you're a *little* jealous." He sauntered toward her.

"Unlike you, I got a sufficient amount of attention growing up to *not* necessitate a career focused on being fawned over by millions of people."

He stepped closer, the heat of his body lapped against her. Should she step back? Remaining where she stood kept her ground but allowed his scent to have its way with her senses like a sneaky cat burglar. What it stole, she had no idea, but August's aroma left her wanting as if something was missing. She stayed put.

"Well, some of us didn't grow up as assured as you.

Perhaps my parents should have taken a lesson from yours. I bet there was a never-ending collage of finger paintings and A-plus papers hung on your fridge as a kid."

Nora dug her nails into her palms at the mention of parents. The image of white construction paper scrawled with a colorful crayon drawing of a small family hanging on the fridge with a state of Missouri-shaped magnet flashed in her vision. *Nope. We don't think about that.* She shook her head as if that would clear the phantom image away.

"You okay?" Concern dipped his smile.

It was the second time in the last four hours that she'd caused a brief crack in August's carefree expression. As much as his endless cheerfulness irritated her, she didn't want to be responsible for stealing it, even for a fleeting moment. It was far better when he just smiled at her saltiness. Although her mood wasn't salty, it was… It was something she didn't want to think about.

"Did you need something, August?" Nora cleared her throat, not addressing his question.

"Tea," he said, holding the cup out to her.

Nora took it, her eyes narrowed at the *Nor* scribbled on the cup. "Usually Derrick brings me tea."

"Most people say thank you when someone brings them something."

She puffed out an annoyed breath. As much as she preferred keeping things professional, rudeness wasn't her aim. The goal was aloof friendliness. Today, she was leaning toward snarky rudeness.

"I'm sorry… Thank you," she breathed.

"You're welcome." The unabashed grin returned to his face. "They were out of your English Breakfast, so I took the liberty of getting you the Jade Citrus Mint. I know how you like your Thin Mint Girl Scout cookies and enjoy your afternoon orange snack, so I figured this would be a good marriage of some of your favorite flavors."

What? She blinked. Did he have a secret dossier of her favorite snacks? If he mentioned that he had a bag of white cheddar popcorn she may wonder if he was in the CIA.

Since she didn't know what else to say, she just repeated "Thank you."

"Anytime." He winked, walking out of the room.

So many people would melt at August Chandler winking at them. The flirtation in that wink would send belly butter-flies flipping. In Nora, it elicited a hot flush not of the sexy variety but of the indignant one. The audacity of *that* man thinking he knew what she'd like. As if he knew her.

She took a long drag of the tea. "Fuck," she groaned as the minty liquid coated her tongue in delicious warmth. He was right.

CHAPTER 4

A Drink with Deputy Douglas

At midnight, the brothers went to separate rooms and shot in complete darkness using night vision cameras. Their only connection to each other and the control center were their walkie-talkies.

August, who had been ghost hunting since he was thirteen, insisted that being alone allowed ghosts to feel more comfortable approaching the living. Nora would just roll her eyes. It wasn't like it was a bar where ghosts approached the living to hit on them. It was ridiculous, but it was good TV and at the end of the day that's what was important.

The paranormal portions of filming were the only time her job felt like work. Shooting at the locations, interviewing experts, and highlighting points of interest in the surrounding area filled Nora with the sense of having an almost perfect piece of cake, the rich taste and smooth texture flooding every tastebud. August and Derrick running around in the dark, jumping at the creaks of what was likely just an old building settling, was like finding a stray eggshell in an otherwise delightful experience.

Her stomach grumbled, and she looked at her watch. It was after two a.m. There'd be no place in Prescott, AZ to get cake at this hour.

"What time is Lucy going on the snack run this morning?" She looked between Dusty and the live footage of both brothers, squinting at the screen where August should be but wasn't. *Where'd he go?*

"I told her to go first thing in the morning," Dusty yawned, stretching his arms wide. "Why?"

"I have something I'd like to add to the snack list." Nora tapped her nails on the table surface. *What mischief are you up to, August?*

He was supposed to be investigating the hotel's bar where the departed soul of Deputy Rafael Douglas, shot in a dispute over a card game, allegedly haunted. The clichéd stories accompanying these locations were laughable. Each seemed to be pulled out of a tattered copy of a paperback that her grandpa would have loved.

She leaned back, wincing just a bit, her back stiff from sitting too long in the hard metal folding chair. "Yeah. Can you add…"

"Chocolate cake," August interjected, causing Nora to jerk toward the door.

His brawny form leaned against the doorframe. A brown cowboy hat obscured his eyes but that big smile of his, quirked in a sardonic grin, was on full display.

Heat inched up her neck. "How do you know what I was about to say?"

"It's the third night of filming." He shrugged as if that was an answer.

Her face scrunched with incredulity.

"You always get chocolate cake on day three."

Dusty chimed in. "You know, you're right. She does *always* ask for chocolate cake on the third night of shooting."

"She also wants a burger for lunch the day before the shoot begins but eats salads, yogurt, white cheddar popcorn, and fruit during filming. Well, except for the cake." August pointed to Dusty.

"Oh! And waffles the morning after the last day of shooting." Dusty returned, as if playing a game of "Who knows Nora's eating habits" ping pong.

Nora blinked. Was she *that* predictable? Also, burgers, cake, and waffles? No wonder her pants were a little tight at the end of filming. Maybe she should skip the cake. Her heart gasped, begging her not to take away the cake. Maybe she'd just hit the gym a little more.

"She also—"

"You're supposed to be at the bar." Nora scowled, interrupting August.

"It's *no* fun to drink alone," he said.

"You're *not* alone, you have Deputy Douglas."

To anyone else looking, his big smile appeared unchanged, but Nora could see the corners pop with playfulness. "If I didn't hear the not-so-thinly veiled sarcasm in that statement, I'd suspect I finally convinced you that ghosts are real."

"Why are you here?" she sighed. "And why are you wearing a cowboy hat instead of the Buffalo Sabres cap you usually wear for shoots?" Double sigh.

"First, I didn't realize you were paying so much attention to my fashion choices."

Heat deepened in her cheeks.

"Second, the hat is to channel the Old West feel and, hopefully, make Deputy Douglas more willing to come have a drink with me."

"But why are you here?" she asked, regretting it instantly.

Strolling to her, he leaned against the table and locked his gaze with hers. "Well, ma'am—" he drawled with a twinge of twang, "—I wanted to sneak a peek at Derrick and Ms. Ruby."

Nora nibbled her lower lip, stifling a bubbling laugh. Her eyes dropped to the monitor showing room *305*. The room had a lingering scent of roses which nobody could explain, and was rumored to be haunted by a late nineteenth century sex worker named Ruby Dallas, who was murdered there by a jealous lover.

"Sleeping like a baby." Nora pointed to Derrick, curled on his side and hugging the pillow as if it were a stuffed animal or a lover.

August turned and bent to look at the screen, his arm brushing against Nora's. The brief skin-to-skin contact ignited a wisp of wildfire that scampered up her spine. Closing her eyes, she willed that fire back down, threatening it with an ice-cold shower if it didn't behave itself.

"Well, that's disappointing," he hummed. "I'd hoped Ms. Ruby would come out to play. It's been far too long since Derrick had a date and I'm sure she'd appreciate a standup guy like my brother."

"Wouldn't we all," Dusty quipped, his head tossed back in laughter.

August wagged his finger. "How would Benji feel about that comment?"

Dusty beamed at the mention of his fiancé. The two had met during the first season, falling head over heels. They'd be getting married after filming wrapped this season. Unlike the field and associate producers that rotated episodes, as a camera operator Benji remained on the crew for the entire season. He'd worked on August's previous projects. Both August and Derrick tended to hire people they'd worked with before, especially for the crew members that remained with them for most of the filming.

"While the good doctor is adorable, he's no Benji Kwon." A warm crimson rouged Dusty's cheeks.

"Well, maybe once Benji is off the market, we can turn our focus to finding someone for Derrick," he chuckled, his gaze fixed on his brother.

Clearly Derrick was a spooner. Nora couldn't remember the last time she'd been spooned. Nora was more the go-to-our-separate-sides-of-the-bed type of sleeper. Peter, the last man she'd been intimate with, said trying to cuddle with her was akin to attempting to hold a feral cat. He'd not been the only one to say that. What he hadn't known was that despite the jitteriness that pulsed in her veins when being held, a longing in her chest to be enveloped as tight as Derrick cuddled that pillow existed. Even if the idea of it terrified her.

"You're like a mother from a Regency Romance novel trying to marry off your brother," Nora teased.

Over the last two years, she watched August wingman or push an unsuspecting Derrick at industry parties, on filming location, or when the crew went out for drinks on the last night of shooting to ask out a potential love interest. He'd tease Derrick on camera about being single and ready to mingle with the lady ghosts. Both brothers were single, but August positioned Derrick to be the reluctant sex symbol of the show. August was just as much the apple of a lusty eye but often deflected the focus to Derrick. It was as if the little brother wouldn't allow himself a relationship until his older brother was happily ensconced.

"Maybe *you're* more Ms. Ruby's type. Perhaps *you* should sleep there before we wrap," Nora cooed with a waggle of her eyebrows.

"Nah, Derrick is the dreamboat."

She shook her head.

August may know all her snacking predilections, but she

knew August. The beauty of keeping people at a distance was perspective. Since meeting in that elevator on her way to the interview for this job, she'd observed much about him. One thing she knew was that his deflection had zero to do with false modesty to garner more affection. The punting of the romantic attention to his brother came from something deeper. Nora wasn't sure what, but she knew that it was something more. *He* was something more.

"There's always the next location." August straightened, towering over Nora.

"Is having your brother be joined in bed by a spirit on camera part of your strategy to get me to believe in ghosts?" Nora smirked, raising her now-lukewarm tea to her lips and sipping.

"Two birds, one fondled brother," August deadpanned.

Nora spat out her tea.

He laughed as he walked across the room and grabbed a handful of napkins from the stack that sat on a small metal cart, piled high with snacks, in the corner of the room. Handing Nora several, he took the rest and dabbed up the wet splotches from the table.

"Thanks," she said.

"Damn, I always wanted to get a spit take on camera," Dusty lamented with a hearty laugh.

Nora grimaced. "Ugh. I've never done that before."

August took off his hat, covering his heart with it. "Ma'am, I am honored to have been your first." He gave her a flirty wink.

"Go to the bar and have a sarsaparilla with your Deputy Douglas, so we can get back to work." Laughing, she shooed him away.

"Fine, but if you see any movement in Derrick's bed call me on the walkie." He plopped his hat back on and turned to leave.

He stopped at the door and looked over his shoulder. Even though she couldn't see under the brim of his hat, she could feel his gaze on her.

"Dusty, tell Lucy to get Diet Dr. Pepper and white cheddar popcorn."

"Night Seven!" Dusty laughed in agreement.

"Night Seven," August said, his deep voice confident and playful.

Nora's forehead puckered. *Two could play this game.* "Dusty, tell Lucy to get pretzels and a jar of Nutella."

August's mouth curled into a sexy smirk. "I do enjoy a salty sweet treat."

Heat tiptoed up her spine at the deep timbre of his voice. It almost caressed against her skin with the teasing promise of being *that* salty sweet treat.

Clearing her throat, she turned to Dusty. "Umm… You should also tell Lucy to get some strawberry cupcakes."

"Oh, *my* favorite!" Dusty placed his hand on his heart.

"That's our Nora. She takes care of us." August's grin beamed brighter. "Ma'am," he tipped his hat to her before slipping out the door.

CHAPTER 5

Predictable Superstition

The empty bag of white cheddar popcorn lay on the table beside Nora. A sharp ache radiated down her back from being confined to the torture device that was the command center's folding metal chair. It was the last night—or, more accurately, early morning—of filming.

Nora looked at her watch. The sun would soon rise, ending their week at the Blackhorse Inn. They'd do wrap-up interviews with the guys about their impressions, break down equipment, pack up, and head back to the hotel for rest. There'd be dinner and drinks tonight. In the morning, Nora would enjoy her waffles and then head back to L.A. for postproduction, while August, Derrick and the rest of the crew went to the next location. Unlike the rest of the crew, the field and associate producers alternated working on individual episodes throughout the season. She was contracted for two more episodes this season.

Nora sipped her Diet Dr. Pepper, rereading the email she'd read three times already today. Each letter mocked her.

Dear Ms. Scott,

Thank you for your interest in the position of Producer with The Great Escape, but we've decided to go with a different candidate.

Sighing, she hit *Delete*, allowing the rejection to join its siblings in the trash folder of her email.

"How's that Diet Dr. Pepper?" Dusty asked, a cheeky grin brightened his features.

Instantly her sipping transformed into gulping. Finishing the last drop, she placed the empty bottle down. "Delicious." It was almost a declaration. Not for the artificial sweetness that coated her mouth, but from the sensation of rightness that filled her with predictability. Despite their teasing about her snacks, her turning down their breakfast invites each morning, or how she knocked on a surface two times whenever anyone said, "hopefully X, Y, or Z happens," she embraced who she was. They may grumble under their breath, but when the unpredictable happened, they came to Nora, who had a plan for every foreseeable and unforeseeable issue.

When the flash flood happened during their first season, stranding them twenty miles from the location, Nora knew alternative routes to get them there. When Derrick tripped last season and smashed his glasses, Nora had a spare pair ready to go. The unpredictable was predictable, because, to quote Grandpa Scott, "The shit always hits, baby girl" and Nora had been learning how to shovel, clean, and step over that shit since she was six.

"Looks like it's almost quittin' time," Dusty yawned, pointing to the monitor.

Beams of early morning sunshine tiptoed into Ms. Ruby's room. Nora shook her head and smiled. The only movement in the bed all night was August, flipping from his back to his side around two a.m. There had been no fondling of this brother either.

Nora bit her lip, watching the sun coax August awake. How strange it was to sit here watching someone sleep all night. To take in the peaceful relaxation of every muscle in his face. A hint of a smile etched his features, even as he slept. Not that Nora was paying *that* close of attention. Well, she was, but for scientific reasons. Only to prove her point that ghosts weren't real.

"Looks like sleeping beauty is up," Dusty said, grabbing his phone. "I'm texting Benji and Raj to head over to do the wrap up interviews with the guys. We'll give them an hour to get themselves dressed. Derrick is already up and…" Dusty whistled, "…doing shirtless pushups. How is that man single?"

"You're as bad as August." She chuckled.

"I wish. Especially with *those* abs." He waved to the second monitor. "Maybe, I shouldn't have had that second cupcake." He sighed.

Nora turned to see August, shirtless, making his bed. A pair of blue plaid pajama bottoms hung low on him. The muscles of his back flexed as he pulled the sheets and blankets tight to the bed. And was that a tattoo on his right shoulder blade?

Grabbing the walkie, she pushed the talk button. "You know the housekeepers will be stripping that bed after you check out."

Turning toward the camera, he grabbed the walkie on the nightstand and held it to his mouth. "I always make my bed."

On the other monitor, Derrick's bed was also made.

"Their mama raised them right," Dusty drawled in his warm East Texan twang.

Nora nodded, a dull ache in her heart. It was silly to have that twinge in her chest, but she did.

Clearing her throat, she hit *talk*. "Get showered and changed. We'll set up for wrap up interviews on the back patio in an hour."

"I have a great spot for us to go to tonight," August said.

For us? The crew. The crew was "us." Nora nodded but then remembered that while she could see him—*so much of him*—that he could not see her. Picking up the walkie she said, "Go get ready. It's not playtime yet, August."

"But you're my *favorite* playmate." His tone was flirty.

Dusty snorted.

Nora glared at both men, which was a feat considering one was one floor up, shirtless, in a murdered sex worker's room.

After both brothers were cleaned up and in shirts, they completed their wrap up interviews for the location. Nora oversaw the rest of the production team packing up their equipment and then spoke with the hotel's manager. They flowed into their typical take-down motions after filming concluded. Benji grumbled about the way members of the crew handled the cameras. Lucy ran around with her tablet. Dusty patted Benji's bicep telling him all would be well with his precious cameras and if not, Nora would have "words" with the responsible party. Derrick sucked the once starry-eyed receptionist into his academic vortex as he talked about late nineteenth century mining techniques. The poor girl who had drooled over Derrick and August all week looked as if she'd rather have a root canal than spend another moment talking to Derrick. August greeted fans that had gathered at the hotel, taking selfies with them and tagging them on his social media, which Nora had to admit was kind of adorable since each fan lit like a chandelier when he did it.

Once everything was tucked away, it would be time to play. August coordinated the crew's celebratory last night of shooting. It was one of the few times Nora lost her sleek ponytail, slipped on a cute outfit, and joined them for a drink.

Nora stood in front of a storefront where a large sign embossed with *Superstition* hung over the doors. "You're taking us shopping?"

Hands in his coat pockets, August smirked. "*You* know me better than that."

Tiny butterfly wings fluttered in her belly at the way he enunciated "you" as if there was so much more to that word than its meaning. Biting her lip, she tried to clamp down her budding smile. She had to admit she enjoyed his planned night outs.

It started after their first shoot, a former brothel turned bed and breakfast in West Texas. After a bumpy week of cameras falling over, drained batteries, and gargled noises on the walkies, all of which August was adamant was para-normal—and all of which Nora knew was standard for a new TV production—he'd organized a crew field trip to a honky-tonk bar complete with a mechanical bull. From then on, at each location, he'd find a unique activity for them to go to.

August led them in. The *woosh* of warm air caressed her face. A hodgepodge of items filled the wooden shelves, and bright light bathed the room in a fluorescent glow. The plank floor creaked beneath the heels of her black booties. When shooting, she stuck to jeans, sneakers, and depending on the weather, a sweater or T-shirt. On non-filming days, she indulged her fashionista side.

Tonight, her hair hung loose, tumbling over her shoulders, contrasting with the red turtleneck sweater dress she wore. Black tights, gold hoops, and pointy-toed booties topped off her outfit.

August led them to an elevator at the back of the store. "We'll be going downstairs."

Nora's pulse ticked up, her eyes searched for rescue, landing on a set of stairs across the small landing. "I'll take the stairs."

"Nora and her steps," Benji teased.

"Well, all those steps make her booty pop in that dress." Dusty snapped his fingers.

"I don't think that's appropriate," Derrick chided.

Nora shook her head, knowing what Dusty would say.

"Well, I don't know if it's sexual harassment as I am not sexually interested in Nora nor what's under that too-tight dress."

Nora cocked her head over her shoulder, shooting a glowered smile at Dusty. "You don't have to be sexually interested to harass someone."

"You're going to make me drive you to the airport tomorrow morning as penance, aren't you?" Dusty groaned.

"Yup." She winked before turning to take the first step.

"Meet you all downstairs," August said, following Nora.

"I've learned my lesson. Hear that, Nora? I didn't say anything inappropriate when I clearly could have commented about Gus taking the stairs to make *his* butt pop in those fitted jeans. Please don't make me get up at the ass crack of dawn to drive you to the airport," he pleaded.

With a laughing headshake, she started down the stairs. The warmth of August's body almost hugged her as he followed. At the bottom, two dark mahogany bars stood opposite each other. Red leather stools encircled each. Tables and chairs, matching the bar's color scheme, dotted the room. Despite the bar being downstairs from what Nora assumed was ground level, floor to ceiling windows lined the far wall allowing for a view of the sidewalk and street outside.

Nora claimed a cushy leather chair in a group of tables near the room's center. "What's the twist?"

"The *twist?*" Head tilted, August's mouth slanted into a lopsided grin.

Nora swatted him with the thick leather menu from the table. "Don't be coy, sir!"

"Someone has rage issues," he teased, taking the menu from her.

Forehead pinched, she plucked the menu back and opened it. "It's all mead."

"Well, except for the tidbits, but there are french fries, so you'll be happy."

Nora tried to hold back her smile, but it was too big. God, she loved french fries. The love for them couldn't be dulled by his pointing out yet another predictable thing about her. She got fries each time they went out for celebratory dinner and drinks after shooting. The one time August picked a place that didn't have french fries was at the end of last season. He'd taken them all to a place where they made their own pizzas and got to bake them in a brick fire oven. August disappeared halfway through, returning with a large order of fries from Sonic. They weren't her preferred fries, but that night was one of her more recent favorite memories.

Nora flipped through the menu. "Derrick will love this."

"Yeah." The elevator pinged and Derrick and the crew got off. "He loves having mead at the Renaissance fair."

"You two and your Renaissance festivals. You're like a giant man-child."

He cocked an eyebrow. "I'm going to get you to go with us one time and dress up."

The Chandler brothers were obsessed with Renaissance fairs. Their parents had taken them as children, and the siblings carried on the tradition as adults. Ever the historian, Derrick geeked out over the sensation of stepping back in time. Nora suspected that August just enjoyed dressing up like a highway bandit in those leather pants of his that left little to the imagination.

The last two seasons, they'd coordinated two different locations due to proximity to a Renaissance festival. Last season, they'd even shot at one to highlight the fair as a point of interest, while investigating a jailhouse in Independence, Missouri.

That was also the one time Nora took a workday off. Being only thirty minutes away from the small town, where she'd grown up, she spent the day retracing her childhood through the small town and sitting in her rental car outside Grandpa Scott's farmhouse. The tire swing he'd hung for her when she was seven spun in the late spring breeze as if a pigtailed Nora was being pushed by grandpa, his eyes crinkled in a big smile.

August went on, pulling Nora from her memories. "One of the interviewees we talked to this week mentioned this place and I knew I had to take Derrick. The crew may hate me, though, because there will be a Dr. Chandler lecture on the history of mead."

Nora grinned, watching Derrick stride over with the rest of the crew. No doubt there'd be a *long* lecture. August would roll his eyes. He'd tease, but he would clank his glass of mead alongside his brother the entire night. It was something she appreciated about him. Despite the teasing and pranks, he was loyal.

"They have mead!" Derrick beamed, scooting in beside his brother.

"What's mead?" Lucy asked, batting her long dark eyelashes.

August smirked at Nora, mouthing *one, two, three…*

"It's fermented honey. Although, you can use other simple sugars. There is this fascinating book about gender and the history of alcohol which…" Derrick droned.

Nora picked up her menu to cover her quiet snickers. Lucy's face turned from interested to regretful to imploring someone to save her as Derrick went on and on. Nora had tuned him out, not registering that he was still talking while she sipped on a raspberry mead and munched on parmesan fries.

"Now, that would be a dream location." August sighed.

"What would be?" Lucy asked, brushing a long dark strand of hair behind her ear.

"Putman House," Nora and August said in unison, their gazes danced for just a moment.

She didn't need to have listened to the last ten minutes of chatter to know what August's dream investigation location was. It was imprinted on her. Each season, as they reviewed their possible locations, it was at the top of the Chandler brothers' wish list.

Lucy's head tilted. "What's Putman House?"

"It's a Victorian mansion in our hometown, built in 1883 and still owned by the Putman family today," Derrick explained, taking off his glasses and cleaning them with a napkin.

"It's a Wyoming County legend." August grinned.

Nora couldn't be responsible for the eyeroll. Since their first episode together, August talked about Putman House. It wasn't the Tower of London, Queen Mary, or other pinnacles of the ghost hunting spank bank that August drooled over. It was a little-known haunted Victorian mansion in a rural village in Western New York.

With a playful chide from his knee bumping hers from below the table, he went on. "There's stories about people getting grabbed or locked in closets, things flying through the air, lightbulbs blowing up, and disembodied voices."

Nora bumped his knee back. "None of which have been validated outside of local lore, because nobody has ever investigated it."

"Nobody's investigated it *yet.*"

Her smile ticked up at the fiery spark in August's eyes.

"Why do you think it's haunted? Was it built on a burial ground or something?" Lucy inquired, grabbing one of the fries and taking a slow bite, drawing attention to her pink glossed lips.

Fresh out of film school, Lucy had joined the team this season. Most of the crew members had worked on the show since the first season. Unlike Nora and more like August, Lucy had a happy puppy energy about her with her brown doe eyes, thick waves of dark curls that were often up in a bouncy ponytail, and bright smile.

"It's more salacious than an unscrupulous contractor building atop a burial ground."

"Gus, they were called carpenters, not contractors, at that time," Derrick interjected, arching an eyebrow at his brother.

He continued. "William Putman built the house for his wife Elizabeth. They lived there for five years until they lost their young son."

"Oh, no," Lucy gasped with all the vigor of a Disney Princess.

Nora imagined that any minute now blue birds would appear and fly around her, singing a sweet lullaby. Biting into a fry, Nora stifled the scowl trying to take hold on her face. If Lucy was the princess, then she was likely the wicked witch. She had the pointy black booties, after all.

"It was dreadful," Derrick continued the story. "William's grief caused a psychological break, and he shoved Elizabeth down the stairs. When servants found her dead body, William was arrested and later hung for killing his wife."

"The house went to William's brother Alexander after the

tragedy. It has remained in the Putman family ever since, and they aren't a fan of the house's haunted fame."

Nora flashed a teasing grin. "Is it famous?"

"Well, in Wyoming County."

"Where's Wyoming County?" Lucy's brows linked.

Nora smirked in triumph. "It's the cow-riddled homeland of our dear August and Derrick."

"Says the woman that grew up on a chicken farm in Missouri."

Their taunting expressions challenged one another. His seemed to say those in chicken houses shouldn't throw cowpies. Hers said "moron."

"Yeah, it would be great to investigate but Mr. Putman would never allow it." Derrick grabbed a fry. "He wouldn't even hand out candy at Halloween because of the rumors about the house."

"Well, Mr. Putman doesn't own the place anymore."

Derrick paused midbite.

August continued, "Mr. and Mrs. Putman retired, moved to Florida, and gave the house to Melody. She's turning it into a bed and breakfast."

"How do you know this?"

"I've messaged Melody a few times and she mentioned it. She's also mentioned being open to us investigating."

"You've spoken to Melody?"

Bemusement tugged at August's lips. "She says hi, by the way."

Derrick threaded his fingers into his chestnut hair. "She did? Oh, hi. Ahh…tell her hi, I mean."

Nora had never seen him get so flustered. He tended to be clueless when August tried to introduce women to him. There'd never been any real interest, but the soft pink on his cheeks at the mention of Melody Putman spoke of a man who was *interested*.

Her gaze fell upon August. "Next season," she said, knowing what gears were spinning in his head.

"But—"

"You have a schedule already. There is already so much chaos and unforeseen things. To throw a change like that at one of the producers is such a dick move," she interjected, pointing her finger at him.

"Dick? I do so adore the sweet endearments you give me, Nor," he said.

"If you're name was Richard, Dick would be an appropriate term of endearment," Derrick offered, dipping a fry into ranch dressing.

Bless his heart. Affection filled her chest for Derrick. How did someone so sweet end up in TV production? The greater astonishment was his ability to remain the embodiment of the good-natured romantic lead of a Hallmark movie.

August cleared his throat. "What if there isn't a next season?" Those puppy dog eyes beseeched.

"Nice try, we're already greenlit for a fourth season," she said.

"*We?* You're going to stick around next season?" He bumped her shoulder with his.

It was a good question. This work was project-based. Most field producers jumped to different shows or moved into a story producer or executive producer role after a few seasons under their belt. In the ten years Nora had been in the field, *Haunted Hideaway* was the longest time she'd worked with the same show and crew.

She wagged a fry at him. "*You* can do it next season. It would be a great season opener, and we can do a whole coming home thing where you two walk us down memory lane of where you grew up. The audience will love it."

"I like the idea of *we*—" he winked, "—doing that next season."

"Me too," Derrick agreed.

Nora tried to ignore the warmth in her chest at both brothers' declaration of wanting her to remain with the show.

"Okay, but what if something comes open this season? Like one of the locations that we've already scheduled somehow drops off?" August mused, placing his hand atop Nora's arm and sending her body temperature soaring.

She dug her red nails into her palm, chastising her body for its relentless reaction to his touch.

"Why would they drop off?" Lucy inquired.

"Perhaps, they're no longer haunted because the ghosts figured out their unfinished business and moved on," Derrick offered.

Unfinished business? Nora's eyeroll was an audible scoff. Didn't all dead people have unfinished business? If ghosts were, indeed, real—which they totally were not—and unfinished business was what tethered them to a world between the living and dead, then why weren't there ghosts everywhere?

Nora imagined there wasn't a single dead individual that didn't have regrets. Something they'd wished they'd done before they left. Someone they'd left behind that they didn't want to. A quiet sadness ached inside her.

"What do you say, Nor? If one of the locations scheduled this season drops out, will you be open to Putman House?" August again nudged Nora's shoulder with his.

"As executive producer that would be your call."

"True, but if it does, would you agree to be the field producer for it? I mean, if you're available and not on another assignment, of course." His tone teetered between bashful and hopeful.

She understood why it was important to him to investigate the place. Putman House had no doubt stoked the flames of his passion for ghost hunting. But why was it so important for him to have her as his field producer?

"There are two other field producers working this season, why not them?"

"Because *we're* a good team." No trace of hesitation hid in his answer.

Listen to your gut, baby girl. Grandpa Scott's words whispered in her heart.

Her mouth tugged up. "Only if you stop calling me Nor."

"Deal…Nor." He gave her a lopsided grin. "Had to get one more in for the road."

She kicked his calf with the point of her shoe.

Lucy skimmed the rim of her glass with her finger. "So, what makes you think Putman House is haunted if nobody has ever investigated it?"

"Diana was friends with Melody and had a few strange things happen during sleepovers. She'd heard people talking at night when everyone was asleep. Once she and Melody woke up to the sound of dishes crashing. They ran downstairs with Melody's parents to find the good china smashed in the dining room," Derrick explained, a wistful expression covered his face.

"Who's Diana?" Lucy asked.

Nora glanced at August, who sat quietly.

"Our sister." Derrick tapped his fingers on the surface of the table as if trying to decide how much more to say. "She was three years younger than me and three years older than Gus."

Was? The tiniest of dips in his smile appeared and her heart sank with his drooping grin. Without thinking, she pressed her knee against his, hoping the contact assured him like a hug. His eyes met hers, gratitude seeming to shine in them.

Derrick continued, "She died when she was sixteen."

The table grew silent. Derrick's face didn't hide the twinge of sadness. Every emotion of the loss shaded his bright features. August appeared unchanged. Only Nora knew he wasn't. Those milk chocolate eyes darkened, telegraphing the grief within. A grief she knew all too well. The one hidden behind whatever mask was chosen to evade the feelings that threatened to consume everything.

Lucy shifted in her seat. The nibble of the corner of her mouth signaled to Nora the words ready to come from the young production assistant. The dreaded "I'm sorry for your loss" comment. That polite statement was akin to a knife plunged into the grieving's heart. A knife left for them to pull out of themselves.

Nora rubbed against the twinge in her heart. The memory of mournful faces saying "I'm sorry for your loss" as she stood beside Grandpa Scott in her black velvet dress blurred her vision. They were waiting for her to say, "Thank you" or "It's okay." The expectation was for her to acknowledge the sentiment. It was about their need to say something for themselves, not her. To feel as if they'd done something to comfort a six-year-old that had lost everything. What comfort are words when your entire world is shredded to pieces? When you are thrusted into a new reality where *they* were gone, and *never* coming back?

She told herself that others meant well. Everyone means well, but it doesn't change what happened. Just as whatever textbook sentiment about loss Lucy wanted to say won't comfort August or Derrick because it's not about them. It was about Lucy's needs.

As Lucy opened her mouth, Nora drained her drink, and announced, "You owe me a drink, August!"

"I knew it!" Benji cheered from the table beside them. "She's still a skeptic. Dusty, you owe me a foot rub!"

"I really thought he had her at this location." Dusty sighed with resignation.

"Not my mulish Nora!" Benji raised his drink and toasted her. "Sorry, Gus."

"Ha!" August hummed. That glint of sadness that had darkened his eyes faded back to his natural milk chocolate.

"I'm not mulish," Nora grumbled, sliding out of the chair.

August stood. "If only Ms. Ruby was into history professors turned paranormal investigators." He wagged a finger at Derrick before turning to Nora. "One day you'll be buying me that drink." He placed his palm at the small of her back and steered her toward the bar.

She both stiffened and melted with his touch. "Keep dreaming, August."

"I do have that overactive imagination of mine to help me be patient for the day I finally win you over."

CHAPTER 6

Maybe it was the Mead

The alcohol danced in her bloodstream as they left Superstition, the soft glow of streetlights illuminating their path. Benji and Dusty lingered behind, no doubt ready to slink down a side street for a quick make out session against an unsuspecting building. They were the first to leave the bar. Derrick remained behind to ensure the rest of the crew got back. Also, he was in a deep discussion with one of the bartenders on the mead-making process.

"So, Derrick got a little flustered when you mentioned Melody Putman. Did they date or something?" She was tipsy enough to ask one of the many questions currently living on her tongue.

August ran his fingers through his dark hair.

Not for the first time, Nora wondered about the texture of his hair. Was it soft and silky or coarse and rough? What would it be like to curl her fingers into those thick strands and give a gentle tug?

"No." A silent laugh crinkled around his eyes. "But I

suspect he's had a crush on her since they were teens. Derrick never acted on it, though. Melody is three years younger, so I imagine my 'always do the right thing' brother thought it wasn't appropriate."

"Why not now? Three years isn't a big difference in your thirties." She bit the inside of her cheek trying not to think about how there were only three years difference between she and August. *He's your boss,* she reminded herself sinking her teeth just a little harder.

"Yeah… Knowing Derrick he's still telling himself it's somehow inappropriate or he's not right for her. There's likely a million reasons pulling him between what he wants and what he thinks is best."

"Poor Derrick," she sighed.

"It's a delicate dance."

She tilted her head. "What is?"

"Allowing for that right time to make your move and missing your chance."

Nora's breath stuttered. Maybe it was the mead loosening her resolve, but in that instant, she wondered what it would be like to kiss him. To raise to her tiptoes and press her lips to his. Did the sweet taste of the blueberry mead linger on his lips? Would the raspberry taste still in her mouth blend with his, their kisses an explosion of berries?

She looked up at the velvety black sky, the moon's glow covered in a haze of passing clouds. Rubbing her hands against her arms, the coziness of her sweater dress heated from the friction, she turned right off downtown's main drag.

"Cold?" he asked. "You should have worn a jacket."

"It wasn't this cold when we left and I—"

The heaviness of his coat wrapped around her, stopping her words.

"Can't have you getting hypothermia."

"But we can risk *you* getting it?" Nora made no movement to relinquish the coat. Instead, she snuggled into it, cocooned in his woodsy summer scent.

"Well, that's why you have two Chandler brothers. There's a spare if you lose one."

The joke dropped like an emotional atom bomb. There'd only been one Chandler sister and now there was none. The other questions tapping from behind her lips wanted to come out in the wreckage of that comment. To ask all the questions about Diana. She was curious, but more than anyone, she understood the toll questions took on the asked.

"It blows my mind that Phoenix is ninety minutes away and it is forty degrees warmer there than here," she said in the most awkward game of small talk ever played.

"You can ask," he murmured.

She gnawed her lower lip. How did he see into her thoughts? It frustrated and delighted her. Not since Grandpa Scott had someone been so in tune with her. Grandpa Scott had always had the ability to assess what Nora was thinking with a single glance or even without looking at all. He'd hear the tone of her steps and just know what emotions whirled within her. "Baby girl, that's some unhappy clumping," he'd said the day she'd come home from school after not winning the class president election.

"I don't want to be rude."

"That's a first." He nudged her with his shoulder. "Just ask."

"How'd Diana die?" The delicious song of her shoes clacking against the sidewalk soured in her ears, knowing she asked one of the questions she hated to be asked.

"Cancer. She'd battled it on and off since she was ten."

"She was sixteen."

He nodded.

"You were thirteen."

He nodded again.

"You started hunting ghosts when you were thirteen." Her footsteps ceased and so did his.

Looking behind them Nora didn't see Benji and Dusty. It was just them among the darkened brick buildings lining the street.

"Yeah," he rocked on his heels. "I started at our house. When Diana was alive, she loved pranking me. She'd hide my sneakers around the house or unmake my bed after I made it. A few days after she died, I found my bed unmade, and I thought it was her. That she was still there. I was convinced and told my parents that Diana was still in the house."

"How did your parents react?"

"Mom and Dad were upset. They thought I was having a breakdown or something."

"Well, your sister had died. You were entitled to a breakdown," she offered.

"Yeah." A thoughtful, yet sad smile dimmed his face. "They made me see a counselor. It made me feel like I was… well, that something was wrong with me. Derrick was a freshman in college, and he'd come back from Syracuse where he was studying. I told him, and he believed me. He bought me a book about ghosts." He looked down at his sneakers and then back to her. "I guess he thought he was helping channel my grief or something."

"Little did he know it would end up with a hit TV show and millions of fans," she said, her mouth lifted into a small grin.

"Yup." He smiled. "So, yes, I hunt ghosts because of Diana."

"Are you still searching for her?"

"No—" he shook his head "—I think whatever her unfinished business was, it was completed after she unmade my bed. Maybe it was to let me know that I was loved and that she'd still be my big sister even if she wasn't there. I don't know, but there were no more Diana sightings after that day."

Nora's heart both swelled and twinged with pain. The idea of Diana coming back just to give her little brother a final message, a last "I love you," in the prankster language they'd spoken when she was alive filled her with both tearful happiness and sadness. The sadness of knowing that Diana didn't come back. That it was likely just the forgetful mind-fuck of grief. In the haze of sorrow, it was easy to believe something *was*, what it wasn't. In all likelihood, it was just a sad little boy who forgot to make his bed.

The delusion was a comfort to August, though. And it was probably one to Derrick, who both believed in and fostered his little brother's belief. Comfort was such a precious gift. Envy pricked in Nora's eyes. The idea of a message from a lost loved one, even a made up one, was the sweetest of gifts. One she'd not have.

"Hey," August said, taking her arm and pulling her to a stop. His right hand gently dashed away a stray tear.

Nora blinked, unaware that she'd been crying.

"What's wrong?"

"I'm fine," she choked, starting to walk again.

"Are you?"

"It's…" The words festered in her throat. There'd been enough sessions with her therapist over the years to know this was only a little about August losing his sister and a lot more about her own loss.

"Nora, what is it?" His voice was as warm as his jacket.

It was reminiscent of being tucked safely in bed where nothing could hurt you. Even the memories that clawed to come out seemed as if they couldn't hurt her. At least, the way he said her name made her want to believe that.

"My parents died," she confessed. It shouldn't feel like a

confession, but it did. As if she stood in front of a judge pleading her innocence or guilt, knowing that the crime of her parents being gone somehow condemned her.

"When?"

"When I was six. My grandpa, my dad's dad, raised me after that."

August nodded. "I should have known. You've never mentioned them. You've only ever talked about Grandpa Scott and his chicken farm."

Again, there was more nodding. It was the easiest thing to do with these types of conversations. The ones where they both understood each other's grief but still tiptoed around it like an emotional mine field ready to go off at any misstep.

Nora closed her eyes for a moment, going back to that day. Her little hand in his big one as he walked her into the farmhouse. The hummingbird wallpaper in the entryway. The yellow curtains in the kitchen. The butterfly bedspread he'd bought for her new bed in her new room in her new house. The pain in her tummy as he showed her these things, telling her this was her home now. That first night when she woke up in the middle of the night crying for her mommy and then the truth that stole away her tears as it hissed, "She's gone. He's gone. They're gone."

"How did they—"

"Car accident," she whispered.

"Is Grandpa Scott still around?"

She shook her head. "He died ten years ago."

The white glow of solar lights outlining the hotel's front entrance came into sight. Benji and Dusty's footsteps grew closer.

"I'd like to hear about them, and your grandpa, if you'd like to share them with me." His words were tentative but coated in tenderness.

What could she say? The memories of her mom and dad were like faded pictures in a photo album.

Nora rubbed the pads of her fingers over the scratched face of her watch. Its tightness around her wrist anchored her. Reaching the entrance, the door *whooshed* open, blasting hot air at them. All the words remained locked within her.

"I'd like to share Diana with you too," he offered, sincerity shined in his warm gaze.

"Share?"

"They're not gone, not completely, if we talk about them. I know Derrick and I haven't talked about Diana before with the crew, but we talk about her with each other and our parents."

"Why hadn't you shared?" As soon as she asked, she knew why. People would do the same math that she'd done, knowing his ghost hunting started with Diana. "Never mind. I understand."

"Some people may distort that story, making it mean something else about Derrick, Diana, and me. I don't care what people think of me, but I do care about what they think about the people I love. My sister is too special to just be a..."

"Ghost story," she finished his words.

He nodded.

"That's why you are so passionate about telling the complete story and not just sensationalizing the macabre."

All the pieces clicked into place. The amount of research both brothers put into each location. The thoughtful approach they took to ensure locations were portrayed holistically with all aspects of what made the place special and not just the ghoulish stories of what goes bump in the night. While they were ghost hunters, they weren't pushing ghost stories, but the entire story of the location and the people that had, and may still be, inhabiting each place.

"Thank you for sharing Diana with me," she said with a grateful smile.

"Thank you for sharing your parents and Grandpa Scott with me." His smile matched hers. "I'd like to share more, and I'd like to be someone you can share things with."

"Like your coat?" She slipped it off, handing it to him.

"To start." He took it, their fingers brushing.

Maybe it was the blast of heat thawing her. Maybe it was her still-buzzing blood tipsy from the mead. Maybe it was the raw emotions that twisted within her. Whatever it was, Nora would hold herself responsible in the morning. Raising her hand to his hair, she brushed her fingers through it. The silken strands hushed all the warning bells going off in her.

"Goodnight, August," she breathed, pulling her hand back down.

"Goodnight, Nora," he murmured, brushing a strand of her hair behind her ear. Licking his lips, his gaze remained transfixed on her.

They'd said goodnight. Her feet should turn and walk across the lobby, up the stairs to the fourth floor, and down the hall to her room. Instead, she remained as if glued to this spot. Glued to him. The desire to kiss him radiated within her. To slide her hands up his muscular body and into his hair, drawing him into a deep kiss. To feel the slickness of his tongue against hers.

"Goodnight you two!" Dusty called, breaking the spell.

Blinking out of the lusty haze that had held her prisoner for the last few minutes, she stepped three steps back. "Goodnight." She pivoted to Benji and Dusty, who stood at the elevator, grinning. "Goodnight." Flustered, she turned back to August. "Goodnight."

A smile lit his face. "Goodnight, Nora."

CHAPTER 7

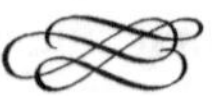

When it Pours Maple Syrup

Mae's brows waggled seductively. "So, you fingered him?"

Nora spat out her tea. "Just his hair!"

Mae's eyes twinkled with self-congratulation. The perverse joy she got out of embarrassing Nora always lit her face with unbridled delight.

"Why do I tell you things!" Nora grumbled, grabbing napkins to clean up her mess. *God, another spit take!*

"Because I'm your sister from another mister. You adore me."

"I do," she sighed, returning to the video chat. Nora had called while she was packing up before heading to breakfast and then to the airport.

Brazil was four hours ahead of Arizona. Mae currently sat on the balcony of the resort she was staying in. A soft blue sky outlined her lean figure. Nora would never get over how stunning Mae was. Grandpa Scott always said that truly beautiful people radiated, and she was radiant.

"You know relationships between colleagues happen *all* the time on sets." Mae said dramatically.

"I'm aware."

With the demanding schedules, relationships and hookups were ever present on set. Nora watched Mae hook up with and semi-seriously date three different women and one man from sets they'd worked on over the last ten years. While other industries frowned upon or made employees declare relationships with HR, in the contract-based TV production world it was the Wild West.

"He's not just a colleague. He's my boss," Nora added, crumbling her napkin and tossing it into the trash.

"Which is hot. Maybe you can play *naughty* field producer and demanding executive producer," Mae purred. "Although, I think you'd be more into being the spanker rather than the spanked. Do you think he'd be into spanking?"

"Mae!" Nora's high-pitched squawk hit decibels that only dogs could hear.

"You and your Midwest hangups," Mae teased.

"You and your former Catholic school rebellious ways," Nora countered.

"If Father O'Brien could see me now." Pride danced on her pink glossy lips.

"I'm surprised Grandma Hoang hasn't sent him a copy of the quarterly Hoang Family Newsletter highlighting all your escapades."

Mae beamed at the mention of the barely five-foot spitfire that was her adopted grandmother. Like Nora, she had been raised by a loving grandparent. However, Mae hadn't lost her parents in a car accident. Her conservative parents had thrown her away. In Nora's mind, there was no other way to describe what had happened. As a teenager Mae had experienced severe depression from denying who she truly was.

At eighteen and three months before her high school graduation, she came out to her parents as trans. It didn't go well. Mae spent several nights sleeping on friends' couches until Ms. Hoang, whom everyone called Grandma, showed up. The choir director at the church Mae had attended since she was five enveloped her in a hug telling her, "You are who you were always meant to be…my lovely girl."

The eighty-three-year-old was Mae's biggest supporter. She'd held Mae's hand through every step of her life over the last fourteen years. Paid for her degree at USC. Marched at L.A. Pride with a *Number One Grandma* T-shirt. Made all of Mae's favorite foods while she recovered from gender affirmation surgery.

While Nora questioned Mae's parents' right to be mourned for, she understood Mae carried a heavy grief for the loss of that relationship. There were different textures to each woman's grief, but at the end of the day, pain was pain. Their pain had bonded them, but their love for one another cemented that bond.

"I'm sure Grandma Hoang would agree with me that you need to hop on that sexy piece of man meat," Mae said, pulling her purple hair into a messy bun.

Nora frowned. "August is my boss!"

"Excuses."

"Mae, I don't like to mix work and personal. It gets messy."

"We mixed."

"That's different. We met when I was a young, impressionable production assistant before I knew better. Also, you gave me no choice. You were all like 'We're best friends now' and made me go to *Buffy the Vampire Slayer* trivia nights with you."

"Like a wild horse, you do enjoy a strong hand." Mae's

expression grew wicked. "Perhaps I should tell August to get all alpha male on you."

The answering middle finger was completely justified. At least in Nora's mind.

"Well, if you're going to *not* get on that delicious man, perhaps you get on a plane and join me. We can finally put the plural on *Girl on the Run*."

Nora knew the invite was coming. Very few calls, texts, face-to-face encounters, or social media exchanges didn't include a moment where Mae asked, blackmailed, or flat-out threatened Nora to join her. For the last two years, in between lucrative jobs shooting commercials, Mae traveled the world, documenting it on her popular YouTube channel *Girl on the Run*.

"Tempting, but I have a contract for two more episodes this season," Nora said.

Mae shook her head. Each shake telegraphed the conversation they'd had a million times. *Why are you waiting, Nora? Take a chance, Nora. Live a little, Nora.*

"Mae, I've got to go. Dusty's knocking. We're having breakfast, and then he's taking me to the airport. Love ya." She blew a kiss.

Mae pretended to catch it and tossed one back. "Alright. I'll send my check-in when I arrive in Argentina. Love you!"

Turning off the tablet, Nora rose and shuffled in her bare feet to the door. "You're fifteen minutes ear…" Her words stopped at the sight of August.

God, what this man did to casual wear was criminal. A grey zip-up hoodie hung loose over his trademark fitted black T-shirt that clung to his musculature the way Nora held onto a pair of Jimmy Choos during a sale. Dark denim jeans molded to his muscular legs. His big smile popped beneath the brim of his blue Buffalo Sabres cap.

"Dusty is taking a later flight, so he and Benji have more

time together. I volunteered to take you for breakfast and then the airport," he said.

"It's a ninety-minute drive."

August shrugged.

"That's a three hour round trip and then you have to head out to the next location. I can rent a car or…"

That smile of his told her he would not relent.

"Fine," she sighed with all the contempt of a surly teenager.

"Are you ready now or…" His gaze dropped to her bare feet. "…did you want me to come back in fifteen minutes?"

It shouldn't feel as if she'd answered the door in slinky jammies, but it did despite the jeans and blouse she wore. Heat crawled up her spine as he stared at her feet.

Thank God I got a pedicure last week. "I'll meet you in the lobby in fifteen," she said, wiggling her red painted toes.

He coughed and moved his gaze back to her face. "Great. I've got a perfect spot for breakfast."

The small café a few miles outside of town had fifteen different types of waffles. Nora didn't often have joy pulsate through her, but it did as she perused the menu. The corner booth they sat in had a tiny shelf with six different types of syrups to drizzle over the waffles. Nora thought she'd died and gone to waffle heaven.

"I can't decide." How was one supposed to choose between peanut butter, chocolate hazelnut, or maple bacon waffles? It was like choosing between three equally cute pairs of shoes. She wanted them all.

"I have an idea." August leaned over with a daring smile. "Why don't we each choose two kinds and share."

"That's so much food."

"Whatever we don't eat we can take to go."

We? Nora's pulse thrummed. The only time she was a "we" was with Mae or Grandpa Scott. It was like a logical angel on one shoulder wagged its finger, saying "not for you, Nora," while a sassy devil that looked a lot like Mae lounged on her other shoulder sipping a skinny margarita purring "go for it." Nora's brain and heart—okay, her lady bits—were in a constant state of tug-of-war around August.

"I'm thinking maple bacon and the berry explosion. You?"

Nora shifted in her seat. "Peanut butter and chocolate hazelnut." Guess she was agreeing to be a "we" for breakfast —but *only* for breakfast. No doubt the Mae devil was fist pumping the air.

They ordered their smorgasbord, her tea, and his coffee and orange juice. A companionable silence settled around them as they sat sipping from their brown ceramic mugs. Both their gazes strolled around the busy café. Servers hustled between tables filled with chatting customers.

Nora had been out with August before but never alone. Not like this, or like last night. The feel of his silky hair still lingered on her fingers, and she longed to be wrapped snugly in his coat again. *He's your boss. He's not for you. You're not for him.* God, that angel was annoying even her. She knew all this, but for some reason her obstinate body wasn't getting the message.

"Why waffles after the last day of shooting?" August asked, stirring cream into his coffee.

"To celebrate the accomplishment."

"Have waffles always been celebratory food?"

Nora leaned back, pressing against the worn brown pleather of the booth. "That and ice cream."

"Perhaps we should have gotten our waffle à la mode."

"That's a little decadent for eight a.m."

"Celebrations should always be a little decadent." His

brown eyes sparkled, punctuating his big smile. He'd taken his cap off once they sat inside. It was something she'd noticed him doing over the last two years. Anytime he wore a hat if he came inside someone's home or sat to eat, he'd take it off.

August's words brought happy memories. A smile stretched across her face. "Grandpa Scott used to say something similar. He'd make waffles for breakfast when we were celebrating something. On my birthday, he'd put a scoop of vanilla ice cream on them. I'd say it was too much, and he'd say 'baby girl, there's no such thing as too much when we're happy,'" she deepened her voice to emulate his twangy gruff accent.

August lifted the mug to his lips, his eyes smiling over its brim. "Grandpa Scott was a smart man."

"He was." Her tone was a little wistful. "He had all these fun grandpaisms that he'd spout."

"Like what?"

"If I said, 'We need to clean this up' or something like that he'd say, 'We?! You got a frog in your pocket?'" she continued in a spot-on impression of her grandpa.

He laughed.

The sound delighted Nora. Beaming she went on, "I remember when a teacher in high school told me to be more realistic about having a career in TV production, Grandpa said 'Baby girl, the only one that can make your dream unrealistic is the good Lord and you yourself, and last time I checked God didn't work at Lakeside High School."

"He really believed in you." August leaned back. "I think my parents were more in the *realistic* camp. They wanted me to consider being a nurse like my mom or an accountant like my dad. It took them sometime, but they got there."

"As they should! You're so talented." How sad that his parents had tried to dissuade him from his chosen path.

"You think I'm talented?" His brow cocked.

She flung her napkin at him. "Oh, shut up. Your obsession with ghosts aside, I can appreciate your talent for telling a compelling story."

Taking her napkin, he wiped his lips. The movement somehow felt intimate, as if her lips, which once touched the napkin, brushed against his. Liquid heat unfurled low in her abdomen at the daydream of her lips coasting along his. The imagined sting of her nipped kisses coaxing him open. The thirst to drink up his coffee-infused kisses pulsed within her.

Stop! Clearing her throat, Nora crossed her legs under the table.

"That means a lot to me. You're so good at what you do. Derrick and I count our blessings you came to work with us and that you stay. I know there are other shows that have been trying to get you to work with them." He grinned.

Ghost shows. The thought sighed through her.

"So, Grandpa Scott called you baby girl?" His gaze swept over her. "I like that."

"You don't get to call me that." She pointed at him. A soft involuntary chuckle escaped her.

"But it's such a good pet name. Even better than the name I'm not allowed to call you."

"We don't need pet names." she *tsked*.

"But you call me August when everyone else calls me Gus."

She sipped her tea. "August is your name, remember?"

He smirked.

"Besides Gus, which I refuse to call you, did you have other nicknames?"

"My mom calls me Sonny Boy."

She shook with laughter.

"I know! I'm thirty-three and she coos 'Sonny Boy' whenever she sees me."

The image of a bemused August being doted on by his mother filled her with happiness and longing. Dr. Unaka would remind her that she was projecting again. She knew that. It was an erratic pain that flared up for no rhyme or reason. She wasn't sure if it was missing Grandpa Scott's deep raspy voice calling her baby girl or that she had no memory of what her mother sounded like cooing a pet name to her.

"Hey." August's warm palm rested on hers. "What were you thinking?"

Nora gnawed on her lower lip. Was she just that transparent or did he have some secret superpower?

"I was wondering if my mother had a special nickname for me." Was she really telling him this? She couldn't blame last night's mead.

"What memories do you have of them?"

She exhaled a heavy breath. "So few. I'm not sure which are real or which are stories from Grandpa Scott."

Though that wasn't entirely true. She could point to one particular memory, knowing it belonged solely to her. The vivid image like a waking nightmare in the memory corridors of her heart. But she didn't talk about *that* memory. Not with Mae. Not with Dr. Unaka. Not even with Grandpa Scott when he'd been alive.

"I get it—" he offered a soft smile "—I was thirteen when Diana died, so I have a whole scrapbook of memories, but I can understand that sensation. My parents, Derrick, and I will share memories that sometimes get jumbled, and I'm not sure if I was actually there or if I've just heard the story so many times that it feels like that." His hand squeezed hers.

Every tense muscle in her body eased with his touch, but her head started packing its bags to run away. This relationship—*or whatever this was*— was a cocktail of confusion.

Annoyance. Lusty inappropriate thoughts. Connection. Fear. So much swirled around their interactions. She'd not pretend she didn't feel something for him, especially in moments like this when he looked at her with so much understanding.

"Waffle time!" the server chirped, depositing their food on the table.

They organized the plates between them. After a fierce debate over which syrups to pair with which waffles, they dug in. He insisted on pecan syrup with the maple bacon waffle.

"How is it?" he asked after her first bite.

The sweet-salty taste exploded in her mouth. She did not want to give him satisfaction that he had been right about the pairing. "It's okay," she offered.

"Sure," he said, unconvinced. He forked a piece of the mixed berry waffle that they'd actually agreed on pairing with traditional maple syrup. "Hmmm." He made a throaty sound of pleasure.

Nora pressed her thighs tight, fighting that clenching in her core at the noises he made. She may need to splash cold water on her undercarriage before she rode in a car with him for the next ninety minutes. She prayed he'd say or do something annoying to quell her lustiness. Otherwise, it was going to be a *long* ride to Phoenix.

Also, she was not going to dwell on how she referred to her vagina as her undercarriage. Those grandpaisms were too engrained in her.

"Try this one," he said, holding out his fork.

She reached across the table with her fork and speared a piece for herself. She'd share food with the man but not eat from his fork. Boundaries had to be drawn. Granted, she'd blurred those lines with last night's running of her fingers through his hair and the far too personal conversations they'd had since, but she could reassert them. They were colleagues. Nothing more.

Smirking, he continued eating.

Both their phones pinged to life, and they simultaneously reached into their pockets. It was an alert that she'd set for one of the locations they'd be filming at. Scrolling through the alert, her mouth dropped open.

"It's burned down," August said, shocked. "Nobody was hurt, but it's gone…"

Nora looked up from her phone. The abandoned hospital they were supposed to film at in May, Nora's next episode with the show, had burned down. Meaning there was no location. Meaning…

August grinned like the fucking cat that got the canary. "Putman House."

CHAPTER 8

Just a House?

The Victorian mansion turned bed and breakfast sat on four acres about a mile outside of the village of Wyoming. After confirming that the original filming location had met its untimely end and nobody was hurt, Nora and August spoke with Derrick. The idea of investigating Putman House brought out a giddiness in both brothers. It made Nora think of her own girlish excitement on Christmas Eve. Only instead of gifts, August and Derrick were preparing to investigate their dream location. It was hard to fight the smile kicking across her face at each man's lit expression as they discussed Putman House.

That same smile curled her lips as Nora eased down Putman House's gravel driveway. As field producer, she'd visit the location prior to production to map out both primary and secondary filming locations logistics and go over things with the property's owners and caretakers.

Her phone pinged with a text from August, *Welcome to Western New York*. Smiling, she replied.

Nora: Just arrived at Putman House. Jealous?

August: Immensely. *Pouting Face Emoji.*

Nora: I also am drinking Tim Horton's.

August: Cruel woman!

A laugh that sounded far too much like a giggle escaped her. She frowned at herself in the mirror muttering, "Really, Nora?"

Nora: I'm going in to meet Melody.

August: Tell her I said hello, but tell her Derrick says *hello* and put extra suggestive emphasis on it.

Nora: Alright, every aunt from a Regency Romance, enough of your matchmaking. Leave your poor brother alone. I'll check in later.

"Check in later?" Nora lowered her head to the steering wheel. What was she doing?

She slid her phone into her messenger bag and got out of the car. Early morning dew filled her lungs as she surveyed the property. A mixture of pine, maple, and birch trees lined the front. Pink rose bushes outlined the large porch decorated with blue-cushioned wicker furniture. Lacey curtains danced in the windows that overlooked the front yard. The house was a strange combo of haunted romance.

It would be perfect to tell the story of William Putman, overcome with grief, killing his wife Elizabeth after the death of their young son. Nora could already picture the opening shot of the house with Derrick's background narration about the story of love gone wrong.

Her black wedge heels clacked against the cobblestone walkway as she walked toward the front porch. The screen door creaked open and a tall man with brown hair, wisps of silver at his temples, appeared in a black suit straight out of an episode of *The Gilded Age.*

"Good morning," Nora said.

"Good morning, miss."

Miss? His diction was so formal. Perhaps that was part of the aesthetic that Melody Putman was going for with her bed and breakfast. It made sense, with the popularity of so many costume dramas like *Bridgerton* and *Downton Abbey.* Hell, Mae had dragged her to a Jane Austen themed vacation rental in Santa Barbara last year.

"I'm Nora Scott. I'm here to meet with Melody."

He nodded. "Oh, yes. Ms. Scott. Ms. Putman is expecting you. I'll direct you."

"You can call me Nora." The formalness of his speech made her rethink the simple black sheath dress and denim jacket she wore. The mid-April day had been surprisingly warm for Western New York.

His forehead puckered as if considering something. "I am Gideon Malone. You may call me Gideon."

Gideon held the door open for her. Nora walked past him. A wisp of cool air kissed her skin, blooming gooseflesh. Ignoring the slight shiver, she stepped into the foyer. Light flooded every corner of the room, leaving no shadows. A delicate fragrance wafted around the room from a vase of white tulips atop a table tucked in the corner. The pale blue painted walls were reminiscent of a perfect summer day's sky.

"This is lovely." Nora smiled.

"This is just the foyer." An almost prideful expression filled Gideon's features.

"How long have you worked here?" Nora asked, following Gideon down a long hallway that snaked along the stairs. August had told Nora that Melody had bought the place from her parents last year and after some renovations opened it in the fall as a bed and breakfast.

"Since the beginning."

"It's great that Melody got a team so quickly. Are you the front desk clerk?"

"Butler," he said with a regal wave of his hand.

"Fancy."

"Indeed," he drawled.

It was hard for Nora to picture a butler roaming around here. It seemed stuffy compared to the floral scented and light draped house. Outside of butlers from TV, she couldn't imagine what Gideon's butlery duties were.

"What exactly does a butler do…" A large thud upstairs caused Nora to jerk. Her head tipped up, peering at the ceiling as if the reason for the noise would appear in the intricate hummingbird shaped crown molding design. "What was that?"

"Guests." Frowning, Gideon let out an exasperated breath. "If you'll excuse me, I'll go check on them. Ms. Putman's office is in there." He pointed to the French doors at the end of the hall. "Just knock and announce yourself. She's expecting you."

"Thank you." Nora turned and headed toward Melody's office.

Through the glass doors she could see Melody sitting at her computer. Sunlight streamed in from the window haloing around her dark curls. No wonder Derrick blushed at the mere mention of Melody. An ethereal aura radiated from her.

"Ms. Putman." Nora knocked as she opened the door. Now she was the one being formal. "I'm Nora Scott."

A giant smile erupted on Melody's pretty face. "Oh, you're August's Nora."

"His field producer," she corrected, stepping into the room fully.

Melody rose and reached out her hand. "Delighted to meet you."

The scent of vanilla and cinnamon danced around

Melody. A lavender dress clung to her soft curves, contrasting with her sun-kissed skin.

"Hope you didn't have trouble finding my office." She gestured for Nora to sit in one of the two Windsor chairs in front of her desk.

"Gideon showed me."

Melody's amber eyes widened. "You met Gideon?"

"He greeted me at the door." Nora's forehead wrinkled. "Is there a problem?"

Shaking her head, Melody sat back in her seat. "Nope. Just didn't realize he was working today."

"Do you have many people working for you?"

"Just a few, but Gideon mainly works overnights." Batting at the air, Melody shifted in her seat. "August speaks highly of you."

"He's great to work with." Nora crossed her legs. "So is Derrick."

Nora wasn't positive, but she thought Melody's smile got just a little brighter at the mention of Derrick. Maybe for this location she'd help August in his attempts to wingman his brother rather than *tsking* him from the sidelines.

Melody shared the story of Putman House with Nora. It wasn't anything Nora didn't already know from the Chandler brothers. There'd been lots of strange things that happened to Melody as a kid growing up in the house. Voices that would be heard when she was the only one home. Doors slamming. Footsteps upstairs when everyone was downstairs. Dishes or trinkets falling off shelves.

"Anything else?" Nora asked, jotting notes on her tablet.

Melody took a deep breath, fiddling with the silver bangle bracelet on her wrist. "This one time we heard yelling and things being thrown. Diana was sleeping over. We got up to investigate, but my bedroom door wouldn't open. We banged and called. My parents' room was down the hall, and I could hear them banging on their door as well."

An icy shiver ripped up Nora's spine. "You were stuck?"

"Not long. Once the noise quieted, our doors opened. When we stepped into the hall my parents were at their door, just as shocked as us. We went downstairs to find my grandma's good china smashed in the dining room."

"Had anything like that happened before?" Every muscle in Nora's body wound tighter. A painful ache knotted in her stomach at the thought of doors that wouldn't open and hands banging to get out.

The image shook away, she grasped for a reasonable explanation. Melody Putman didn't seem like the type to make up stories to sensationalize things. Over the years working with ghost hunting shows, there'd certainly been many people that did that in hopes of getting the notoriety of being on TV.

"There were a few times doors wouldn't open, but it never lasted long. It always seemed to correspond with some loud commotion. I like to think it was the ghosts keeping us safe while one of them was having a tantrum."

Nora huffed a soft laugh.

"You're a skeptic." Melody's right brow ticked up.

"That I am."

"No wonder August likes you so much. He loves a challenge," Melody laughed.

God, the desire to ask more buzzed inside Nora. What did that mean? Like, did he like her or *like* her? Was the appeal winning her over or did he enjoy being around people that challenged him? *Stop mentally sputtering about your hot boss!*

Clearing her throat, she changed the subject. "Are those your mom and dad?" Nora pointed to a picture of a beautiful woman with long grey dusted curls and a tall blue-eyed man with silver-streaked auburn hair.

Twisting in her seat, Melody picked up the silver framed photo. "Yup. They live in Ocala, Florida. Mom was an attorney, and dad was a teacher. They retired last year."

"How do they feel about you turning Putman House into an inn?"

"They're concerned, but what parents aren't?" Melody set the frame down. "I'm sure yours worry about you traveling the country for your job. You know how parents are."

The sting of the words shot through Nora. "How about a tour?" She stood, smoothing down her dress.

"Sure." Melody popped up. Twisting, she grabbed a long white cane from the corner.

"Wha…" She stopped herself before she said something disrespectful.

"It's okay." Melody's soft laugh eased Nora's tension. "I'm legally blind. I have my central vision but no peripheral. The cane ensures I don't run into or trip over anything."

"Have you been…" Nora shifted foot-to-foot. How indelicate was she being?

Melody's laugh deepened. "It's all good. I'm usually someone's first experience with a legally blind person. I have an eye condition called retinitis pigmentosa. I was diagnosed when I was eight. I think that's why Diana and I were such good friends. I was the only legally blind kid in our class, and she was the girl with cancer. We were both outsiders and often underestimated," she explained, leading them out of the office and down the hall.

"Did you become friends after she was diagnosed with cancer?"

"No, before. Diana was one of the only kids that treated me like everyone else. Even before the cancer, we were friends. She had this big heart. I remember her coming up to me in homeroom pointing at my Sailor Moon T-shirt and saying, 'I'm totally Sailor Jupiter.' Then she declared we'd be best friends."

Nora's lips lifted into a big smile. "My best friend Mae did something similar."

"I don't think I've ever had as good of a best friend as Diana." Melody stopped at the stairs, a wistful expression etched on her face.

"She sounds so special."

"She was. Derrick and August were—*are*—just like her. Whenever I see them, it's like no time has passed."

"What were they like as kids?" Nora couldn't help herself.

"August was ever the little brother, pestering Diana and me with a million questions, but he always had a big smile on his face. Derrick…" A soft crimson kissed her cheeks, "…he was quiet and sweet but protective of his siblings. Even of me. Guess I was his little sister by proxy. When I was a freshman and Derrick was a senior, he once beat up a ninth grader who was picking on me in PE because I used a ball with a beeping noise in it, so I could hear it and play basketball with everyone else."

"Derrick beat someone up?" Nora's mouth dropped open.

"Yup."

It was decided. She'd team up with August to facilitate this coupling. That story was too adorable. Clearly, Derrick had pined for Melody for far too long. This was like romance novel-level shit. Mae would swoon when Nora told her this story later.

They walked through the house. Nora snapped pictures and made notes for potential shots and people to interview. She'd meet with Derrick and August later in the week via video conference to formalize a plan. The brothers were currently shooting at a former school in Utah.

Putman House was impressive. Its main floor featured a

large sitting room for guests, a formal dining room, a kitchen, a day room, and Melody's office. Three bedrooms and a library made up the second floor. More bedrooms and a former nursery that Melody converted into a common area for guests dominated the third floor. A narrow set of stairs—which Nora did not appreciate—led to a large attic that spanned the entire top floor.

Putman House was perfect. With its blend of antiquity and modern luxuries like WiFi enabled flatscreens hung opposite four-poster beds it was ideal for a girls' weekend or romantic getaway. Melody, who lived in a carriage house apartment on the property, had overseen every aspect of renovations to convert her childhood home to the quintessential sweetly chic country inn.

No wonder August loves this place. Contentment sighed through Nora. She suspected it wasn't just about the alleged ghosts, but the essence that wafted through Putman House that intrigued August and Derrick. At that moment, she was equally enamored with this place as the Chandler Brothers. Something about Putman House felt as if Nora slipped on an old favorite sweater that had almost been forgotten about in the back of a closet.

"Since we'll be closed to guests, there will be space for your crew to stay onsite during the shoot. There are few hotel options around here unless you drive to Batavia. I'm assuming you want to be close to Putman House for shooting," Melody offered.

Nora looked around, taking in the landscape paintings dotting the robin's egg blue walls. Putman House was lovely and had more character than the generic hotels the crew typically stayed in, but some may appreciate the distance. With the long hours on set, it was nice to have a break from the location. Not to mention there were some in the crew that subscribed to the belief that ghosts are real and may not enjoy sleeping at an allegedly haunted inn, no matter how cute its vibe.

"I'll take that into consideration. Thank you," Nora said, following her down the hall.

Walking along the second-floor hallway, Melody stopped in front of the library as her phone went off. Slipping it from her dress pocket, she frowned. "I have to take this. Do you mind?"

"Not at all. I'll check out the library." Nora grinned.

Melody shuffled down the hall. "Melody Putman," she said, answering the phone.

Nora ducked into the library. Early afternoon sunshine illuminated the room. The faint smell of lavender greeted her. A plush leather couch sat across from a fireplace. Shelves lined with books filled much of the wall real estate except for some landscape paintings in ornate gold frames. It was almost out of central casting for post-dinner brandy and cigars in a period drama.

"This will be perfect for Derrick to interview Melody," Nora mused, tapping the note into her tablet.

"Who's interviewing Melody?" A quiet voice startled Nora.

Spinning on her heels, Nora placed her hand on her heart. A woman in a pink silk robe over a long white night-gown stood at the window. Her long blonde hair pulled back in a loose braid, wayward tresses spilling out. Nora shook her head, swearing the woman hadn't been there a moment ago.

She blinked. "Excuse me?"

The woman turned from the window and studied Nora.

Fidgeting with the skirt of her dress, Nora stared back at the woman. Whatever the woman seemed to be weighing over, Nora hoped she'd be found fitting. The woman appeared to be around Nora's age, but a maternal vibe radiated from her.

"Whose interviewing Melody?" the woman repeated.

"It's for a TV show."

The woman arched a brow. "Like Kelly Clarkson?"

"Not exactly," she laughed. "How do you know Melody?"

Unless Melody really leaned into the casual look for staff, which Nora doubted, this woman was a guest and not an employee.

"I've known Melody for years." The woman stepped closer. "What is this TV show?"

"Oh…" Nora bit her lip. She wasn't sure if Melody was telling people. There were typically press releases when they were filming and before the show, but they hadn't officially agreed nor signed anything yet. "I'll let Melody tell you about it."

The woman's face pinched.

"I'm Nora."

"Beth."

"Are you a guest here?"

Beth turned back to the window. "It's lovely here, isn't it? I adore what Melody has done with the gardens."

Nora stepped beside her to look out the window. Goosebumps bloomed across her skin. Even with her jacket an icy shiver crawled up her spine. Rubbing her hands against her arms, she followed Beth's gaze. A small bench sat below a wooden arbor draped in leafy green vines. Rose and lilac bushes lined a small cobblestone path looping through the backyard. The path started at the back porch ending at a grassy lane leading into the thicket of trees at the edge of the yard.

Nora pointed. "Is that a walking trail through the woods?"

"It is. Bill and I used to take so many walks there." There was a tiny quirk of her lips, while her eyes remained a little sad and distant. It was as if the memory both pained and comforted her.

"Who's Bill?" Nora cringed immediately. "Sorry, that's rude of me to ask."

"Is it?"

"Well, we don't know each other and…" Nora gestured with her hands as if the motion explained everything.

"How else do people expect to get to know each other if they don't ask questions?"

Nora nodded. One couldn't fault the logic.

"My grandpa always said a new friend is one hello away." Nora smiled fondly.

"Your grandpa sounds like a very wise man." She moved her gaze back to the window.

Nora's eyes followed. Melody appeared, hands on hips, talking to a tall man in gray trousers and an undershirt stretched over a muscular body. Nora tried to make out the man's face, but he turned his back to Melody and stomped away.

"Bill was my husband," Beth murmured.

"Was?" Nora closed her eyes. "I am sorry."

Was could mean anything. It could mean divorce. It didn't have to mean death, but something in Beth's voice telegraphed that it was the latter and not the former.

"It was a long time ago," Beth said, moving away from the window.

Pivoting, Nora watched as Beth glided to the door. She wanted to say something. Anything. To offer comfort, but what comfort was there when you've lost someone? The pain of loss never went away but for a few moments talking about Grandpa Scott over waffles with August made her feel close to the happy memory of life with him instead of the sadness of one without him.

"You and Bill used to go on walks there?" Nora asked, motioning out the window.

A small smile lifted her lips. "Yes. When we were first married. He'd take me on long walks in the evening. We even had picnics there. There is a clearing down the trail. Perfect for couples."

"I'll have to take your word on that," Nora chuckled.

"No suitor for you?"

A loud guffaw belted from Nora. "Suitor?"

Beth batted the air. "Your generation."

"Beth, I think we're the same age."

Beth's mouth flexed into a smirk. "So, there's no one, then."

"I'm focused on work."

Excuses. Mae's chiding comment echoed inside her.

"Bill was like that. He was focused on his business. He'd had no interest in marriage."

Nora arched a brow. "Until you?"

Beth raised her left hand looking at the simple rose gold band on her finger. "Until me."

"He must have loved you a great deal."

"At that time, he did." Her gaze flicked around the room.

What did that mean? Nora's curiosity piqued. Gnawing at her lower lip, she debated. Ask or not? Beth had invited the questions. How else could they become friends? Wait, did Nora want to become friends? This was a complete stranger. Befriending someone at first sight was more a Mae thing. Nora needed a vetting process and a six-year trial period before committing. Outside of Mae, Nora didn't have a lot of close friends. Not even a lot of not-close friends.

"I should go to my room. It was lovely meeting you, Nora. I look forward to seeing you again."

"You too," Nora said, her gaze drawn to the window by a deep voice grumbling.

The man that had been talking to Melody reappeared from the trees.

"Who is that?" Nora asked, turning back to find that Beth was gone.

The lavender aroma faded away and her goosebumps subsided. The fresh coolness disappeared, leaving the room stale and warm. Nora looked back out the window, watching the man. As if sensing her, he peered up and for a beat they stared at each other in a wordless conversation. A mix of sadness, anger, and longing twisted his expression.

"Sorry about that," Melody announced, walking into the room.

"It's all good. I was talking with Beth." Nora turned away from the window.

"Beth was here?" Melody scanned the room.

"Yeah. She went back to her room." Nora looked back out the window, but the man was gone. "I saw you talking to someone outside. A man. Who was that?"

"Oh, he works here." Melody motioned with her cane to the door. "Let's finish the tour and we can talk logistics."

CHAPTER 9

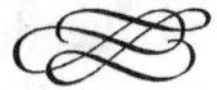

Travis Olson

"You're a sexy bitch!" Mae crooned as Nora stepped out of the black SUV.

Shimming her hips – just a bit – Nora beamed. She knew better than to argue with the fashionista that was Mae. Modesty of the false or even of the very real type would not be tolerated. Mae championed her friends, embracing all their "take a bow" moments. The silky emerald dress that hugged Nora's curves and flowed at the knees, paired with strappy silver heels was a total bow-worthy outfit. Between the outfit and her hair styled in loose waves that cascaded past her bare shoulders, sexy confidence surged within her. It was the perfect look for the Destination Network's annual renewal party.

"Look who's talking, gorgeous!" Nora walked up the steps of the restaurant to greet her.

Mae's purple hair was swept up in a topknot allowing her lovely face to be on full display. Gold chandelier earrings and dramatic red lips popped against her skintight satin backless black halter jumpsuit. Gold stilettos added at least four inches to her tall, lean figure.

"Someone's showing off their 'ready for summer' bod with that sexy number," Nora teased, kissing Mae's cheek.

"And you haven't even seen how it accentuates my luscious booty," she giggled, jiggling her backside.

The two laughed and headed inside. Parties—well anything—were always better with Mae for Nora. It was nice to have her in person and not just as an image on screen. Mae had flown back to L.A. to serve as director of photography on a few commercials before she jetted off for a month-long Australian tour. It was perfect timing for her to be Nora's date for tonight.

Each year, the network held a party for all the new shows they picked up and current shows they'd renewed. Most of the partygoers would be show hosts, executive producers, a few directors, and a sprinkling of field producers. A lot of the party was the typical schmoozing of industry people. TV was fifty percent experience and eighty percent who you knew. The math didn't add up in the real world, but in the TV world it made sense. While Nora didn't frequent many of the industry parties, she'd take advantage of the few she attended to make connections and push her ultimate goal of doing something beyond paranormal shows.

Nora and Mae made their way through the room lit in the colorful glow of paper lanterns. Guests sipped cocktails at a series of low and high-top tables scattered across the marble floor. Grabbing a glass of chardonnay for herself and a merlot for Mae, they claimed a high-top in the corner of the room allowing them to scan who was there without being in the center of things. It ensured Nora could see without being seen.

"See anyone we know?" Mae asked, sipping her wine.

"Not anyone we know."

"Anyone we *want* to know?"

"Depends. If you mean potential connections…" She scanned the room. "…nobody. If you mean someone for you to get your flirt on with, check out that Glen Powell look-alike at three o'clock."

Mae turned, pretending to wave at someone. "Yes, please." Playful wickedness glinted in her eyes. "What about you?"

Nora waved her hands dismissing the question. "I'm focused on one person and one person only."

"August Chandler," Mae purred with all the dramatics of a horny cat.

"I'm here to make connections…for *work*."

"Let me guess, we're looking out for Travis Olson."

"Yup."

The only other show more popular than *Haunted Hideaway* on the Destination Network was *Great Escape*. Six years ago, the former teenage heartthrob Travis Olson, who a teenaged Nora and legions of fans had drooled over on the high school vampire drama *Dark Shadows High*, rebranded himself as host and executive producer of the wildly popular travel show.

Great Escape was Nora's dream job, and she had already been rejected for it twice. They traveled the globe to not just the well-known tourist spots but also explored the lesser-known parts of the world. Each week they brought these places, people, and cultures into the homes of millions of people, many of whom wouldn't otherwise have access to them for various reasons. Financial. Health. Disability.

Baby girl, with a click we can go anywhere. Grandpa Scott's words whispered inside her.

"I thought they already had their producers lined up for this season. That girl I was seeing last year is a boom operator for them and will be leaving to shoot the first episode in two weeks," Mae said.

Nora tapped her fingers on the table's smooth surface. "Yes, but I've heard a rumor one of the producers already got fired."

"Wow." A breathy laugh tripped out of Mae. "Fired before shooting begins. That's shockingly impressive."

"My hope is I can convince him to give me a shot. I heard it just happened, so they haven't put out the position yet."

"So, you'll dazzle him with your big old field producer and Destination Network fangirl brain, and he'll hire you before interviewing anyone else for the position."

"Exactly." Nora grinned, lifting her glass of wine. The confidence etched on her face did not match the swirl of nervous energy inside her.

After getting her first season under her belt as a field producer, she'd started applying for positions with more traditional travel shows. Rejection after rejection found their way into the trash bin of her email.

"You know," Mae paused, her eyes soft but determined. "… If you'd join me on my YouTube show you could avoid chasing being a producer for a travel show and *actually* be a producer."

A sigh rolled across her entire body. "That's a new record. You made it a whole twenty-five minutes without pointing that out."

"It just makes no sense. You want to produce travel shows, so come do it with me. Let's be our own bosses and fuck these privileged white boys that run things."

"There's no guarantee with a YouTube Channel. With a show like *Great Escape,* doors will open for me to produce other travel shows and rise to the executive producer level."

Mae's face scrunched in annoyance.

"I know it doesn't make sense to you, but it makes sense to me. It's been my dream since I was a little girl."

Mae reached across the table and squeezed Nora's forearm. "You want to bring the world to everyone, but you don't need Travis Olson, the Destination Network, or anyone else to do that. All you need is you."

"And you." Nora smirked.

"That goes without saying." Mae made a dismissive gesture, their gazes locked in a show down. "Fine—" she sighed "—Remind me what Travis looks like again."

Gratitude lifted the corners of Nora's lips. Mae would huff in frustration, but at the end of the day she was her true-blue sister. She'd *always* have her back. They were ride-or-dies and she'd always drive the getaway car.

"He's about six foot with blond cropped hair and gray eyes."

"So, a white boy," Mae chuckled.

Nora laughingly nodded.

"Ten o'clock." She pointed a red manicured finger.

Nora casually turned. In a gray suit that clung to what Nora knew was a muscular body thanks to the many episodes featuring a shirtless Travis, he stood at a high-top talking to someone.

No wonder the show was so popular.

Spinning back to Mae, her heart raced. She gripped the stem of her wine glass to calm her nerves. It was one thing to talk about approaching Travis Monroe about being his next field producer, but it was a whole other thing to actually *do* it. This seemed like a good idea when she'd swiped the red lip stain onto her lips before leaving her condo. Now, it felt like the *worst* idea ever.

"Nora," Mae said, grabbing her arm. "You are a badass bitch. You are a goddamn goddess that men fall to their knees to worship. You march over there like Queen Boudica charging into battle and show him why it would be a fucking mistake for him to not hire you."

Mae's reassuring squeeze settled the butterflies drunk fluttering in her belly. "Thank you." Nora smiled.

"Do you want me to go with you?"

"Nah." Nora batted the air.

"Okay. You go get him." Mae tipped her head toward the Glen Powell look-alike whose gaze was fixed on her. "I'm going to go get *him*."

"Do you want me to go with you first?" Nora peered between Mae and the Glen Powell look-alike flashing bedroom eyes at her friend.

It was never a good idea for any woman to approach men they didn't know alone, especially for a trans woman. Nora and Mae made it a habit to approach possible romantic partners, even just for simple flirts, together to suss out safety for one another. On the rare occasion they did go home with someone precautions were taken. Locations shared. Photos of the man taken. Any man that protested found themselves left.

"I'm good. Just some public flirting. If he screams creep, I'll come to you. Otherwise, meet at the bar in thirty?" Mae jutted her chin toward the bar in the far right of the room. "Same thing goes for you. If Travis Olson turns out to be in the Harvey Weinstein fanboys club, you sachet your booty to me."

"Deal."

Moving through the crowd, Nora's heart thumped with each step.

You got this, baby girl. She could almost hear Grandpa Scott. Before every test or track meet, he'd tell her she had this. It was never a wish for good luck, but a certainty that she had what it took to succeed.

Just as she reached Travis's table, the man he was speaking to slipped away. Travis stood, sipping an old fashioned.

"Why hello," he greeted, his smile almost blinding her with its wattage. The actor turned TV host had made countless sexiest and beautiful people lists.

Tucking a piece of hair behind her ear, she inhaled. *You are a badass bitch.* "Nora Scott," she said, placing her glass on his table. "Mind if I join you?"

His eyes swept down her figure. "Nice to meet you. I'm Travis Olson."

"I know."

Laughter bubbled out of him. "Most women like to pretend they don't know who I am when they approach me. Maybe they think it's more of a turn-on for celebrities if they pretend nobody knows them. I like your honesty; it's refreshing."

Turn on? "Oh, I'm not approaching you for *that.*"

Even if she had daydreamed about his car breaking down in front of her house the night of the homecoming dance and taking her to said dance, she wasn't a sixteen-year-old girl anymore. She was a thirty-year-old woman. The current daydream was less Travis giving her a kiss in the middle of the high school gymnasium and more him giving her a field producer job.

A slight frown dragged down his lips. "That's too bad. So, why are you approaching me, Nora Scott?"

"I hear you need a field producer for *Great Escape.*" She fixed her eyes on his and stood tall.

"News travels fast," he said and sipped his drink, the ice clanking against the almost empty glass.

"I've been in TV production for ten years. The last two years I've been working as a field producer for a top-rated Destination Network show. I have the experience you need." On the outside she may have looked confident, but what he didn't see was the slow drip of sweat rolling down her back.

She was doing this, though. Stepping outside of her

comfort zone. Nora had always followed the process. Oh, she'd made connections like everyone else, but she'd never approached anyone and point blank said, "Hire me."

Placing his now empty glass on the table, he asked, "What show?"

"*Haunted Hideaway.*"

One brow ticked up. "The ghost show?"

"Paranormal investigation."

"That's not really what *we* do. We're a travel show. We're not about the things that go bump in the night." His tone was dismissive.

Her teeth dug into the inside of her cheek, biting back the indignation as she continued, "It's more than that. It's a travel show with a paranormal component."

"A *travel* show?"

"It's very travely." She winced. *Travely? Really?* The memory of August saying sciencey and explaining how words become words bolstered her to lean into it. "Yeah, travely. We explore various parts of the United States. While we do paranormal investigations, we also feature different points of interest in the community we're filming at. We highlight not just the tourist and ghost stuff, but lesser-known history and culture. Just like you."

He tapped his fingers against the table, his gaze darting between Nora and the room. "It's not quite like us."

"Have you watched an episode?" she asked, sipping her glass of wine. The gesture offered the appearance of casual indifference while calming her frying nerves.

His face twisted. "Well…no."

"Then you can't say we're not like you. I watch your show and mine. Even the episodes I don't produce. I think if you watched an episode, you'd see that I'm right. *Haunted Hideaway* is different than the grotesquely sensational ghost hunting shows out there. At the heart of this show is a story about two brothers exploring the country together. Just like your show is about your adventures around the world."

God, she wanted to high-five herself. Even if he laughed her out of the room, she knew she was right. It was true. August and Derrick had created a paranormal show that was travely. She could imagine August's big smile at her use of that word.

"And you think you'd be the right producer for me?"

"She'd be the best damn producer you'll have. You'd be a fool not to hire her."

Nora's heart jumped into her throat at the sound of August Chandler's voice.

CHAPTER 10

Just a Kiss

Nora's pulse quickened. First, at the knowledge of him having witnessed her pitch to Travis to get a different job. Second, at the sight of him standing beside her. A charcoal jacket stretched over his broad frame. Her eyes strolled down his body. The way the fabric hugged every muscle should be illegal. Her eyes stopped at his feet, clad in his signature black Converse.

A small smile curved her lips.

Smirking, his brows raised playfully as if saying, "Yep, sneakers."

She was aghast when he'd shown up at their first network renewal party after getting picked up for their second season, wearing sneakers with his suit.

"August. Nice to see you again," Travis drawled. "One of your producers was just lobbying me for a job."

"She's not one of my producers. Nora is *the* producer."

She warmed at his praise. Maybe Mae was right, she had a praise kink.

"Don't you have multiple producers?" Travis's right brow quirked.

"Yes, but none like Nora. We'd be just your run-of-the-mill 'what goes bump in the night' show without her." Nodding at her, he continued. "Nora has guided us to be both a paranormal investigation *and* travel show."

Brow creased in thought, Travis looked from Nora to August. "This is a first. Never have I witnessed a fellow EP go to bat for his producer like this. When someone is as good as you say, we tend to want to keep them."

"I'd never stand in someone's way." A rare stern expression spread across August's face.

"Yeah… I'm aware of what a boy scout you are," Travis said wryly before jutting his chin toward Nora. "If you're right this could save me the hassle of interviewing. Send me over a few episodes that you've produced. I'll watch and if the show lives up to being like ours but with ghosts…" he huffed a quick dismissive laugh, "…then I'll give you a shot. The producer we fired was scheduled for our shoot in Cape Town in July. Will that work for you?"

"Yes," August answered quickly.

Nora's head jerked to him. July was when they would shoot the last of her three episodes for the season.

"Excellent." Travis slipped a card out of his pocket and slid it over to Nora. "Send me three episodes."

Nora took the card. "Okay." Her voice was steadier than her heartbeat.

"I'm not going to pretend I'm not disappointed you weren't approaching me for *that*." He winked, repeating her words from earlier. "However, this may be even more of an intriguing proposition."

August clenched his jaw. "I hope you're not one of *those* executive producers."

"Relax, boy scout." He patted August's shoulder. "I'm not

like that. It's just an inside joke between Nora and me." Turning to Nora, he grinned. "I look forward to watching your episodes."

"I look forward to proving you wrong about *Haunted Hideaway*," she said, slipping his card into her black clutch as he walked away laughing.

"Dick," August grumbled.

Nora's eyes widened. She'd *never* heard August call anyone a name. Let alone a dick.

He turned. "What was that *that* comment about?"

"He thought I approached him to hit on him." Nora fiddled with the silver bracelet on her wrist. She missed the anchoring weight of her watch, but it didn't go with her outfit. "I told him I wasn't, though. I'm not interested in him."

The fire of his stare ignited every nerve in her body. She sucked in a breath and commanded her body to cool down. It did not listen.

"You didn't have to do that," she said.

His grin ticked up.

"I mean... Thank you." She bit her lip. "Most executive producers wouldn't do that."

"I'm not like most executive producers."

"You're not like most people." *Oh my god! Did I say that out loud?* She dug her fingernails into her palms.

His smile got bigger.

"You said I'd be free in July. That's when we're supposed to shoot my last episode of the season. Am I fired?"

"Never," he scoffed. "If you're offered the job and you want to take it, I want you to know that I...*we* won't stand in your way. I know paranormal shows aren't your passion. I know it's something you've fallen into. If there's a chance for you to do what makes you happy, I want to help."

The earnestness in his words dripped through her like

warm honey. Not only did he not stand in her way, but he supported her. He went to bat for what she wanted. He didn't tell her to give up or do it in a different way.

"Thank you for that…for believing in me."

"Of course," he placed his hand atop hers.

The impulse to step closer and eliminate the inches between them pulsed within her. To discover the feel of his arms wrapped around her. To lean into his supportive embrace. His hands trailing down her body, claiming every inch.

"Is *Great Escape* your passion?" His question knocked her out of her lusty haze.

"Yes. Well, not that show in particular but what it represents."

"What does it represent?"

"Did you ever watch *On Tour with Jack Stevens* when you were a kid?"

"That British guy?" A furrow formed on his brow.

"Grandpa Scott called him the nobleman because he sounded like someone from a *Masterpiece Theater* program. We'd watch his show every Sunday and talk about all the places we'd go someday…" She swallowed thickly. "…But we never went."

"Why?"

"When I was eight, grandpa was diagnosed with ALS. It progressed and over the years he lost more and more function. He lost his ability to walk. Then speak. The last few years of high school he was in a nursing home. No matter what was happening with him physically, though, we never stopped exploring the world together, one episode at a time."

Emotion filled her chest with the memory. Sadness at grandpa's body breaking down. Happiness that, no matter how the disease deteriorated him, he remained ever her loving grandpa. Sorrow that he wasn't there to see her take one more step toward their dream.

August threaded his fingers with hers. "Who did you stay with after he went into the nursing home?"

"Until I was eighteen, I was in foster care. My mom's parents had passed before I was born and neither of them had siblings, so there was nobody else."

Nora's gaze turned away, not wanting to see the pity she knew would be there. Whenever anyone heard her full story, it always reared, except with Mae.

"But you were still able to see him? To watch your show together?"

Nora's attention moved back to August. No pity. No sadness. Only understanding swam in his chocolatey pupils.

"One of the families from the church we went to became my foster parents. They made sure I got to visit him as often as I wanted. Even when I went to college, I drove back every Sunday to watch travel shows with him. By that time the Jack Stevens show was off-air, but there were new ones for us to explore the world with."

"This is why you're *the* producer. You're driven by your heart to offer more than just a TV show to people; you want to bring them the world." His hand squeezed hers.

Anchored in this moment by her hand wrapped in his, Nora fought the urge to drift away. To escape from revealing herself just a little more to him and he to her. He was a good man. A man that believed in her. A man that held her hand, telling her how special she was.

Slipping her hand out of his, she raised it to stroke his cheek. The stubble dusting his face was both rough and smooth against her fingers. Lowering her hands, she raised to her tiptoes and pressed a soft kiss against his cheek. She didn't give in fully to her urge but enough to settle the impulse.

"Thank you," she murmured.

Throat bobbing, August just stared at her.

Grabbing her clutch, she turned and walked away. If she stayed, she knew that unquenched impulse would take control. And she'd let it.

CHAPTER 11

Romantic Antics

Kelly Clarkson's music belted in the rental car as Nora eased up Putman House's gravel driveway. Their weeklong shoot at the bed and breakfast began tomorrow. Nora, who was staying on site, was arriving early to do her typical filming pre-check. The rest of the crew and both Chandler brothers would arrive later today.

The brothers would also be staying on site. The rest of the crew were uncomfortable with sleeping at the allegedly haunted house and were staying at a Bates-looking motel in the next town over. Nora would rather take her chances with imaginary ghosts than the very real probability of bed bugs from the roadside motel everyone else was at.

It had been four days since the Destination Network's renewal party. Four days since she'd kissed August. Granted it was on his cheek, but she'd kissed him! Besides work-related texts there'd been zero interaction since then.

Parking the car, she opted not to think about this being the first time she'd see him since she walked out of the party. Instead, she thought of the message from Travis Olson confirming receipt of her episodes and that he'd watch them this week. Although that didn't settle her stomach either.

Grabbing her messenger bag from the passenger seat, she slipped out of the car. Focusing on the task at hand allowed her to move away from both men pulling her into anxious pieces. One with the key to her professional dreams. The other…

"Ms. Scott." Gideon stepped onto the porch. "I mean, Nora."

"Gideon, nice to see you again." She waved.

"Nora!" Melody burst from the front door. Her dark curls bounced in a high ponytail.

Since meeting a month ago, their emails, texts, and phone calls about the filming morphed into something more like friendship. Just like Mae, any type of relationship other than friends with Melody was impossible. Where Mae had simply declared them besties, Melody's magnetic sweetness pulled Nora in. While at Putman House, she'd be staying in Melody's guest room.

There'd be no filming or investigation of Melody's carriage house apartment. Even if there had been reported activity in the carriage house, Derrick was adamant that there'd be no infringing on Melody's private space. It was the most alpha-male Derrick had ever been during planning sessions.

"I should go check on…" Gideon's brow puckered. "…check on…things."

"Good idea," Melody said. "I'll help Nora get settled in."

With a tight smile, he turned and walked back into the house. After Nora grabbed her suitcase, Melody led her to the carriage house. The former garage space was renovated with a large entertainment room on the first level. A small bar, blue leather sectional couch and matching oversized chair, and four-person table greeted them as they walked in.

"There's a laundry nook in the corner." Melody pointed. "Since I don't drive, I figured I could maximize this space for entertaining. I'm going to host a little drinks party for the crew tonight. Nothing too fancy. Just a few tidbits, beer, and wine."

"That's sweet of you," Nora said, following Melody through a door to a set of enclosed stairs that led to the second floor.

Fresh eucalyptus caressed Nora's senses as they walked into the apartment. The scent's source was found in a glass vase on the center of the granite kitchen island that separated the kitchen and living room space. Black-framed photos of different famous queens dotted the pale blue walls.

"Is that Queen Latifah?" Nora mused, pointing at a picture between framed photos of Queen Elizabeth I and Cleopatra.

Melody beamed. "Sure is! She's been my favorite diva since I saw her in *Hairspray* in high school. My mom had all her CDs from back in the day, so I went down an early nineties music rabbit hole the summer I turned seventeen."

"I feel that way about Kelly Clarkson. My grandpa loved those singing competition shows. He'd rooted for Kelly and even called in to vote for her when she was on *American Idol*. He'd always have her music playing around the farmhouse and we'd sing a long while doing chores."

"I love her show. I take my lunch break at eleven each day to watch it," Melody laughed, guiding Nora to the guest room.

Both bedrooms were off the main living room, with a small bathroom between them. Nora's room overlooked the backyard, offering a view of the trail that looped into the thicket of trees at the back of the property. A creamy duvet stretched over a queen-sized bed. Fresh yellow daisies sat atop a light wood dresser. Instead of queens, the walls were bedecked with framed pictures of castles. Melody explained they were all actual castles in Europe that she planned on visiting one day. She'd gone to a few over the years, but once Putman House was on more stable footing, she wanted to visit more.

"That's why you're all here," Melody said, a quiet hopefulness in her tone.

"I know a number of places we've investigated have seen an increase in tourists after the show airs, but I'd imagine with how beautiful your bed and breakfast is and the limited hotel options in the area you'd have no trouble getting guests."

Melody fiddled with the hem of her blouse. "One would think."

"Has it been a challenge attracting guests? I know you had some people here when I was here in April."

Melody's eyes met Nora's, her mouth opening and then closing as if weighing what to say.

"Melody!" August's voice drifted in from the living room.

"Oh, I told him to come up when he and Derrick arrived. Let me go greet them." Standing up, she glided out of the room.

Sounds of the happy reunion waltzed into the room. Tapping her fingers against her jean-clad thighs, Nora debated. Finish unpacking or go out and greet? The aftermath of a kiss on the cheek shouldn't be awkward, but it was. How to greet him? A handshake? A wave? A hug? Her body temperature ticked up at that last one. Sucking in a deep breath, she shut her suitcase and headed to the living room.

August stopped mid-swinging hug of Melody. His eyes

met Nora's from across the room. Heat crisscrossed her body with their joined gaze. Her breath stammered with the charged air between them.

"August," she breathed.

"Nora." His mouth slanted into a lopsided grin.

"August," she repeated and then cringed. "I mean—" she gestured to Derrick who stood beside Melody, "—Derrick. Hi. I already said 'hi' to August. Hi…Derrick."

Seriously? She dug her fingers into her palms. She acted as if she'd pressed him against the wall and tasted every inch of him, not offered a chaste kiss against his cheek.

"Sorry. Long trip." She tugged at the end of her ponytail.

"Of course." Derrick nodded and crossed the room. "Glad you made it safely," he said, hugging her.

Embracing Derrick back she said, "I hope your trip from Kentucky was uneventful."

The brothers' last episode was shot at a former bourbon distillery outside of Lexington. Since there weren't actual rooms on site, they'd spent the week in tents on the property.

"I'm happy to be in the land of running water and flushing toilets again," he chuckled, releasing Nora, and stepping back.

August tipped his head to Nora. "I know it was a long trip for you, but I hope it was good," he said, slipping his hands into his pockets.

"It was." Nora's jittery fingers traced her watch.

Why was this awkward? She wanted to convince herself that nothing had happened. That wasn't true, though. Something had shifted between them, like a curtain lifted, revealing each of them to one another.

"I should go do the final walkthrough," Nora blurted.

"Oh yeah, you've all got work to do before tomorrow. The bed and breakfast is empty. No staff or guests this week.

Well, except for me and Gideon. He'll pop in and out to check on things," Melody explained.

"Thank you, Melody," Derrick said, combing his long fingers through his hair.

"I'm going to walk to the store in town to pick up a few things for tonight. I'm hosting a small drinks party for your crew. Seven sharp. Downstairs. While you're not shooting in the carriage house, I've told Nora the downstairs entertainment space can be used by crew for their breaks," Melody went on, brushing a wayward curl behind her ear.

"You're so lovely," Derrick murmured and then winced. "I mean, that's so lovely of you."

August's smirk met Nora's. The awkwardness in her washed away by their shared nonverbal agreement about the plan to help Derrick woo Melody or vice versa. Nora was equal-opportunity wooing.

"You know Derrick, I don't need you for the walk-through," Nora said with a mischievous grin.

"Yeah. It would be nice if someone accompanied Melody into town. You could walk or take the rental to get a few things, like Nora's Diet Dr. Pepper and white cheddar popcorn." August winked at Nora.

"And pretzels and Nutella for August," Nora sassed, her tease-filled stare tethered with August's.

Even if this was about orchestrating alone time between Melody and Derrick, it felt more flirtation than matchmaking. Both she and August were flexing with their knowledge of the other. Their playful banter caused a swoop in her abdomen.

"I could drive you," Derrick said, clearing his throat.

"That would be nice, but I wouldn't want to take you away from work." Melody fiddled with the thin bangle bracelet on her delicate wrist.

Adjusting his glasses, a soft crimson swept across his cheeks. "If I was needed, Nora would tell me."

August slapped his brother on the back. "It's settled. You two go shopping, while we—" He pointed to Nora and then to himself. "—do the walkthrough."

We? Those ruthless belly butterflies could not be fought.

CHAPTER 12

Flying Couches

"**S**o, I see you're joining me in the ranks of meddling Regency novel mothers." August bumped Nora's shoulder with his, their gazes locked on Derrick holding the card door open for Melody.

"Just this *one* time. They're too cute not to try to hook up." Nora faced him.

Amusement played in his features. "They are like adorable puppies."

"They blush when either is mentioned in front of the other." She turned toward the front door.

August followed, grabbing the door with one hand and resting his other at the small of her back to usher her into the house. The heat of his palm spread a warm fizzy sensation through her. The feeling was reminiscent of the first sips of a hot cup of tea on a cool morning.

"You should have seen him when she walked into the living room. He stopped moving and had this look of pure admiration and panic on his face. It was something out of a sappy romcom." He chuckled.

At that moment, Nora feared that she may also be something out of a sappy romcom. Every inch of her body ignited at his touch. This was no good. She needed to regain her footing and focus on work. Slipping from his touch, she bound up the stairs.

"We should block the library for tomorrow's interviews, so we can let Benji know how to set up in the morning," she said, reaching the second-floor landing.

Once in the library, she moved to the other side of the room and as far away from August as possible. Her body couldn't be trusted near him. Each time August got close to her every nerve ending tingled. Her fingers itched to caress his soft stubble. Her lips twitched to taste him. Her body both wound tight and completely relaxed in his presence.

"Which episodes did you send to Travis?" August asked, shoving the couch across from the chair to set up a better shot for the interview.

Almost no executive producers and certainly no hosts ever got this hands-on. But neither Chandler brother was above any job on set. Moving furniture, picking up snacks, cleaning up trash, or settling the nerves of a fresh-out-of-school production assistant. They did it all.

"The Fort Niagara episode. The one at the Galveston Hotel." She helped him straighten the couch. Her breath caught with the quick brush of his hand against hers as they worked. "The Halloween special from Tombstone." A breathy quality captured her voice from the lingering effect of the contact with his skin.

Their gazes mingled. Both quiet for a beat.

"Those are good ones." He swallowed thickly, his stare moving from her eyes to her mouth and back.

Nora's heartbeat quickened. The air between them crackled. Moving just a few inches would end the longing, the not knowing. Their lips could touch. Nora could thread her fingers into his silky hair. She could pull him into a deep kiss. She could press the softness of her body against his hard edges. She could ball her fists into the fabric of his T-shirt, guiding him atop her on the couch. Her legs wrapping around his hips…

Breathless, she stepped back. "This should work. We should…" Her eyes darted around again. "Shit, I left my tablet on the porch."

"I'll get it," he offered, placing his hand on her shoulder.

Their eyes locked and his breath grew ragged. Something pulsed between them, wanting and needing to be released. They were on the cusp of something, but neither seemed ready or willing to step off the cliff.

He drew a deep breath and swallowed hard. "I'll be back." He turned and walked out the door.

The air in the room was suddenly suffocating. Nora moved to the window and opened it. Several gulps of fresh air filled her lungs and untwined the tensing muscles of her body.

As she looked outside, a rustle in the tree line drew her attention. The auburn-haired man she'd seen her first day emerged from the woods wearing the same slacks and undershirt. Mumbling something to himself, he paced the length of the backyard.

"What's he doing here?" she asked aloud.

"Who?" A soft voice startled Nora.

She turned to see Beth, wearing that same pink robe and white nightgown, her hair pulled back in the same loose braid. If Nora wasn't sure that it had been a month, she'd swear it was that mid-April day again. Both Beth and that man looked exactly the same.

So had Gideon.

Mouth slack, she pointed at Beth. "What are you doing here? Melody said there were no guests."

"Well, I'm not a guest." Beth crossed the room to where the couch had been moved. Her eyes narrowed, hands on hips. "Who moved this? Melody never changes anything without my blessing."

"Why would Melody need your blessing?"

"It's my house."

"It's Melody's house." Nora tilted her head.

"She cares for it now, but it's Bill's and my house. Well, technically he had it made for me as a wedding gift."

"Bill? Your dead husband? Wedding gift? The house was built in the nineteenth century." Nora's words were slow and deliberate.

"I don't like this couch here," Beth said, her face pinched.

The lone lamp in the room surged with bright light.

"Melody is at the store, but she'll be back—"

Beth blew out a heavy breath. "Kindly move the couch back or I will."

Nora moved closer to Beth as if approaching a wild animal. The woman was in her pajamas in the middle of the day saying a house built in 1883 was built as a wedding gift for her. Clearly something was wrong. Nora's eyes flicked to the closed door, willing August to appear and help her calm Beth.

"Beth, why don't we—"

"Fine! I'll move it." With a flick of her wrists, she gestured to the couch.

The couch slid across the hardwood floor and slammed into the wall, barely missing Nora.

"Oops... Sorry." Beth cringed.

"What the fuck?!" Nora screamed, her breath ragged.

"You'd think after over a century I'd get a handle on this. I truly didn't mean to have the couch come your way. I hope you're okay." Beth stepped closer, reaching out.

Jumping away before Beth could touch her, Nora scrambled to the other side of the room. "How did you move that without touching it? What the fuck was that?"

"That type of language really is uncalled for," Beth scolded.

"So is almost killing me with a couch!"

"And they thought women of my day were melodramatic." Beth rolled her eyes.

"Your *day*?"

Beth ignored the question and continued, "It was an accident. If I wanted to do something, I would do something like this." She motioned with her hands.

The vase from a small end table flew across the room and smashed against the wall, porcelain shards clattered to the floor. Nora shrieked.

"Oh, calm down. It didn't even come near you." Beth batted the air. "I always hated that vase. It was a gift from my mother-in-law. Dreadful woman." Beth crossed her arms over her chest, a look of pure pride etched on her face.

"Nora!" August burst into the room, taking in the scene. "Are you okay?"

"And you said you didn't have a young man. He's rather handsome," Beth crooned, waggling her eyebrows.

"What...the...fuck is ha...ha...happening?" Nora clutched her stomach, her breath coming in hiccupping gulps

This wasn't real. It couldn't be. Had Beth really moved the couch and the vase with just a flick of her wrist?

"Beth!" Everyone turned as the man from the woods appeared out of nowhere. "Are you okay?" he asked, rushing to her.

"It's not like anything will hurt me," she said, tossing her hands into the air.

Nora blinked rapidly. "Did he just…come *through* the wall?" Nora breathed. Each thump of her heart rattled like a runaway jackhammer. Her vision blurred. She took one step toward August before her world went black.

CHAPTER 13

Caught

A warm palm stroked along Nora's cheeks, and she opened her eyes to see August hovering over her.

"Easy," he said, helping her to sit up.

Nora's gaze drifted around the room. August sat perched on the edge of the couch. The broken pieces of the vase still lay scattered along the floor as proof that it had not been a delusion. The room was empty except for them.

"When I thought of you hovering over me on the couch, this isn't what I meant," she said, dazed.

"Excuse me?" Amusement crinkled around his eyes.

"Oh my god, I said that out loud," she whined, covering her face with her hands.

"Nora! Are you okay?" Melody cried as she and Derrick ran into the room.

"I think I fainted." Nora moved her hand to her head. "Did I hit my head?"

"No, your young man caught you. It was rather romantic. He whisked you into his arms calling your name. It was like something out of a novel," Beth gushed, clutching her hands to her chest.

"I told you to wait outside," August growled, his arms coming around Nora protectively.

"Don't speak to her like that. This is her house," the auburn-haired man snapped, storming through the wall again.

"Oh, hush Bill. He's just protecting his young lady. Something you'd know nothing about," Beth huffed, turning her narrowed gaze to a scowling Bill.

"What was I just doing?" he gritted through clenched teeth.

"A little late."

Tossing his head back and letting out a frustrated snarl he shouted back. "When will you let this go?"

"When I'm no longer dead!" she shouted back, balling her hands into tight fists.

The lamp on the end table surged to full brightness before the bulb exploded.

Beth pulled an apologetic face. "Oops."

"Aunt Elizabeth and Uncle William, you promised." Melody let out a long breath.

"Sorry," both said with sheepish grins.

"What is happening?" Nora pleaded, taking in the scene. Still pressed in August's arms, she turned her beseeching stare to Melody. "Please, explain."

"Meet William and Elizabeth Putman. My great, great, great uncle and aunt...and the ghosts haunting Putman House."

Realization sobered Nora to reality. Beth was Elizabeth Putman, and her Bill was William Putman. The man that was executed for murdering his wife. Imagine not just being murdered by your husband, but ending up a ghost in the very home he'd killed you in. With him as your fellow phantom.

"Haunting." Bill scoffed. "It's my house."

"Technically mine. You gave it to me as a wedding gift," Beth corrected.

"I don't think you two are helping." Derrick cleared his throat, placing a hand on Melody's back.

"It's a little familiar for you to rest your hand on her back." Bill glared at Derrick, who immediately removed his hand from Melody.

Melody went on, "I'm sorry Nora. My aunt and uncle had promised to make themselves scarce this week, so you'd get no evidence." She looked between Derrick and August. "I'm so sorry guys. I lured you here under false pretenses. I thought if you investigated and found nothing that it would end the rumors about Putman House being haunted."

"But it *is* haunted," August said.

"One cannot haunt their own house," Bill grumbled.

"I know it was wrong to deceive you, but I was desperate to make potential patrons more comfortable staying here."

"Don't apologize. You were thinking like a business-woman." Bill beamed looking at his niece. "You're a Putman after all."

"Thank you, Uncle William." Melody turned to her uncle and aunt. "Would you two give me a few minutes to speak privately with Derrick, August, and Nora?"

Nora shook her head, watching both Beth and Bill disappear through the wall.

"Is Gideon also a ghost?" Nora asked.

Melody nodded. "Yes. He was the original butler. He died a few days after Aunt Elizabeth."

"Are *you* a ghost?"

"No!" Melody laughed. "I promise you. I am very real."

"I think it's safe," Derrick said, after poking his head out the door and closing it. "I don't see them in the hall."

"Safe? Are they dangerous? You said none of them were dangerous." August's hold on Nora tightened.

Stepping forward, hands out, she assured, "They aren't dangerous. I just didn't want to talk about this in front of them. I lied to them. I knew there was *no* way they'd make themselves scarce. Aunt Elizabeth is too nosey, and Uncle William is too protective of her to not make an appearance. I think you understand protective men," she said, a small smile aimed at Nora.

Nora looked at August, whose arms still wrapped around her. Her instinct was to wiggle out of them, but she was honestly enjoying his embrace. The safety. The belonging. The support. It all twined around her. It wasn't just being in someone's arms, but *his* arms.

"I wanted you all to come here to help them move on…to find out what their unfinished business is. They've been stuck here for over a century. Gideon is such a good man, and I'm afraid he's stuck here because of them. None of them are at peace. My aunt and uncle have been in a marital disagreement this entire time, and Gideon has played their referee."

"Marital disagreement?" Nora's lips pursed. "Didn't he kill her?"

"She has a point." August jutted his chin at Melody.

"I don't think so. Aunt Elizabeth never saw who pushed her. Uncle William has always contended his innocence. Plus, the way he looks at her—" a soft starry gaze shimmered in her eyes, "—a man that looks at someone like that could never hurt them. Even with my limited vision, I can see that. Plus, this might seem as far-fetched as ghosts, but I've always had a strong sense of people…their energy. I believe he's innocent. I want to help them, and I think the only way is to help them come together. I think that's their unfinished business and once we do that Gideon will also be free."

The room grew quiet. Was she right? Had Bill been falsely executed for his wife's murder?

"You knew about this?" August addressed his brother, anger lining his forehead.

"I just found out. Melody explained things to me on our way back after you called us." He and Melody looked at each other. "I think we should help. It's why we got into this."

Nora's brow creased. "What was the thing with the light and Beth's ability to move things? Do Gideon and Bill do that too?"

"No. Just Aunt Elizabeth. Her emotions get the best of her and have an impact on things. We go through a lot of light-bulbs," Melody half laughed, half sighed.

"She's a little poltergeisty. All the more reason we should help," Derrick persisted, staring at August.

"But if we film them, we'll make Elizabeth, William, and Gideon into an oddity. I know this is the dream for all para-normal researchers to capture fully manifested ghosts, but if we can't help them move on, I don't want their afterlives to be spent like animals at a zoo," August cautioned.

Nora threaded their hands, squeezing tight. "I know." Her heart swelled with his concern for this bickering ghost couple. "Let's go get some fresh air and discuss this."

August nodded.

"I'm really sorry, Nora. I promise I didn't want you all to find out like this. I planned on talking to the three of you today. Gideon knew what I was doing, and he was going to help me explain. I'm so sorry." Melody's eyes brimmed with regret.

Slipping out of August's embrace, Nora moved to Melody. "I know." She wrapped her arms around her. Like Melody, she knew people. Grandpa Scott always told her to trust her gut and her gut knew Melody was a good person driven only to help.

Taking August's hand, Nora led him through the house to the backyard. The rest of the crew hadn't arrived yet, which she was grateful for. Both for the ability to walk hand-in-hand and to have time to figure out what to do. They followed the grassy trail into the woods. She shook her head remembering Beth's statement that it was the perfect place for couples.

"How are you doing?" he asked, as they reached a small clearing.

"Well, I owe you a drink."

His laughter filled the air.

"I like when you laugh." It appeared that she was going to say *all* the things that had once hid within her.

"I like your smile," he said, tracing the outline of her lips. "Nora, I'm sorry." He pulled his hand away. "That was—"

"Don't be sorry. I'm not sorry." She took his hand and pressed a tender kiss to his palm.

"Are you sure?" His throat bobbed.

She wasn't, but she didn't want to fight it anymore. If ghosts were real, then so was magic, luck, and all the other things he'd encouraged her to believe in since they met. At that moment, she wanted to believe that the pull between them was real. That there was a possibility of a world of August and Nora. In a world where ghosts existed, couldn't that also exist?

"I am. I hope I'm not misreading things." She lifted to her tiptoes, circling her arms around his neck.

"You're not. I've wanted to kiss you since the day we met on that elevator. I've fought it every day since. I didn't want to be *that* executive producer."

"Do you still want to fight it?" she asked, lips inches from his.

"No," he breathed.

"Then kiss me."

Slowly, his mouth met hers. It was sweet and tender. His hands trailed down to her middle, pulling her body flush against his. Nibbling on her lower lip, he opened her up to deepen their kiss. The sweetness of his coffee and mint taste left her wanting more. She ran her fingers up and threaded them into his dark hair to pull him even deeper.

The sweet kisses melted into a hungry frenzy. She wanted to consume every ounce of him. Even more she wanted him to drink up every last ounce of her. He lifted her, and with three quick steps, Nora found herself pushed up against a tree, her legs wrapped around his waist. He kissed down the column of her throat, grinding his growing arousal against her.

"August," she gasped, as his hips moved against hers.

"Yes?" he hummed before nipping at her throat.

"Please...don't stop..."

He pushed her harder against the tree. Her fingers dug into his shoulders as he hit that place that she needed him with just the right amount of delicious pressure, spooling her tighter and tighter.

"Oh...my..." she whimpered with release.

Waves of pleasure rippled through her, jellying her limbs. It had never happened that quickly. She wasn't sure if it was the last two years of emotional foreplay between them, but she'd never been able to just let go like this. Orgasm had always been a slow chase for Nora with sexual partners. Something had held her back from just letting go in the past. Wrapped in August's arms, she could just fall, knowing that he'd catch her.

Breath settling, Nora leaned her head against the tree trunk. Her body remained pressed tight between the rough bark surface and August. One of his hands gripped at her waist, while the other roamed over her body.

His lips quirked with boyish pride. "I like that noise you just made for me."

"I like what you just did to *make* that happen," she murmured, and buried her face in his neck.

"Are you okay?"

Raising her head, she nibbled on her lip. "Yes and no. I want this. I've been fighting this for a long time too…"

"But?" He arched a brow.

"You don't want to be *that* executive producer that takes advantage of his crew. I don't want to be seen as someone that sleeps with the executive producer to get ahead."

"Nobody would think that about you. You're—"

"A woman in a male dominated industry. An industry that, despite the MeToo movement, has light years to go with how women are treated compared to men."

"Are you saying—" concern twisted his features, "—you want to pretend this never happened?"

"No." The words sprinted out of her without consulting her brain.

Trust your gut, baby girl. Grandpa Scott was right. Her gut trusted this. Trusted August. Also, there'd be no going back to a world before kissing him. After tasting him and experiencing how perfectly their bodies came together, there'd be no going back to yesterday.

"I want to keep kissing you." She skated her fingers along his jawline. "I would also like to do *other* things to you."

He made a throaty humming noise. "Yeah." His gaze burned bright with wicked agreement.

"I just want to keep this between us. Well, you can tell Derrick because, let's face it, I will be talking to Mae about this. But when the crew is around, we go back to our normal selves."

"And when they aren't around?" His tone was playful.

"We do this." She took his mouth in a deep kiss.

"I told you this trail was perfect for couples," Beth's voice purred.

August lowered Nora's feet to the ground, hiding his erection by turning into her body.

Nora wagged her finger at Beth. "You need to stop sneaking up on me, or I'll get a priest to exorcise the house."

Beth raised her hands in defeat. "Fine. I was simply coming to apologize. I truly do feel bad for scaring you. It wasn't my intention. My emotions get the best of me. Also, I know Melody really likes you and I didn't want to cost her a new friend. She doesn't have very many and..."

"We're good." Nora looked to August and back to Beth. "As long as you stop sneaking up on people."

A sassy smirk kicked across Beth's face. "Sure, as long as you admit that he's your young man?"

Nora patted a grinning August's cheek. "He's my young man."

"Now August, what are your attentions with Nora?" She crossed her arms, arching a brow.

August coughed.

Beth roared with laughter. "I'm just joshing you. I am fully aware that things like this happen all the time. I may have been born in 1858, but I was around for the roaring twenties. Oh, and don't get me started on the sixties."

"Beth, can we have some privacy?" Nora rubbed the center of her brow.

With a playful curtsy, Beth glided away.

A bemused August sighed. "What are we going to do about them?"

"I actually have an idea."

CHAPTER 14

Trust Your Gut

The rest of the crew was supposed to arrive by two, so Nora didn't have much time to brief everyone on the plan. Melody gathered the ghosts to join the living in the library. The couch had been moved back to where it had been. All evidence of what happened was swept away with the broken vase pieces.

"Ms. Nora, I am dreadfully sorry for keeping my not being alive from you," Gideon said, strolling in.

"It's alright. I never told you I *was* alive, so we're even." She winked.

Leaning against the side of the couch, she watched as the rest of their small band of conspirators came into the room. When Melody entered, Derrick rose from his chair like a lovestruck man from a period piece greeting the woman that held his heart.

August nudged Nora's shoulder with his. "You ready?" he murmured.

Beth and a stern-faced Bill appeared in the room. While

Gideon entered rooms through the door, the Putmans seemed to have no desire to engage in false pretenses. They really embraced their ghostly ways.

"So, I've been summoned to my own library," Bill grumbled.

"Yes." Nora said, her spine straight.

Smiling, August pushed his hands into the pockets of his jeans. No doubt to keep his hands to himself. After Beth left them alone in the woods, his hands trailed down Nora's body as she explained the plan to him. No doubt future meetings for planning episodes or discussing edits would prove far more interactive with this new dynamic of their relationship. His weren't the only exploring hands. Hers had slipped beneath the fabric of his black T-shirt, reveling in the contraction of his back muscles as she whispered her plan into his ear between kisses.

She pushed the memory away and spoke, "We're going to tackle this head on. Melody has brought us here to help you uncover your unfinished business."

Bill scoffed, his face drawn into a sour expression.

Nora couldn't disagree with him. While today had made her question the truths she had once held tight to, she still didn't believe in the idea of unfinished business. If that theory was true, wouldn't experiencing ghosts like Gideon, Beth, and Bill be an everyday occurrence?

Wouldn't they still be here? She shook off that thought.

There had to be some other explanation for why these three still inhabited this place. They weren't the only deaths at Putman House. Derrick's research packet showed that Melody's great-grandmother and grandfather died on the property, and they didn't haunt the house.

Someone else would have to figure that out. Her goal was to film the show without exposing Gideon, Beth, and Bill's existence, find some way to help Beth control her emotions, broker peace between the feuding couple, and destroy the Putman House's haunted reputation. Simple.

"For the next week, while the crew is here and we're filming you'll keep your promise to Melody and make yourself scarce. You can hang out in the woods together or—"

"You can come to the carriage house," Melody offered.

Beth gaped. "Melody, that's your personal space. Your sanctuary. We promised your parents we'd never go there unless it was an emergency."

Nora peered at Melody. No wonder Melody's parents were concerned about her opening the bed and breakfast. It would be hard to keep this long-held family secret with guests traipsing in and out of a house full of ghosts.

"Just for this week. It's what is best," Melody insisted.

"No." Beth shook her head. "I won't break a promise to your mother. I like her too much. She's my favorite of the women that have married into this family. Beside your mother and me, the Putman men have had terrible taste in wives."

A tiny snort escaped Gideon.

Derrick cringed. "I do remember your Grandma Putman not being very pleasant."

"She was terrible." Melody smiled weakly.

"We won't come into your space. Nora, tell us when and where we should be, and we'll do that. Anything to help our Melody. Right Bill?" Beth motioned at her husband.

"It's my house!" he let out a loud breath.

"You're barely in here anyways. You're always stomping around outside, so it won't be a big loss."

"I'm outside because each time I come inside you have a fit, exploding lights or smashing something." He shot her a stern expression.

The wall sconces flickered.

"Mrs. Putman." Gideon's caution was gentle.

Closing her eyes, she let out a loud breath. "What else, Nora?"

Gesturing between Beth and Bill she said, "Then there's that. Beth, we need to find a way to get your emotions under control."

"Good luck," Bill snarked. "She's always had a temper."

Beth glowered at him. The lights surged bright.

"Well, you're not helping." Nora scolded.

"Thank you, Nora." Beth tipped her head up with an air of haughty vindication.

"You're no better either." August wagged his finger at Beth.

"Ha!" Bill grinned. Then, seeing his wife's face, he spun to August. "Son, I told you not to speak to her like that."

"Always after the fact," Beth muttered.

Nora took in Bill's stricken face. It was fleeting, but his eyes blazed with regret. Turning his back to his wife, his stare moved to the window.

In that moment, Nora knew that Melody was right. Bill didn't kill his wife. The hurt and longing that swam in his expression spoke of a man tormented by not being with the woman he loved. It could just be regret or remorse, but the flutter in her belly told Nora it wasn't. Her ever-present need for logic stood in conflict with the idea of gut instincts, but she still trusted them. They hadn't failed her yet.

Nora crossed her arms over her chest. "Every morning at seven a.m., you will meet me in the clearing for one hour."

"For what?" They said in unison.

"Therapy."

"What?" They gaped.

August nodded. "Nora knows what she's doing. Trust her."

Did she? It was likely that she was just winging it, but his belief bolstered her. She'd been in therapy since she was six.

She had been seeing her latest therapist Dr. Unaka for the last seven years. Twice a month, Nora sat on his couch, sipping a cup of tea and talking. Sometimes about actual issues. Other times about the mundane. Sometimes she'd leave drained like an oversqueezed orange. Other times she'd leave as light as the Santa Ana breeze. She knew all the tricks for how to handle emotions and deal with grief.

"I'm sorry, Nora but you're not a therapist," Derrick said, his tone was tentative and apologetic.

"Correct. It will be a mutual aid group." Nora dropped her hands to her sides and turned to August. It made sense when they discussed the plan in the clearing. Was this a huge mistake? Perhaps it was just the post-orgasm endorphins clouding her judgement.

August slipped his fingers in hers. Each gentle squeeze of her hand coaxed her to proceed.

"Mutual aid group therapy…for grief. For those that have gone through it. I'll run it."

Beth's lips pursed, a slight tremble in her hands. The room's lights exploded. Everyone's cell phones buzzed violently. Bill looked between his wife and Nora.

Lightening flashed in Bill's expression. "How dare—"

"For those that have died," she cut off Bill's objection.

She imagined they assumed she was going to force them to talk about their son Willy's death. She wouldn't. It may happen naturally, but she wouldn't push them to face something they weren't ready to face. She understood the slow trail of grieving loved ones. Even if it had been well over a century since their son died, it was clear they may not yet be ready to talk about that.

Her gaze flicked around the room. It was filled by people that knew grief. That had all lost someone they loved. A child. A friend. A sibling. A parent. A grandparent. Gideon, Beth, and Bill had, no doubt, lost generations of people they loved. What might it have been like to spend all this time in this house watching the births, lives, and deaths of everyone they loved over the years? They clearly loved Melody. Nora couldn't fathom the many, many layers of grief that wrapped around the three ghosts in the room.

"What greater grief than dying?" Melody said.

"How are you going to run it? You've not died," Gideon's brow wrinkled.

Nora swallowed. "But I did."

Mouths dropped open. Eyes blinked. Breath stuttered.

"If you want to know my story, be at the clearing at seven tomorrow."

CHAPTER 15

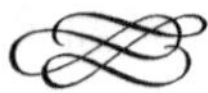

Torture and Chardonnay

The room was quiet until Gideon cleared his throat and announced that he would be there in the morning.

Nora watched Derrick and August have a wordless conversation. Derrick's wide eyes seemed to ask, "Did you know?" But he didn't. Nobody knew except Grandpa Scott, Mae, and Dr. Unaka. It took almost two years of therapy with Dr. Unaka for her to talk about it with him and four years of friendship with Mae before she'd confided.

Unspooling her fingers from August's, she excused herself to go meet the crew. She needed to break away and get back into work mode, reclaiming her badass demeanor.

"Wow, this place is gorgeous!" Dusty let out a long whistle and hopped out of the van. "This would be the perfect place for a wedding."

"We're not getting married at a haunted bed and breakfast," Benji tutted, opening the back of the van to start unloading equipment.

"But you two met at a haunted hospital, so this is a step up," Raj chuckled.

"You are weirdly glowing," Dusty said, tilting his head and studying her. He was like a bloodhound sniffing out on-set romances. He'd quickly spotted Raj's secret relationship with Jane, the production assistant from last season, so no doubt he'd suss out what was happening between she and August if she wasn't careful.

"There's a walking trail in the woods, and I just got back from a quick jaunt," she said, smoothing down her low ponytail.

"Ugh, you and exercise. You're as bad as Gus," he grumbled.

Nora nibbled on her lip. There would be time to daydream about *exercising* with August later.

"Don't overexert yourself with your exercise. You look all flushed," Benji said, wagging a finger.

"Okay, dads." She waved them off. "I've emailed the locations for setting up the X-cameras and the shots for tomorrow. Lucy, come with me. I'll show you where our command center will be."

After instructing Lucy on the setup of the command center in the day room on the first floor, she went over the scheduled shots for the next day. In the morning, Dusty would take the lead while they filmed some points of interest in the village. This would give Nora time to stay behind and run her "We Died" support group. She'd need to work on that name.

Around six, the crew wrapped for the day, allowing them time to head back to their motel to shower, change, and come back for the drinks party. When Nora walked into the carriage house, Melody and Derrick were in the kitchen preparing food.

"How did it go?" Melody's bright smile was akin to a cool

glass of water on a hot summer day, refreshing and comforting.

Apprehension had knotted within Nora with each step towards the carriage house, wondering who would be there and what they would say. She imagined there were questions. Hell, she'd have questions if someone announced, "Oh, by the way, I died." She just didn't know if she was ready to answer them.

Gnawing on her lip, she debated saying something. They deserved something. So did August. Her eyes darted around the room half expecting to see him leaning against a wall, hands pushed in his pockets, smirking at her. He was not. Disappointment fluttered in her belly.

"Where's August?" she asked.

Melody's big smile made it obvious that she either knew or suspected something. "He had to run an errand."

"Do you want some help?"

"Nah, you go shower and change." Melody made a "scoot" motion with her hands. "Plus, I have my sous chef." She hip-checked Derrick.

"Of course," he said, a flirty lilt to his voice.

Perhaps she and August wouldn't have to try too hard to make this match happen. The two appeared to be falling together organically.

"Thank you," Nora said, her heart swelling. "Not just for…"

Derrick looked up from the bell pepper he was cutting. "When you're ready to share, we're here. And even if you never share, you're still our Nora."

Grateful, she walked over and kissed both their cheeks before heading to her room to shower and change for the party.

An hour later, she stood in front of the mirror for a final check of her look. A pale pink goddess-style maxi dress hugged her breasts and flowed over the soft curves of her hips. Her long hair hung straight and loose. White gold dragonfly earrings dangled from her ears, a gift from Mae's trip to the Canary Islands last spring. She slipped into a pair of white wedges and headed downstairs. Derrick and Melody had already set up and the crew was there.

"Look at you, lady!" Dusty hooted as Nora walked into the room. "You clean up well."

"So do you." She motioned to his short sleeved blue plaid button up and yellow bow tie.

Like Nora, Dusty always dressed for the occasion. They'd both grown up in small farming towns where your "Sunday Best" was pulled out for special events or parties. It was something they'd bonded over after they'd first met. She'd grown up on her grandpa's chicken farm in Missouri, and he'd been raised on his parents' cattle ranch outside Pagoda, Texas. Though, his style was more southern garden party or church potluck with dockers, loafers, and a colorful collage of coordinated button ups and bow ties.

"You can take the boy out of Pagoda, but not the Pagoda out of the boy," Benji chuckled and pressed a tender kiss to Dusty's cheek.

Grabbing a glass of chardonnay, Nora scanned the room. Everyone was there, except for August. She didn't want to be *that* girl, but she was totally being *that* girl. What was this errand? Was it just an excuse to leave? Was he upset with her about learning that she'd died with everyone else? Should she have told him first? This is why she didn't do relationships. Too much self-doubt.

"Gus!" Lucy exclaimed.

August appeared at the door, a large brown paper bag in his right hand. He tipped his head in greeting and strode into the room, a black T-shirt and dark jeans molded over his muscular frame. His gaze met hers from across the room, and a giant grin erupted on his face. The butterflies went wild in Nora's stomach.

Her smile matched his. *Okay, so he's not mad at me. Guess I was being silly. Oh, Mae is going to torment me for this.*

He deposited the bags on the bar where Nora stood sipping wine beside Melody. "I had to get something important for our get together," he announced, pulling out two large white containers. Playfulness twinkled in his features as he opened the containers.

"French fries!" Nora squealed with all the delight of a child.

Melody nudged Nora in the ribs. "And they say flowers are how you woo a lady."

Nora rolled her eyes. *Guess, she really can read people.* It was clear that Melody suspected there was something—whatever this something was—happening between Nora and August.

Taking a plate, Nora scooped up several fries and perched herself at the end of the bar. While everyone else mingled, she munched. True to the "Let's be normal" promise they made earlier, August moved through the room, chatting with everyone, while Nora remained solo eating her fries and sipping wine at the bar.

"You must be excited to finally investigate Putman House," Lucy said, placing her hand on August's bicep.

Nora bit hard into a fry, reminding herself that Lucy was a toucher. She'd seen her do the same thing to Derrick, Benji, and even Dusty.

"Yup." August lifted his bottle of beer to his lips.

"You're far too cool for the night before investigating your dream location," Benji added. "I thought you'd be like Nora the night before a sale on Jimmy Choo's."

"I don't think anyone gets as excited as Nora does about shoes." He winked at her over his shoulder, sparking a happy zing across her body.

"I don't know how she walks in those. I'm more a sneaker girl. I rock my Sketchers even with dresses," Lucy giggled, motioning to the pink sneakers she'd paired with a white T-shirt dress.

She shouldn't be jealous, but she was. Lucy was everything that Nora wasn't. She was a soft, warm breezy day. The cool girl that Nora was not. God, Mae would chide her for comparing herself with another woman and for calling another woman a "girl." Hell, she'd wag a finger at herself. But Lucy's Disney-princess vibe made more sense with someone like August. Nora thought of herself as the woman at the start of every Hallmark movie that the hero breaks up with for the Lucys of the world.

Baby girl, don't question people who see you for the special girl you are. Question why you don't see it.

Grandpa Scott was right. That big smile that spread across August's face each time his gaze met hers across the room cemented that truth. Even now, he looked past Lucy and straight at her.

"I'm grabbing another," August said. "Anyone?"

Lucy batted her eyelashes. "I'll take another Labatt."

"You got it." Slipping behind the bar, he reached into the fridge and pulled out two bottles of beer. Bending across Nora to grab the bottle opener, he whispered, "You look gorgeous."

"Thank you." Her response was barely a whisper.

"This is torture," he murmured, turning to toss the bottle caps in the trash behind him. "I want to touch you."

His words prickled heat along her body. Had it only been seven hours since he pressed her up against that tree? The burning need rioting through her spoke of years without his touch, not hours. Although hadn't it been? Hadn't they denied themselves this for years?

"I want to touch you too." Her murmur was breathless.

Looking at the large black and white clock hanging on the wall that inched closer to nine, she knew the party would wrap soon. The team would meet at seven a.m. to head out to film at some of the offsite locations. Any minute now Dusty would announce "Pop-pop needs to go to bed," calling the night to an end. Once he did that and the crew headed back to their hotel, Nora would...

"Pop-pop is tired kids!" Dusty yawned dramatically.

Just a Walk before Bed

After everyone left, Derrick, August, and Nora helped Melody clean up. Once the entertainment room was cleared of discarded cups, plates, and platters, the little foursome found themselves in the apartment kitchen. Melody rinsed dishes, while Derrick loaded them into the dishwasher.

Every muscle in Nora's body spooled tight with the urge to kiss and touch August. Even some she'd had no idea existed. Each time he moved past her, the heat of his body licked against her skin, igniting a forest fire of want within her. He hadn't touched her yet making her unsure if he told his brother, so she'd kept her distance. She was ninety-nine percent positive Melody had sussed it out, or else her nosey aunt spilled the tea.

"We're almost done, so if you two want to go to bed, we've got this," Melody offered, a wink in her voice.

Make that one hundred percent.

August's sneakered feet shuffled foot-to-foot. His long

fingers raked into his dark hair. "Okay…uh…goodnight." He looked at her and then the door and then back to her again.

Their gazes met in a wordless conversation. Hers saying, "Don't go," while his seemed to implore her to come with him.

"Goodnight, August." Nora's words were a soft breath.

With a quick nod, he slipped out the door.

Excusing herself to her room, she sat on the bed, tapping her fingers against her thigh. It was useless to think that each tap had the power to soothe the want that surged through her veins. It was more than wanting him. It almost felt like she couldn't breathe properly until she pressed herself against him and gulped up his kisses.

This is stupid. You're like a horny cat. She let out a shaky breath. For two years she'd kept her distance. She'd been able to push down those rogue butterflies. Somehow the moment her lips pressed against his, any restraint she'd had blinked away.

Fuck it! Jumping up, she ran out of her room. "I'm going to go for a walk," she announced.

"Now? It's late." Derrick gaped.

"Just around the property. I have my phone." She waved her cell like it was a weapon, moving to the door.

"Have fun," Melody almost crooned.

With each step toward the house, Nora's heartbeat sped. This was crazy. She should be cool about this, but all she wanted was to bury herself in him. She hoped that just one more kiss would calm the need that turned her bloodstream molten. As her shoes slapped against the steps toward August's room, something told her it would never be just one more kiss with him. That she'd unlocked something that couldn't be tucked back away.

Her hand barely knocked before the door swung open, and he pulled her into his arms. "Thank god," he breathed.

Their mouths crashed together with consuming need. He lifted her into his arms and her legs wrapped around him as he turned, kicked the door shut, and walked them to the bed. Never breaking their kiss, he laid her down and lowered himself atop her, settling between her legs. Each touch scorched against her burning skin.

"I want you so bad," he panted, pressing hungry kisses down her throat to her collarbone.

She found the hem of his shirt and tugged it off. She'd seen him shirtless before but not like this. Not where his sculpted chest hovered over her, close enough to touch. Not where she could inhale his delicious scent. Not where she could press her lips to his chest.

"You're so beautiful," she hummed, tracing his well-defined muscles.

A boyish smile, somehow both bashful and sexy, stretched across his face. "If I'm beautiful, you're stunning."

He sat back on his heels and pulled her up to straddle his lap. Taking her lips in a slow deep kiss, he gripped her ass kneading each globe and causing her to whimper.

Heat pooled at her center, cascading across every inch of her. She slipped the straps of her dress down and pushed it to her waist, revealing her lacy white bra.

Licking down her throat, his hands reached for the clasp. His hands halted and he looked up at her. "Is this okay? I want to make sure that you want this. We can stop."

Cupping his face, she smiled. "Yes. This is *very* okay. I want this...I want *you*." She dipped her head, claiming his mouth with hers.

Eyes dark with desire, he unclasped her bra and slipped it

off. Skating his hands over her skin, he rubbed his fingers over her pebbling nipples. A sweet ache filled her breasts as he took a taut bud and sucked gently.

Her head lulled back. "Please…don't stop."

"I'm just getting started," he murmured against her skin.

He kissed a slow trail from one breast to the other before taking her other taut peak in his mouth. With a flick of his tongue, he teased her until he relented to her tiny whimpers and sucked the needy bud. Back arched, her fingers wove into his hair. He groaned with her gentle tugs and then responded with a hardened suck of her nipple. She writhed against him, chasing needed friction to ease the building tension.

His kisses and touch teetered between bruising and feather light. It was perfect making Nora both feel worshipped and unbreakable. Somehow, he knew what notes to strike to coil that pressure low in her belly just a little tighter.

"I want more," she whined, the need spooled to the point that she feared she may combust..

"And I'll give it to you," he said, his voice was low and laced with wicked promise.

He slid her off his lap and laid her back on the bed. She raised her hips, and he pulled her dress the rest of the way off.

Running his fingers along the front of her damp panties, his smile turned wolfish. "I want to taste you."

The want flooded every inch of her. "Yes." Her entire body craved to be consumed by him.

Dragging down her panties, he tossed them aside and pulled her to the edge of the bed. With a wicked glint in his dark gaze, he bent between her legs and inhaled deeply. "So sweet."

His praise surged pleasure within her. "Please," she whimpered as he placed a nipping kiss on her inner thigh.

"Please what?"

"Taste me…" She bit her lower lip in anticipation.

"Gladly." His throaty reply made her entire body sing. His tongue rasped down her center. "Fuck—" he peered up at her, his eyes almost black, "—I take that back. I don't want to just taste you. I want to fucking drink up every bit of you."

"Then do it," she breathed.

And he did just that. He took her clit in his mouth, rolling it with at first gentle pressure and teasing licks but with each dig of his fingers into her thighs he sucked harder. Head tossed back, she moved against his working mouth. She sank her teeth into her bottom lip to quiet her cries. It was too good. The pleasure wound every muscle with a vise-like grip causing the edges of her vision to grow black. Her breaths came in heavy gulps and she feared she may break into a million pieces.

"So fucking good," he growled between sucks.

It was filthy and reverent. Somehow, he both made love to her and fucked her with his mouth. His feral moans as he drank her up sparked awake every one of her nerve endings into tiny fireworks bursting inside her. This was as much for him as for her. That knowledge making her drunk. The wave built with each lick, suck, and roll of her clit until he slid his finger in to find that sensitive spot on the inside of her wall, tipping her over the edge.

"August!" she screamed, clenching her legs around his head and riding out her climax.

He rose, unbuttoning his jeans and pushing them down. The rather impressive arousal tented his boxers' fabric.

"Please tell me you have a condom," she said, breathlessly sitting up on the bed.

"That was part of my errand. I didn't want to be

presumptuous, but I wanted to be prepared." He pulled a box of condoms out of the top drawer of the bedstand.

"I love that you were prepared." She smirked, watching his boxers drop to the floor.

He was breathtaking. The hard planes of his sculpted chest. The cut ridges of his torso. The teasing trail of dark hair that led low to his cock, thick and veiny. Something almost feral coursed through her veins at the sight of him, like a primal need to consume and be consumed by all that raw masculinity.

Licking her lips she moaned, "Now, I want to taste you."

"And I want that too, but I won't last…and I *need* to be inside you. At least this first time."

Her lips ticked up at the idea of "first time," implying many, many more times. This one time with August wouldn't be enough. Despite the orgasm she'd just had, her body burned with a craving for him.

Rising to her knees, she took the condom from him. Opening the package, she pulled it out and rolled it onto him. A ragged breath escaped him with her touch.

"How do you want me? Dealer's choice," she said with all the seductiveness of Aphrodite.

"Are you real?" His breathy question was disbelieving.

She nipped his lips. "Very much."

"You on top," he said, laying on the bed.

Reminiscent of a stalking tigress, she crawled over his body. Taking his length in hand, she eased herself onto him. She rocked slowly at first, the fullness spreading sparks of pleasure within her like bonfires.

Hands braced on his chest, she increased her momentum. His hips thrusted up, meeting hers in a tantalizing slow dance.

"You feel so good, baby," he moaned.

"I want you deeper," she commanded, grinding her pelvis against him.

Gripping her waist, he flipped them. Her legs wrapped high around his back. The angle deepened his position within her, the deeper and harder thrusts tightening the decadent pressure enveloping her core. He slipped his hand between them to stroke her where she needed him most.

Her nails dug into his back as the climax took her. "My... god!"

He continued moving inside her, prolonging her pleasure, and chasing his own. With an unintelligible barrage of curse words, he grunted with his release.

"Look...at you... You're so...beautiful," he panted, his sweat kissed face lit with a goofy post-orgasm grin.

"Ditto." Her grin, no doubt, matched his. "Why did we wait so long to do this?"

"Because I'm a moron, remember?" He bent and pressed his smile to hers.

"My moron," she said instinctively.

"Yeah..." He caressed her cheek.

Something warm and gooey filled her chest, making it hard to speak. The idea of him being her anything was too tempting. Part of her wanted to run away. It was her default mode with men. No promises beyond mutual needs met. At that moment, that part of her was a mere whisper drowned out by the thump, thump of her heart in his presence telling her to stay.

He nuzzled his nose with hers. "Let me take care of the condom and I'll be right back."

As he lifted off her, she sat up and moved to get off the bed. "I should probably get dressed and—"

August shook his head, wrapping his arms around her. "I'd like to hold you for a bit before you run away. It's only eleven. The crew won't be here until seven a.m., so we have time."

"Why, August Chandler, are you a snuggler?" she teased.

Kissing her forehead, his chocolate eyes sparkled. "Very much."

Silently laughing, she shook her head. "Alright. Let me use the restroom and then we can snuggle."

It wasn't *that* surprising that August was a snuggler. He gave golden retriever energy, after all. What was more surprising to Nora was that she was finding herself wanting to snuggle.

In the bathroom, she took care of her needs, freshened up just a bit, and headed back. Slipping back into the room, she found August already in bed waiting for her, a sated expression anchoring his features. With a soft smile, she slid beneath the pale blue duvet beside him, his strong arms pulling her into his chest.

"I should have asked, but do you like to snuggle?" His hands glided down her back.

"Not really." She ran her fingers in the light dusting of hair across his chest. "I've always felt claustrophobic when men tried to cuddle me. Like, I'd get all hot and have trouble breathing."

In the past she'd just complain about being too hot or needing to get up in the morning. Anything to escape.

"Do you want me to let go?" he asked, his hands raking into her hair.

"No, but…" She worried her lower lip. "Would you loosen your hold but not let go?"

Despite the gentle current of anxiety prickling along her nerves, the sensation of his bare skin against hers was too addictive. His warmth cocooned her in a sense of safety. The sound of his heartbeat lulled her like a soothing lullaby. In his arms, she knew if she needed to pull away, she could.

He'd let her go, if she asked. That knowledge soothed the ripple of anxiety. Even if the truth that she may never be able to pull away from him pulsed within her.

"Is this better?" He loosened his grip, but his arms remained around her.

"Yes." She melted into his embrace, the last flicker of anxiousness extinguished.

"Good." He placed a tender kiss on her temple.

"I could get use to this." She nuzzled against him, inhaling deep his mixed scent of cologne, sweat, and her.

"I could get used to this too, but if you need me to let go just say so. Otherwise, I might never."

The confession filled her with happiness. Why had she waited so long to do this? Why had she denied them—denied *herself*—this feeling?

"So, claustrophobic…" he paused, his fingers drawing soothing circles along her skin. "…Is that why you avoid elevators and get uncomfortable in rooms with no windows and a shut door? You don't want to feel trapped?"

Nora swallowed hard. He'd noticed. Of course he had.

"Yes."

"I've noticed that sometimes you flick this—" he tapped at the rubber band on her wrist "—when we're in small places. Does it help?"

"At times. It gives me something else to focus on besides the anxiety swirling inside me," she said softly. It had been a trick the school psychologist had suggested after a panic attack seized Nora on a school trip to a corn maze, causing her to curl into a ball and hyperventilate.

August's head tilted down, his eyes studying her. The unasked questions visible in his soft expression.

Taking in a deep breath she spoke, "You can ask me…I want you to ask me."

"Was it your parents' car accident? Was that how you died?"

"Yes." She closed her eyes. The memories splashed over her like an icy wave. "We were coming home from dinner. It was Pizza Palace. I loved it because mom and dad let me get a personal pizza. I felt so grown up picking my own toppings. Even though I only ever got pepperoni. That's still my topping of choice."

His long fingers combed into her hair. The reassuring gesture anchored her to him. So often, she'd run away rather than share herself. In that moment, she didn't want to run. She wanted to stay, even if what she was doing mirrored running towards something. Something with this man.

"I don't remember much. A drunk driver hit us, and the car flipped and went off an embankment. I remember not being able to get out. I remember my mom's voice calling me. Then it was dark….so dark. I called for my mom…my dad, but they didn't answer. I heard someone say, 'It's not your time, little one,' and then I saw a man's face over me. I guess it was the paramedic who revived me. They're not sure how long I was gone for, but when they found us, none of us had pulses. They worked on all three of us, but I was the only one they revived."

Hot tears stung, blurring her vision. Burying her face into his chest, she tried to hide the tears. She tried to hide the truth of her fear. The fear that although alive she was still dead inside. The echoes of past relationships hissed inside her. *You have no heart, Nora. You're dead inside, Nora. You're cold, Nora.*

And it wasn't just men she'd dated, but even friends and colleagues. Part of Nora worried that while she may have come back to the world of the living that day that an important piece of her remained in the world of the dead—her heart. Even now, cocooned in August's warm embrace, the fear rippled within her.

"Hey," he murmured, tucking his hand below her chin, and guiding her gaze to him. He lowered his head, kissing the corners of her eyes, then her tear-stained cheeks, and finally her lips. "Thank you for sharing this with me." His gaze almost reverent as he stared at her. "Thank you for sharing so much of yourself with me."

"You want me. Not just this…" she motioned to her naked body. "…You want all of me."

"I do."

The proclamation both eased and ramped up the fear. She didn't know if there was more to her. Did she have a heart to give? For the first time in her life, she wanted to find out. Fear still rattled within her that this may end like other failed attempts at relationships. But she'd already gone farther with him than with anyone else. If ghosts were real, then maybe so was her heart and its ability to open.

"Don't get me wrong," he chuckled. "I want more of this." A devilish smile played on his lips as his hands skated down her naked body. "But I want *this* even more." He placed his hand on her heart, which thump-thumped in reply. "When I first met you on that elevator, I was instantly attracted to you. You're gorgeous. Whether dressed up in a pretty dress or all sweaty in your workout clothes. And you're especially pretty when you're naked in my bed."

She laughed.

"But it's so much more than that. You're brilliant, talented, you keep me on my toes, you're passionate, nobody makes me smile and laugh like you, nobody's smile steals my breath like yours, and despite what you think, you're warm and kind. You may not be the bake cookies and make home-made cards for birthdays kind of person, but you're thoughtful in all the important ways. Like how you always indulge Derrick's nerdy historian ideas or how you called in a few favors to get Benji and Dusty the same commercial jobs during our hiatus so they could work together."

He kissed a different part of her after each declared attribute. Her cheeks, lips, chin, below her ear, and neck were all assigned a different reason he was drawn to her. Each word and kiss sent a buzzing along her veins reminiscent of drinking crisp champagne, leaving her a little happy-tipsy.

With a grateful smile, she raised her hands, cradling his face. "I tried to fight it, but I wanted you from the moment you complimented my shoes."

A lazy grin split his face.

"I know I've acted like I wasn't impacted by you, but I was. I used every excuse to fight this pull to you. I've never had any type of relationship with someone that I actually..." She closed her eyes. Why was this so hard? The words banged around inside her, but seemed to flee the moment she went to speak them.

"With someone that you actually want to be in a relationship with?"

Nora nodded. It was true. Mae told her that she'd use any excuse to deny the attraction to August because she was scared. God, she was so scared. It was easy to roll into bed with someone that she saw no future with. Hell, she'd never invited a man to her place. She'd go to theirs, get her itch scratched, and go home. She'd never linger in their arms after.

"When we met on the elevator, did you notice my panic when the elevator got stuck? Is that why you started talking about ghosts? We're you trying to distract me?"

"Yes."

"I knew it. I was so conflicted about you that day. I thought you were the competition and when you said good luck, I thought you were being a douche canoe."

He barked with laughter.

"But you were so kind and adorable with your earnest belief that ghosts were real…"

"Which I was *totally* right about."

"Yes. Yes, I know. I owe you a drink."

"I'd rather take you to dinner." He smirked.

She nibbled on her lip. "I'd like that… A lot." Her lips lifted in a big smile.

"Actually—" his eyes twinkled with mischief "—can I take you to lunch tomorrow? We'll be back by noon from our morning of shooting, and then we're on break until seven."

"Ummm…" Her pulse ticked up. "…. Aren't you and Derrick having lunch with your parents?"

One of the perks of this shoot for the Chandler brothers was it being in their hometown, allowing them to see their parents. It also gave them a chance to showcase some of their favorite things from the area. Several locations had been scouted for them to shoot at during the daylight hours, letting both brothers share something personal about themselves and highlight some lesser-known tourist spots. Lunch, though, would be a personal thing with no cameras. No crew. Just them and their parents.

"Yes, but Derrick is bringing Melody, so it wouldn't be weird if you came. Also, I'd like them to meet you. Properly." He swiped his thumb along her jaw.

Meet his parents? The chaotic thump of her heart drowned out the air conditioner's soft hum.

On the surface, meeting a man's parents twenty-four hours after you started seeing him seemed fast. However, they'd known each other for over two years. And technically, she'd already met his parents. She'd spoken to them on several occasions when August answered their video chats in the middle of meetings or filming.

"Wait? Melody?" She gaped. "Has Derrick made his move? They did appear awfully chummy when I left the apartment tonight."

"God, I hope so." He laughed. "I'm not sure. My mom invited Melody when she knew we were investigating Putman House." He traced her lips. "So, is that a yes?"

"Yes."

A giant smile kicked across his face.

"Well, I should meet your parents. You are my young man, after all." She batted her lashes.

He captured her in a long kiss, wrapping his arms tighter around her.

Melting into it, she allowed herself to let go. To just revel in the sensation of safety and belonging enfolding her.

Their kiss slowed and he pulled back. "Stay with me tonight. Please."

She longed to say yes. "Not tonight. I will go to lunch, though. You can tell Derrick and your parents that I'm..." she searched for what to call herself.

"My Nora?"

The flutter in her belly kicked up with that. "Your Nora." A sweet claiming, which she did not object to. "I still want to keep this quiet with the crew, though. At least for now. After filming, we can figure things out."

"I understand."

"I appreciate that." She licked her lips. "And to show my appreciation, I'd like to leave you with a parting gift."

Nora slipped out of his arms, kissing down his body. His breath shallowed with the downward movement of her lips. Looking up at him through hooded eyelashes, she flashed a sultry smile before taking his growing erection in her hands and placing a chaste kiss at the tip. Delight filled her at the working muscles of his throat in reaction to her hands stroking him.

"Oh, my Nora," he groaned as she took him into her mouth.

CHAPTER 17

Group Therapy

You really can Google anything, Nora thought. Tips for facilitating conversations with survivors of near-death experiences filled her phone. Gideon, Beth, and Bill weren't *survivors*, but the suggestions may still work. They'd all died and come back in different ways. Nora came back to life and the three ghosts returned as...well, ghosts.

Slipping her phone into her pocket, she paced in the small clearing, the late spring sky already a soft blue. The morning soundtrack of chirping birds, rustling leaves in the gentle breeze, and babble of the small brook sang in her ears. So much life around her as she prepared to meet with the dead. It was like a rejected Alanis Morrisette lyric.

"You ready?" August's deep voice drew her attention.

"I hope so."

Part of her wondered what the hell she was doing. She was a television field producer, not a therapist. Especially not one to the not-so-recently passed. When Grandpa Scott told her that she could do anything, he may not have envisioned this.

Stepping close, August looped his arms around her waist and tucked her into his firm chest. "What words of wisdom would Grandpa Scott have for something like this?"

Thoughts of her grandpa always soothed her jitters. After last night's second round of toe-curling sex, she laid in August's arms talking. Something about those strong arms folded around her unlocked so much. She told him about grandpa sitting by her hospital bed, taking her to his farm, his little nuggets of wisdom, and how he'd hung a tire swing for her in the old maple tree in the front. Hours were spent swinging or just sitting there with a book about a faraway place that she wanted to visit someday. The entire time, August's fingers combed through her hair as he listened with a contented smile on his face. Luxuriating in his embrace and encouraging smile, Nora didn't creep away until nearly two a.m.

Her face scrunched. "I don't know if Grandpa Scott would have advice for facilitating a death mutual-aid group for ghosts."

His arched brow seemed to question that statement.

Running her fingers across the scratched surface of her watch, she closed her eyes. What *would* Grandpa Scott say about this? There'd been so many nuggets of grandpaisms that she clung to. *Trust your gut, baby girl. A new friend is just one hello away. Never trust cat people.* From the age of six to twenty he'd been her entire world. The steady compass guiding her on life's journey. In so many ways, he still was.

Opening her eyes, she tipped her head up to August. "If you don't know how to fix the car, listen to its engine."

The memory played in her vision like a waking dream. *Bent over his pickup, her hair coiled in two cinnamon roll buns during the Princess Leia phase she'd indulged in after grandpa showed her the original Star Wars trilogy. Smudges of oil dotted her denim overalls. The scent of oil and his vanilla coffee creamer filled her nostrils. With his dexterity failing from the ALS, he'd started teaching her things that should have waited until she turned sixteen. By fourteen, she didn't just know how to change the oil, but she also knew how to drive the truck on the dirt road near the farm.*

His blue eyes, the same as her dad's, twinkled as he guided her through the parts of the engine, reminding her to listen. "Just like people, if you listen long enough, you'll know what's wrong. Engines, they need you to fix them, but people, sometimes they just need you to listen."

The memory faded and she breathed, "Just listen."

"Grandpa Scott for the win." Dipping his head, he pressed a slow kiss.

It seemed odd that only twenty-four hours ago she lived in a world with no knowledge of the feel of August's full lips against hers. That she'd never tasted his sweet mix of coffee and mint kisses. That every muscle in her body hadn't sighed happily when enveloped in his safe arms. It was now the world she inhabited, and it would take a crane to pull her away from this world…from this man.

Baby girl, your heart will always recognize its match. Even if your brain fights it.

Something fluttered in her chest. She wasn't sure if it was the remembered grandpaism or August's whispered, "My Nora," that caused it.

Shaking off the feeling, she cleared her throat. "You should get going. You have to leave for filming, and I have ghosts to deal with."

"You have ghosts to deal with," he repeated, his smirking mouth inches from hers.

"I appreciate your restraint in *not* reminding me of my 'ghosts are a product of an overactive imagination' stance." A wicked smile tugged at her lips. "Although I do have a greater appreciation of your imagination after the things your surprisingly filthy mouth said last night."

Her core clenched with the memory of his voice rasping into her ear the delicious ways he wanted to devour every inch of her as he thrust into her from behind. She'd never have suspected such a delightfully depraved mind behind that boyish smile. She may have lingered a little too long in the shower this morning, her hands coasting along her body, envisioning the future pleasure promised in his dirty words.

August's fingers slipped beneath the hem of her T-shirt, skating along her smooth skin. "I've had two years to dream up so many things I'd like to do to—and with—you," he purred as his fingers tiptoed higher.

The scent of lavender spiraled around them, chilling the crackling fire within Nora. Tilting her head to look beyond August, she sighed, "Beth."

Beth's face contorted in an apologetic grimace. "I promise that I wasn't sneaking up. You said to be here by seven."

"I should go," August mumbled. "I'll pick you up at twelve-thirty for lunch." He placed a quick kiss on her cheek before stepping back.

"Oh, don't hold back on my account." Beth's salacious lilt almost sang.

With a soft laugh, he turned and strode down the grassy path to the house.

"Tell me everything!" Beth squealed. "I promise I wasn't eavesdropping, but I heard you two last night. I haven't heard noises like that come out of the bedrooms in the house since the night Melody was conceived!"

"You listened to us?" She gaped in horror. "Oh my god, did Derrick hear us? Oh no!" Had they been *that* loud last night?

In the past, sex had never been like the romance novels Mae made her buddy read. Sure, there were a few panted breaths and pleased sighs. There were orgasms, but never like what she'd experienced with August. Her body still hummed from the pleasure August wrung out of her last night.

Beth bent close, her voice dropping to a whisper. "Derrick didn't come back until after midnight. By that time the second round of your cries of passion had subsided."

"Cries of passion?" she guffawed. "Aren't you a Victorian ghost lady? Shouldn't you be all clutched pearls about this?"

With a swat of the air, Beth dismissed Nora's comment. The cold wisp of air spread gooseflesh down Nora's arms.

"That is such a stereotype. We enjoyed sex as much as anyone else. The fifties were more buttoned up than *my* day. If you only knew what Bill and I did against that very tree you're leaning on…"

Nora immediately took a step away from the tree of ill-repute. "Wait? Derrick? After midnight? Where…" Realization washed over her with Beth's wide eyes.

"Please don't say anything to Bill. He gets a little overprotective of the Putman women. Especially our Melody. She's the first granddaughter…well, *ever.*"

"Derrick was with Melody?" No doubt Nora's smile was equal to Beth's in its salacious nature. "Go Derri—"

Beth slapped her hands over Nora's mouth. "Hush. They're coming."

A shiver pulsed from where Beth's hands were. They didn't feel like hands. It was like an icy breeze settled on her face. The prickling cold scampered along her body. The sensation akin to one's foot falling asleep. Only this was the entire body.

A sense of déjà vu rolled through Nora at the touch.

"Ms. Nora." The edges of Gideon's dark eyes crinkled with an open smile as he entered the clearing.

A scowling Bill followed.

The articles she'd googled all talked about the forming, storming, and norming phases of setting up groups like this. They suggested establishing group rules with clear agreed upon boundaries. Experts said to spend time introducing each other. But they didn't have time for that. Nora was only here for a week. The groups discussed online had weeks, months, and, even sometimes, years to do that.

Fuck it! Trust your gut.

"Let's all share how we died," Nora said, looking at each ghost.

"We all know how I died…" Beth glared at Bill. "…Bill threw me down the stairs."

"I did not!" he hissed, his fists clenched at his sides.

"Said *every* convicted killer ever." Her tone was mocking.

"You didn't even see who pushed you." He spun, and the cold air *whooshed* off him. "You may not have even been pushed. Perhaps you had one too many nighttime sherries and fell down the stairs. Lord knows you needed your little *helper* to fall asleep back then," he sneered.

Anger flashed in Beth's eyes.

"Mr. Putman. Mrs. Putman." Gideon's head tipped back to the sky as if beseeching for patience.

"Why don't we stick to what we know. Only what we saw. Not what we suspect," Nora suggested.

"Agreed," Bill gritted, his glowered face fixed on his wife. "I was hung for a crime that I did not commit."

Beth's death stare could combust someone with its intensity.

Nora closed her eyes, readying for another squabble between the Putmans. Perhaps this was a bad idea. Maybe they didn't need to come to terms with their deaths but undergo intensive marital therapy. She wondered if Dr. Unaka did postmortem marriage counseling.

"I had a heart attack," Gideon announced, his rapid speech akin to a trotting horse.

Nora flashed an appreciative smile. No doubt Gideon had perfected running interference between the Putmans. Imagine the punishment of being stuck playing referee for one's former employers for eternity.

Why were they here? Nora stroked her watch. What was it about Putman House that pulled them back? Why could they be seen as clearly as any living person? Was there something special about them? About this place? Or had Nora seen ghosts all along, but not realized it? That mysterious cowboy from the Blackhorse Hotel flashed in her memory.

She pushed on, "Gideon, you died in the house?"

He nodded.

"So did Beth…but Bill, you didn't. Yet, you're here." She knew from Derrick's research that Bill was hung at the county courthouse a town over.

Nora turned to Bill. The spring air blew a soft breeze that should ruffle his thick auburn hair, but it didn't. None of them were impacted by this place, but all bound to it.

Why, though? The question swirled inside her.

"Lucky me," Bill grumbled.

"Maybe this is your penance for pushing me down the stairs," Beth hissed.

Nora let out an annoyed breath.

"Fine. *Allegedly* pushed me down the stairs."

"What about you? How did you die?" Bill's question dripped with dismissiveness.

Tugging at the end of her low ponytail, she sucked in a breath. "My parents and I were in a car accident. The medics tried to revive us, but only I woke up."

Beth's eyes brimmed with emotion. Gideon's formal smile twisted with pained remorse. Even Bill's scowl smoothed.

"How old?" Beth's voice was soft.

"Six."

Beth and Bill's eyes met in a wordless conversation. Swallowing hard, Beth turned her stare from him. Her jade eyes darted around the small clearing.

"Oh, Ms. Nora, I am dreadfully sorry," Gideon murmured.

"You lost them?" Beth croaked. "Both of them? Who raised you?"

"My grandpa." With an anchoring touch of her watch, she went on, "It's fine, though. It happened a long time ago. Well, not as long as for you all. I've had a good life. Grandpa Scott was good to me. He was—"

"Not them." Bill's interruption was gruff.

A fire ignited in Nora's belly. Her eyes narrowed at Bill. Maybe it was the pity in his expression. Maybe it was the dismissive accusation that somehow Grandpa Scott hadn't been enough because he wasn't them but at that moment she wondered how she could slap a ghost.

"But he was there when they couldn't be. That's what matters," Gideon added, clearing his throat. "Parental love comes in many shapes."

With a wistful smile, Beth nodded. "Just like you and Agnes."

"Who's Agnes?"

"Gideon's niece. He'd raised her from the time she was ten, after his sister passed. She worked for us as a kitchen maid. She was a sweet girl," Beth explained.

Warmth spread in Nora's chest. She'd taken an instant liking to Gideon, and now she knew why. He was the Grandpa Scott for his niece.

"It's wonderful she had you," Nora offered with an appreciative smile.

"I had tried with Agnes...to be there for her. She was so lonely after my sister died...and..."

Bill placed a large hand on Gideon's shoulder. "You were there for her. Agnes was very lucky to have you. Don't be so modest. You would have done anything for that girl."

"What happened to Agnes after you passed?" Nora asked.

Gideon shook his head. "She left Putman House and...I don't know."

Something about that caused a dull ache in her heart. There was no ghost of her sweet grandpa, but she could imagine the sadness of his spirit sitting on his favorite recliner wondering what became of her. She'd never thought about how the dead might miss the living. All her grief had been steeped in what she'd lost, not what those she lost may be grieving.

But they're not ghosts, they're gone. The thought was an icy chide.

Nora tapped on the face of her watch. Gideon grieved his once living and now long-dead niece. The Putmans grieved their dead son. All four of them shared that common bond of grief. Not for the life they'd lost and got back in different ways, but for those they'd lost. Nora was given a second chance to live with actual life, while they were given an afterlife. Was it a second chance or a punishment? Why had the three come back? Something tethered them to this place...to each other.

"Ms. Nora," Gideon said, pulling Nora out of her head. "What shall we do next?"

It was a great question. She was charting a course with no map. In the last twenty-four hours, her life had gone wildly off-script. She was terrified, but her gut told her to go with it.

"Ah..." She clicked her tongue. "What happened when you died? Like what do you remember from that moment to ending up here?"

Gideon's thick fingers brushed along his chin. "It was

dark. Then I was standing over my own body in the parlor. Then I saw Mrs. Putman."

"Were there any lights or voices?" Nora asked.

He shook his head.

"There weren't for me either," Beth added. "I remember Bill…ah…*someone*, "she quickly corrected herself, but the iciness in her features spoke volumes, "…pushing me over the railing. The next thing I knew I felt the impact and then blackness. Just like Gideon, I was then standing over my body. Then Bill ran down the stairs saying how sorry he was. Then the servants appeared."

Bill was sorry? Wanting to avoid another argument about Bill allegedly killing Beth, she ignored that internal question and quickly asked for clarification. "None of them could see you?"

"No. I'm not sure why but I wasn't able to make myself be seen. Not then, at least. We can make ourselves unseen at times. We call it going quiet."

"We were quiet for a long time out of respect for Mr. Putman's brother's family, when they took over the house. We'd slip up from time-to-time," Gideon added.

"Especially with the children." A sheepish smile spread on Beth's face.

"Beth couldn't help but make herself known to the children of Putman House." Bill's tone was almost playful as he looked fondly at his wife.

Nora's head tilted. "Is that how Melody knew about you?"

"Yes. We all agreed to only show ourselves to the children when they were very little. Like imaginary friends, to help them if they were sad, lonely, or scared. We hadn't shown ourselves to Melody since she was seven, but when Diana died…"

Bill started to reach for his wife but stopped himself and yanked his hand back.

"Diana? August and Derrick's sister?"

"Such a lovely girl. Always laughing. Melody and Diana had filled the house with so much life," Beth chuckled, shooting her husband a wry grin. "They even made Bill smile from time to time."

"Mr. Putman loved those girls. He would push them on the swing set." Gideon beamed.

Beth turned to Bill. "You did?"

"They never knew it was me. I'd remain quiet and push as they swung. They'd giggle. No doubt they thought the extra speed and height was from their own momentum."

"I didn't know you did that."

The Putman's gazes mingled for a moment. Something passed between them that Nora couldn't quite make out, so she remained quiet allowing the wordless exchange to continue.

After a long beat, Beth turned back to Nora. "Melody was devastated after Diana died. It was hard for Melody to make friends as a girl. The village is small and that sometimes comes with small-minded people."

"Ms. Melody was different, and she lived in a house that was..."

"Different," Nora offered.

Beth stepped closer to Nora and her lavender scent spun around them. "For a long time, Diana was Melody's only friend. When she died, Melody was so lonely. So sad. We'd promised we'd not appear but—"

"Mrs. Putman can't ignore someone in distress."

"She never could." Bill stared at his wife, a wistful longing in his eyes.

"You mentioned promising Melody's mom to not infringe on her space. How did they know about you if you made yourself scarce?"

Bill huffed a quick laugh. "Beth."

Beth crossed her arms over her chest, an indignant expression on her face. "She was worried about her daughter, so I wanted to assure her everything was fine with Melody."

"The current living Mrs. Putman would hear Melody talking to Mrs. Putman and thought that Melody had…ah…"

"Dropped her basket." Beth jumped in, filling in Gideon's words. "I had appeared to Melody to comfort her, and then to her mom to, well, comfort *her.*"

"Tell them why you appeared to Melody's father." Bill prompted, laughing.

"Stationery was not an appropriate sweet sixteen gift. The Putman men are clueless about gifts," she tutted.

"You never minded *my* gifts."

Even Nora's cheeks heated at the suggestive nature of Bill's retort. If ghosts could blush, Nora imagined Beth's cheeks would match her own.

"That's why we are no longer quiet. We started showing ourselves to help Melody and we continue to do so. She's such a special young woman and we're very protective of her," Gideon explained.

"She needed us, and I think still does. We do want to help her. We…I don't mean to make things difficult for her," Beth said, wringing her hands. "I know how hard it was for her growing up here in this village."

"Melody is a Putman. She's special and some people in this village were jealous of that." Bill almost growled, his jaw clenched. "Those little bastards were lucky I was confined to this property or else I would have—"

"You're trapped here?" She knew that but hearing them confirm it still jolted her.

"We all are. None of us can go beyond the property line. When we try there is an invisible force that holds us back," Gideon said.

Nora tapped her foot against the grass. "Bill, what happened when you died?"

If Gideon and Beth had died on the property, it made sense they were here and trapped. But why was Bill there? How had he died at a jail one town over, only to come back to Putman House?

"I'll spare you the graphic details. It went black and then as if blinking my eyes awake, I was in this clearing." He motioned around.

"Any light? Voices?"

He shook his head.

"Had you seen light and heard voices? Is that why you keep asking?" Beth's expression turned thoughtful.

"It was dark. There wasn't light, but I've heard some people with near death experiences say that. I heard voices, though." Nora closed her eyes, hearing a soft voice in her memory saying "Not yet, baby," and a more gruff one shouting "Go back!"

"Whose—"

Nora's alarm interrupted Beth's question. "That's time," Nora said, yanking her phone out of her pocket to silence it. "I think that was a good start for today."

Was it? She had no idea.

Bill's slight eyeroll confirmed he wasn't impressed. Thank goodness for Beth and Gideon's placating yet encouraging smiles.

She had no clue what she was doing, but the little foursome made it an entire hour without Beth going poltergeist on anyone, so it was a win. "Homework!" she announced.

Dr. Unaka always gave an assignment between sessions. The ghost trio weren't the feelings-journal types, but there were things they could do.

"For one hour today, you must spend time by yourself focusing on the day you died. Remember everything that occurred within the hour of your death. What you were thinking. What you said. What others said. What you saw. Smelled. Tasted. Heard. Anything that may help us figure out why you are all here."

"So, you can figure out how to banish us from our own home?" Two angry lines creased down Bill's forehead.

She shook her head. "No, so we can figure out why you're here and how to free you. If you're trapped here, then that means this place is your jail."

"And jail didn't end well for you last time," Beth quipped.

CHAPTER 18

Ghoul Talk

"So, how much heat was he packing?" A teasing sultriness played in Mae's features as she beamed from the tablet.

"I tell you ghosts are real and August's penis is what you focus on?"

After group therapy, Nora called Mae and debriefed about everything. As she ran the curling iron through her hair, she listened to Mae's "Oh Mylanta's!" grow higher pitched with each bombshell. Ghosts were real. She'd not only kissed August but had earth-rattling sex with him... Twice. She'd facilitated a support group for the ghosts.

"Lady, please—" she made a dismissive wave with her manicured fingers, "—my aghast face is reserved for truly unbelievable things. Ghosts aren't in that category, but you finally ending your self-induced sex drought where you refused to go for August, even though you've *totally* pined for him since you first met him like a heroine from a Brontë novel, while choosing to *not* get your lady rocks off with anyone else is far more fascinating."

"I never pined."

"Oh, I can't have him because he's my boss but secretly I'm in love with him and have quiet Midwest masturbatory sex thinking about him going down on me and then brewing me a cup of tea," she mocked, doing an impression of Nora.

"I'm not in love with him." It was a half-hearted guffaw.

In love with August Chandler? The thought scoffed within her. Outside of her parents, grandpa, and Mae, she'd never loved anyone. She had a strong like of August, but nothing more. Even if something fluttered in her chest at the mere thought of him.

Mae rolled her eyes. "Enough deflection. Give me the goods on his goods!"

"Fine." Nora smiled wickedly and pointed at the fat round curling iron. "His penis is a weapon of multiple orgasms."

"I knew it!" Mae squealed, her high ponytail bouncing with each cheering clap.

"It was *amazing*, but now I'm meeting his parents and I've never done that. I need your help. Parents *always* love you."

"That's true. Several of my ex's moms still invite me to family dinners." Mae leaned back against the headboard of the bed in the hotel she was staying in. For the next few days, she was shooting some commercials in San Diego. "So, he told Travis Olson he'd be a fool to not hire you, gave you multiple orgasms, insisted on cuddling, and is now introducing you to his parents?"

Nora nodded, clasping the silver dragonfly pendant around her neck.

"Yeah, so this is clearly not just a casual fling for him either."

It wasn't. Nora wouldn't pretend it was. She'd seen enough

on-set hookups. They'd run hot and heavy until the last piece of equipment was packed away. Then they'd fade into black. It happened all the time, but there was never a meeting of parents.

Hell, this was new territory for Nora. In none of her past romantic relationships had she met the parents. It wasn't just meeting August's parents but desperately wanting them to like her. To approve of her. To want her to be part of their… She shook off that thought.

"How do I look?" She stepped back, allowing Mae to see her entire outfit.

It was a simple pale blue sundress with white lilies that flowed over her curves. A soft white cardigan and tan wedges amped up the "I'm a nice girl; I swear that I don't swear" vibe that Nora was going for. Her hair was styled in loose curls.

"You look ready for a church picnic. You're perfect!" Mae grinned.

Nora smiled, grabbing her pink lip stain off the dresser.

"Have you heard from Travis Olson yet?"

"Uhh…"

In the blur of her life since yesterday, she'd forgotten about it. She hadn't even checked her email since yesterday morning. Tossing the lip stain back on the dresser, she grabbed her cell from the bedstand, pulled up her email and scrolled. "Not yet."

Mae wrinkled her nose. "How are you *not* compulsively checking your email every five minutes? Isn't this your dream job?"

"I've been a little busy. Also, it's barely been four days since I sent him my reel."

"You've been a little happy." An almost smug expression lit Mae's face.

"What does that mean?" Her face scrunched.

"It means that I haven't seen you smile that big or be so animated talking about things since…well, ever."

"That's not true," she scoffed. "I just hadn't had good sex in a long time. It's just the orgasm afterglow."

"While I never doubt the power of a good trip to O-town, especially *multiple* ones, I don't think it's just the sex. You're still Nora, but you seem lighter somehow. Like, you had this big smile on your face when you told me about the Putmans and Gideon, and how you and August are shipping Melody and Derrick, and even about the shoot for this week. It's like you're actually letting yourself enjoy life. You've always held yourself back. You'd walk up to the edge of life's pool and dip your toe in but would never jump. And now, suddenly you've cannonballed into your life."

It wasn't meant to be cruel, but somehow the words stung. It felt too close to Peter's parting shot when she ended things with him. *You have no heart, Nora.*

Choosing not to address Mae's comment, she grabbed the lip stain and finished applying it.

"You also opened up to August and the ghosts about what happened to you. You never open yourself up like this," Mae went on, her voice as soft as a blanket.

Nora fiddled with the edge of her cardigan. "I know."

"And it's scary to be so open with others. To let them know all of you."

Nora met Mae's eyes, understanding shimmered in the brown irises. She and her best friend may have different paths, but each twist, turn, and rut brought them to each other. Both knew what it was like to lose people they loved. To be scared to let others in because of that fear. Only Mae never let the fear control her, to stop her from living. Like Nora had.

"I want to be as brave as you are," she confessed.

"You are. You just forget it from time to time."

"Good thing I have you to remind me."

"Good thing." Mae's entire being almost twinkled.

"I love you, Mae," Nora breathed.

As staunch as Nora was that she wasn't in love with August, she was as resolute with the love she had for her best friend. Mae came into Nora's life just as Grandpa Scott had left it. Despite her hesitancy, Mae's steady effervescence broke through Nora's defenses to form not just a friendship, but a sisterhood.

"I love you, too," Mae murmured, the warmth in her expression caused a gooey sensation within Nora.

"Knock-knock," Melody said, poking her head into the half ajar bedroom door. "Nora are you ready?"

"Is that the mythical Melody?" Mae cooed, as Melody walked into the room.

"Is that the legendary Mae?" she chuckled.

Neither woman had met each other, but both had heard lots about the other from Nora. Watching Melody and Mae gab like old friends, it was hard to believe what Beth had shared about her niece. Her radiance pulled you in like a bee to a rose petal. How had the people of this village not gravitated to her? To only see her disability and not all that she was. How was Melody able to look past that and come back to start a business in a place where she'd never been accepted? The biggest question was why?

"They are adorable together. Derrick says they are all stolen glances across the room and have been like that for years." Melody's musical voice pulled Nora out of her head.

"Speaking of Derrick, what's going on between you and *that* scrumptious scholarly sex god?" Mae's mouth quirked into a teasing grin.

Soft crimson rouged Melody's cheeks. "We're friends."

"Friends?" Mae arched an eyebrow. "Enough with the pining! If what Nora has told me is true, he's been infected with a case of 'Hot for Melody' for years."

"Mae!"

"He has?" Melody's eyes widened. "He's never said anything, nor made a move."

Mae pinched her nose. "You ladies may be into the only two heterosexual white boys in TV production that are actual gentlemen."

"Sorry for my friend, Melody. She doesn't know when to *not* say the things in her head." Nora scowled, crossing her arms over her chest.

"I blame Grandma Hoang, who taught me to speak *my* truth." Mae cringed. "Although, sometimes I need to *not* speak other's truths. Sorry."

"I'm not." A big grin brightened Melody's face. "I've suspected but wasn't sure. Derrick has always been sweet to me, but I thought it was out of a sense of big brother affection."

"Beth said you were together until after midnight last night. He didn't make a move?"

Melody shook her head sadly.

"Oh, Derrick," Nora sighed. "He may be too much of a gentleman and may need a gentle push to—"

"Fuck her into the mattress like August did with you last night." Mae cut in with a suggestive waggle of her eyebrows.

"Mae!"

"Oh, I've missed girl talk. Tell me everything!" Melody bounced on her feet like a giddy schoolgirl.

"Did someone say girl talk?" Beth glided through the wall. "Give me the dish, girlfriends."

"Holy fuck! Did she just walk through the wall?" Mae's voice hit an octave that could only be heard by canines.

"More importantly, did you just say 'Give me the dish, girlfriends?'" Nora pointed at Beth, who met her with a cheeky smile.

"Aunt Elizabeth likes to watch Kelly Clarkson with me. And *a lot* of Bravo."

"Just because I'm dead doesn't mean I can't be hip with the times."

"Did the Victorian ghost lady just say 'hip with the times?'" Mae scrunched her forehead.

Shaking her head, Nora placed her hands on her hips. "Beth, what are you doing here? I thought you didn't want to trespass on Melody's inner sanctum unless it was an emergency?"

"It *is* an emergency. I was called for a fashion consultation to help Melody turn the eye of her reluctant gentlemen caller." Beth motioned to the sleeveless sundress Melody wore. "I think I did a smashing job. It really accentuates her *assets*." She gestured to Melody's breasts.

"It is a *drop-dead* gorgeous selection," Mae quipped.

With an overdramatic curtsy, Beth preened.

"Mae, this is Mrs. Elizabeth Putman. Melody's aunt and one of the ghosts of Putman House. She goes by Beth," Nora said.

"Shave my head and call me Vin Diesel. Ghosts are real," Mae deadpanned.

"I thought ghosts were more believable than me getting together with August?" Nora's right eyebrow cocked.

"Oh, they *totally* got together! I heard her cries of passion." Beth held up two fingers. "Twice last night. He must be an excellent lover. She was *very* vocal."

"Aunt Elizabeth!" Melody said, aghast.

"Oh, I like her. She's sassy." Mae winked.

After the strangest girl talk session in history, Nora hung up with Mae. Giggling like teenaged girls, she and Melody headed downstairs to meet the men Beth had dubbed their *dreamboats*. Most of the crew were back at their motel or out for lunch for an extended break until six p.m., when they'd return to resume filming.

Entering the entertainment room on the carriage house's

first floor, Nora found both Chandler brothers and Lucy. Derrick sat, nose in a book, on the small couch. August sat beside Lucy at the table looking at something on the laptop. Her big brown eyes were a little starry-eyed as he pointed to the screen, explaining an editing technique.

Conflicting feelings fist-fought in Nora. Her heart swelled at how he'd patiently spend time with different crew members, especially the production assistants, teaching them both TV production and paranormal investigation skills. However, the heart swell did not negate the spark of jealous heat crawling up her neck at Lucy's hand rested on August's bicep.

For a moment, she wanted to pull Lucy by her curly hair and say, "Not yours to touch!" Instead, Nora balled up her hands into fists, reminding herself that it had been her that August spent last night with. It had been her that he'd kissed sweetly in the clearing this morning. It had been her that he'd asked to meet his parents.

August looked up, his grin breaking across his face like a brilliant sunrise. "Ladies."

The giant swoop of her belly was reminiscent of gymnast cartwheeling across a mat. *Yep, there was no need for that little bit of jealousy.* The spark in his gaze telegraphed that his eyes were only for her.

Derrick looked up from his book, his stare dropped to Melody and his breath stuttered. The canary yellow sundress's bodice hugged her ample breasts and flared out at the waist in a sexy girl-next-door silhouette.

"You're gorg…uh…" A flustered Derrick stood up, dropping his book. "Hi."

A small snort escaped Nora at Derrick picking up the book only to drop it again. He was such a goner for Melody.

"We should get going. We need to meet Mom and Dad soon." Derrick motioned around the room.

"Oh, you *all* are going?" Lucy tugged at a dark curl. "I didn't realize *Nora* was going with you." An almost sour accusation coated the question.

Why'd she say my name like that?

Nora shot August a panicked look. As much as she wanted to claim him and tell Lucy to keep her Disney Princess hands off her man, she didn't want the crew to know. Not yet. They needed a plan to navigate a world where they dated and worked together.

"I'm seeing Derrick and we're having lunch with his parents today. They already know me, but not as Derrick's girlfriend." It came out a little high-pitched, but Melody continued, "Nora is coming with me to help make it more casual."

Nora's lips curved in an appreciative smile at Melody, who no doubt was trying to help. During girl talk, she'd shared with the ladies that she and August were keeping their relationship quiet until after this shoot.

Once Nora returned to L.A. to edit this episode, she'd have time to process and figure out what this meant. More importantly what this meant for her future with the show. Even if Travis Olson didn't offer her a field producer job on *The Great Escape*, she couldn't stay with *Haunted Hideaway*. There weren't industry rules about this, but there were optics.

"You're seeing Derrick?" Derrick's brow creased. "I mean…Uh…Yeah. Me, I'm Derrick. You're seeing me."

August raised his hand, covering his snicker.

"That's really nice of you, Nora." Lucy's tone was surprised.

It wasn't an unusual reaction. Nora knew she could be standoffish, which painted an image of her as cold and unfriendly. Not the image of someone that would accompany a friend to a "meet the parents" lunch. Her hand went to her watch, wrapping her fingers around its surface remembering Grandpa Scott's words that "Kindness has many faces."

"Nora has a big heart and takes care of people," August said, his stern stare fixed on Lucy.

"I didn't mean it like that. I know Nora is nice." Lucy fiddled with the hem of her T-shirt.

"I know you didn't," Nora assured.

"Thanks." Lucy's smile was tight. "I should head back to the motel. Gus, thanks for being so sweet and going over that editing strategy with me." Her delicate hand rested on August's arm. She turned to leave and tripped over a chair, almost tumbling.

August's arms shot out, catching her. "Easy. You okay?"

"Yeah—" her lips pursed, "—I could have sworn that chair was pushed in."

Melody sniffed the air before bending close to Nora, whispering, "I don't think Aunt Elizabeth likes Lucy."

The faint aroma of lavender flittered around the room, signaling a "quiet" but present ghost. A flash of flickering light appeared behind Lucy and August, drawing Nora's attention. A self-satisfied smile beamed from Beth's face.

Winking at Nora she mouthed, *I got you, girl,* before she disappeared.

CHAPTER 19

Meet the Parents

The car eased down the sloping hill toward the Chandler brothers' childhood home. Nora and August sat in the back, their fingers threaded, deep in a wordless conversation of long glances and grins each time Melody slipped flirty comments into her conversation with Derrick, and he reciprocated, somehow turning the phrase *historical significance* into the most adorable flirtatious thing Nora had ever heard.

"I guess that *Flirting for Dummies* book I got him for his birthday is paying off," August murmured against the shell of her ear.

The yellow Dutch colonial house sat tucked beside a large pond, like something out of a quaint Netflix drama about a small town. Leafy maple trees flanked the driveway, and lilac bushes in full bloom framed the cobblestone walkway leading to the oversized front porch. A white porch swing danced in the gentle spring breeze.

"This place is so pretty," Nora gushed, getting out of the vehicle.

August strode around the back of the car, taking Nora's hand. "We Chandler men like pretty things."

A snort escaped Nora.

"I swear that sounded more smooth and less sexist asshole in my head."

"So, this is happening. You two really *are* together." Derrick motioned at them. "When August told me today, I was half expecting it to be a practical joke, like the time he'd convinced me that Dusty was the wayward son of Eastern European aristocrats."

"That may still be true. We haven't disproven it," August teased.

"Kids!" A tall man strolled down the front steps, arms outstretched.

Even if she'd never seen pictures of Fred Chandler or took in his grinning face on video chats with his sons, she'd know instantly who he was. He was an older version of both brothers. Derrick had his chestnut-colored hair, minus the salt and pepper at the temples. August's big smile was identical to his dad's.

Unsurprisingly, Fred was a hugger. When August introduced her as "His Nora," Fred swept her up in a tight squeeze.

Gemma Chandler bounded outside and enfolded her sons into her arms. "Look at my handsome sons and their beautiful lady friends. Melody it's so good to see you." She squeezed Melody. Pulling back, she turned to Nora. "Nora?" she cooed, taking her hands. "You're even lovelier than on the face chat."

"Mom, that's FaceTime."

"Don't get smart with me, August." She playfully nudged him.

Fred looked at his watch, letting out a long whistle. "Well, Gus that's a new record. You're home less than five minutes and your mom has already Augusted you."

He grinned. "Nora calls me August, so it has new connotations for me."

The butterflies collided in a crush-drunk dance as he smiled at her.

The Chandlers led them through the house and onto the back patio. The six of them sat around a glass table laughing and enjoying Gemma's grilled haddock tacos, black bean salad, and a spicy rice dish.

Besides dinner at Grandma Hoang's when Mae and Nora were both in town, it had been at least fourteen years since she'd last sat around a table having a family meal. As a kid, it was just her and grandpa for the holidays or Sunday dinners. He'd always make it special. Even if it was just the two of them, he'd get the whole turkey rather than just a small breast for Thanksgiving. They'd eat all variations of something turkey for several days after, but it was totally worth it.

"I love that you ladies are eaters," Gemma praised, motioning her fork between Melody and Nora, who sat on opposite sides of the table.

Nora sat beside August, his arm draped over the back of her chair when he wasn't eating, as if it was the most natural thing for him. The gesture filled her with a sense of rightness, like she belonged here, belonged with him…belonged to this family. Dr. Unaka would have a field day with the feelings roaming within her at this lunch.

"That reminds me, Mom did you—"

"Sonny boy, are you new? Of course, I did. You asked me." Gemma's grin was wide.

"You're the best." August winked.

Nora turned to him. "What?"

"You'll see." He picked up his fork, mischief played in his features.

Effortless conversation filled the table. Melody talked about her plans for Putman House, including community events like concerts and high tea in the garden for guests and village residents. Nora imagined much of that may rest on how successful she was at helping Beth get control over her poltergeisty outbursts.

"When Putman House was first built, it was the center of so much for the village. Aunt Elizabeth and Uncle William…" Melody halted at the perplexed looks of Gemma and Fred. "…I mean, my ancestors hosted community events and parties at the house before everything happened. Generations of Putmans closed off the house. I want to make it what it was, what it was always meant to be. A place for the village's celebrations—its life."

"A place where everyone is welcomed," Derrick added, resting his hand on Melody's forearm and squeezing.

Realization sighed through Nora. The girl that had never quite been accepted was creating a place where everyone would be welcomed. Melody was taking a place that the village had shunned or whispered ghostly stories about and showing it for what it was…a place for life.

Gemma placed her hand on her heart. "That is so lovely, Melody."

"Well, Melody is lovely," Derrick murmured. "I mean—" he shifted in his seat "—it's lovely."

"Speaking of lovely." A cheeky expression popped on Fred's face. "Why don't I help my lovely wife take the dishes in. You kids stay put, because I may take advantage of being alone in the kitchen with your mom and try to cop a feel."

August snorted.

Derrick blanched. "Dad!"

Fred flicked his son's nose. "You could learn a thing or

two from me boy. Forty years of marriage and I think your mother is more in love with me today than on our wedding day."

"Come on Casanova, make me swoon by loading the dishwasher," Gemma quipped, piling the dishes on a tray.

"I see where you get it from." Nora smiled as Gemma and Fred shuffled into the house.

"I hope we're like them," he said, placing a soft kiss on her lips.

Us? Like them? Someday? Nora blinked. Those belly butterflies did not know what to do. Half of them swooned. Half stood still, gaping.

"I think it's funny we're all in our thirties and still referred to as kids," Derick chuckled.

"I suspect to parents we're always kids. My mom actually licked her finger and wiped a smudge off my cheek when I signed the escrow paperwork for Putman House." Melody shook her head and chuckled.

August's arm looped around Nora, tucking her into his side. She wasn't sure if he did it because of the mention of parents or just because he always seemed to be touching her since yesterday, at least when the crew wasn't around. Either way, it was welcomed. She leaned in and rested her head on his shoulder, listening to Melody giggle about the time her mom showed up at the very fancy NYC hotel that she worked at in a *I have the World's Greatest Daughter* T-shirt with a cake to celebrate her promotion to manager.

There'd been many moments in the last twenty-four years that Nora daydreamed about what her parents would think of her life. Would they be proud? Would she have lived up to the things they hoped for their daughter? Would the man and woman that Grandpa Scott described as a vibrant rainbow bringing color into any room that they stepped into agree with the gray that, until recently, was Nora's life? A growing pit in her stomach told her no.

"A six-foot-four birdy told us that it's someone's birthday," Fred announced, coming back out from the house with a yellow paper birthday cone hat on his head.

Nora swallowed hard. The erratic drumbeat of her heart pounded. Her eyes darted between the smiling faces at the table.

"I told you that you'd see soon." August leaned close, a smile on his lips.

Nora's pulse raced as she looked back at him, her eyes wide, and head shaking. The whites of her knuckles glared with her tightened grip of the table's edge.

"Nora?" Concern flashed in his expression.

"Happy birthday to you…" Gemma sang, following Fred and carrying a chocolate cake.

The flames of the lit candles swayed in the gentle spring breeze.

Everyone, except August, joined in singing to Nora. Turning away from August's worried stare, she schooled her face in a blank expression. Her teeth bit into the inside of her cheek, trying to force a placid smile.

You can do this. Just smile.

A grinning Gemma rounded the table, placing the cake in front of her. "Voila!"

As the last note was sung, Fred cheered, "Blow them out!"

Closing her eyes, she sucked in a breath. *Don't cry. Don't cry.* Opening her eyes, she blew out the candles.

"I made it this morning. It's chocolate cake with a hazelnut ganache. August said you love chocolate cake." Gemma beamed.

"I do. This is so… Thank you," she croaked. Her vision blurred as the battle with those fucking obstinate tears was lost. Standing up, her chair shot back, almost tipping over.

"I'm sorry.... I need…uh…to use the restroom. Excuse me." Then she turned and ran into the house.

God, it was rude to abruptly leave the table after someone brought a birthday cake to you. Normal people didn't react like that, but the anxiety that coursed overcame her ability to be proper. To smile and accept the sweet gesture. To sit at a table and celebrate what should be celebrated, not mourned.

She beelined to the bathroom at the end of the short hall that ran between the kitchen and living room. Once safely behind the closed door, Nora stood at the sink.

"Don't do this. Not here! You're stronger than this," she whimpered, clinging to the sink but avoiding her reflection in the mirror.

Straightening, her gaze flicked to the closed window. Pushing the curtains aside, she unlocked the window and opened it. The fresh spring air filtered into the room, filling her nostrils. She inhaled a deep breath, held it for a count of three, and then released. She repeated the action, trying to settle the torrent of emotions snarling inside her. Embarrassment. Anger. Guilt. They clustered in a knotted mess within her.

A gentle rap came at the door. Wiping away the tears, she tried to make her voice sound normal. "I'll be right out." It was the trademark voice of someone crying in the bathroom.

"Baby, can I come in?" August's tone was soft and coaxing.

Can he? Mae's words from earlier echoed. Part of living was doing it with others. It was letting people in. Hell, even the ghosts of Putman House knew that. Didn't they show that with their interactions with Melody? Their willingness to share their stories with Nora? In the last twenty-four hours she'd taken the first steps down this path.

"Yes," she said, pivoting to face the door.

August stepped in and shut the door behind him. He said

nothing, just pulled her into his firm chest, allowing her to melt into his embrace.

As the tears subsided and her rigid muscles relaxed with the gentle strokes of his hands along her spine, she tipped her head up to him. "I'm so sorry. Your parents must think I'm the worst."

He slid a hand to her face, swiping away lingering tears. "Nope. In fact, my mother blamed me for ambushing you with a surprise for your birthday. I think they already like you better than me."

She sniffled. "It's not your fault. You didn't know. I haven't celebrated my birthday…since…"

Realization flashed in his eyes. "Is that when the accident happened?"

"Yes."

"Oh, my sweet Nora." He kissed her temple. "I'm so sorry."

"You didn't know, because I didn't tell you. I don't tell anyone anything. Dr. Unaka says it's my Achilles' heel." She sloshed a hard breath. "After the accident, it was just too hard to talk about them. It hurt too much. There were so many questions. So many pitying looks. So much judgment. I just stopped talking about it and anything else. To the school therapist. To friends. To anyone that wasn't grandpa."

His hand went to her chin, guiding her downcast gaze back to him. "That might have been true at one time, but you've told me things. Not everything, but important things. You're telling me this now. You opened the door, and let me in."

"The last man I dated told me that I was dead inside. That I didn't have a heart."

Angry lines formed on his face. "That asshole."

Nora shook her head. "It hurt when he said it because it's something that I've feared. Like I may have been revived that day, but that a part of me was still dead. Like I'm not fully capable of being alive…being warm. Others have said something similar at times."

But hadn't there been a seed of truth in their accusation? She'd held others at a distance. It took her two years to tell August about her parents. It taken her six years to open to Mae and even her own therapist whose entire existence in her life was based on dealing with things. Hell, the crew teased her about not joining them for meals until the end of the shoot. Outside of Melody's drinks party and the post-shoot outing tradition, she'd not joined.

Peering back at August's patient expression, she opened. "At first, I told Grandpa Scott I didn't want to celebrate my birthday because it hurt too much to think about them. I remember my mom was a good hugger. I remember Dad's booming laugh. In all of grandpa's stories, they were so full of life. How could I celebrate that day? It was the day I lost them. As the years went by, it became less about them and more about me." A sharp pain radiated inside her chest. "Like it reminded me that I shouldn't be here. That it should've been me and not them. That *they* were the ones with so much life inside them."

August clasped her face in his large hands, his eyes boring into her. "You have so much fucking life in you, but the grief…the guilt is clouding your vision. I saw it that first day I met you. The way your eyes lit when we met. Women who are dead inside don't have eyes that shine brighter than the North Star. Women that are dead inside don't have smiles that leave you forgetting your own name. Women that are dead inside don't make you burn for them… And I am fucking on fire for you Nora."

Nora's breath stuttered.

"You are the sun. I know I sound like a cliché from a romance novel, but it's true. The moment you stepped onto that elevator I was pulled into your orbit. Dead things can't do that."

Lifting to her tiptoes, she claimed his mouth in a slow, thankful kiss. Every unspoken word expressed with each press of their lips. *Thank you for reminding me that I am alive and making me feel more alive than I ever have. Thank you for being patient with me while at the same time holding out your hand to help me into the pool.*

Mae said that Nora had cannonballed into life's pool, but she knew she was still in the shallow end. However, August was a strong life preserver. She knew he'd not let her drown. Even better, he'd not let her get out of the water.

CHAPTER 20

Nap Time

August had not been kidding that his mom blamed him. When they emerged from the bathroom, a frowning Gemma met them, her hands on her shapely hips.

"What did *he* do?" She glowered at her bemused son.

"Why do you think I did something wrong?" His response was less protest and more snicker.

"Because I raised you and have many stories of being called to meetings at your school. May I remind you of the time you were suspended after you kidnapped a calf from Jackson farms and snuck it into the principal's office? We had to pay to replace Mrs. Lincoln's carpet!"

"You what?" Nora guffawed.

With a shrug and smirk, August appeared the ever-unrepentant cad.

"I know. Where did I go wrong with him?" She tossed her hands up, but her expression was loving.

"The bovine kidnapping aside, I think you went pretty

right with him," Nora offered, tilting her head up in an appreciative smile to August.

"Oh, I *love* her," Gemma gushed and then lightly swatted her son's head. "Don't fuck it up, Sonny Boy!"

A sense of belonging coursed through Nora's veins. She'd made a spectacle of herself, yet this woman stood here embracing her. She didn't pretend nothing happened. She acknowledged it but didn't push for a reason and proceeded to teasingly blame her son. It was the oddest and sweetest reaction to a meltdown.

"I am really sorry about earlier. The cake was so kind. I just got overwhelmed…I…"

Gemma pulled Nora into a tight hug. "Honey, we all have stories and when you're ready to share, I'm here to listen. I'll even supply the chardonnay. But if you're not ready to share yet, that's okay. Doesn't change the fact that you may be too good for my son and that if he messes this up, I plan to keep you and send him packing."

Reminiscent of waking sunflowers – the blooms outstretched – a smile erupted on Nora's face. She closed her eyes and melted into Gemma's jasmine-scented embrace. The Chandler brothers were carbon copies of their kindhearted parents. A quiet hope bloomed in Nora's chest that she could keep them all, especially their son.

She was falling hard for him. She'd been falling for him since his first winking smile on that elevator, but meeting his parents sent her into a freefall. Despite the fear of crashing to the ground, she tentatively let her arms out.

Gemma pulled back, clasping her hands with Nora's. "Now, let's go have cake and tea. Fred has pulled out the photo albums, so we can properly embarrass our sons with naked baby pictures and photographic evidence of August's unfortunate boyband phase." Her face contorted into a grimace. "He had frosted tips for three months in eighth grade."

"Frosted tips?" Nora snorted.

"I may have a video of him lip-syncing 'Bye, Bye, Bye' during an eighth-grade talent show."

"Mom! let's not scare her off. I have a certain sexy man mystique to maintain."

Gemma and Fred's ability to embarrass their sons was epic. Never had she seen both brothers' faces so red. By the time they left, Nora's cheeks hurt from smiling and stomach ached from laughter. Despite her emotional hiccup, it had been a good lunch. Gemma and Fred wrapped each of them in tight hugs. Leftover chocolate cake in hand, they headed back to Putman House.

Neither Melody nor Derrick asked about her meltdown. As the car rolled down the country road and Forest Blakk played in the background, it nipped at Nora. Not that they didn't ask, but that she didn't say. Gemma was right. Everyone had stories and they chose when to share them. Exhaustion seeped into her bones from not sharing and keeping people at a distance.

Fingers linked with August's in the back seat, she sucked in a steadying breath. "When I was six, I died in the car accident that killed my parents. It was my birthday. They'd taken me to Pizza Palace because it was my favorite, and I could have a personal pepperoni pizza." It flew out of her mouth at the speed of a sprinting cheetah.

The car grew quiet. It was the kind of silence that was almost loud with all the unasked questions the made the air thick.

Derrick looked back at Nora through the mirror's reflection.

"You don't need to say anything. I know I just dropped a bomb on you all. I just wanted you to know...to know me."

August raised their intertwined fingers to his mouth, pressing a tender kiss on her knuckles.

"Thank you for trusting us with this." Melody turned, reaching to squeeze Nora's knee.

"Yes, thank you," Derrick echoed.

They drove for a few minutes in a companionable silence. It was such a different quiet than earlier. This one was almost reverent. As if each honored what Nora had done. Not what she shared, but the act of her opening up herself more to them.

Derrick cleared his throat. "Is Pizza Palace still your favorite?"

Nora's brow knit. "What?"

"It's a serious question. We always get Dominos when we order pizza for the crew, and I feel bad that we didn't get your favorite."

The entire car erupted into loud giggles, snorts, and guffaws. Only Derrick would worry about someone not having their preferred pizza.

Melody raised her hand to his cheek. "Oh, Derrick."

Arriving back at Putman House, they split up. Melody went to her office to catch up on some work. Derrick headed to his room for a nap. They had three hours until the crew came back. Both brothers would want a catnap before a night with little to no sleep.

Walking toward the carriage house, August bent close to her ear and almost purred, "I propose a joint nap."

Nora's senses hummed with the promise of August in her bed.

"Only napping." He kissed below her ear.

"Suuure."

Once upstairs at the carriage house, they headed to her room. Placing her purse on the dresser, she turned and watched August undress. His back muscles flexed as he yanked the T-shirt off, revealing his tattoo. It was the only ink he had on his muscular body.

"Why a snowflake?" she asked.

"Get in your napping clothes, join me in this bed, and I'll tell you." He pushed down his jeans, tipping his head to the bed.

"Wait, napping isn't code for sex?"

He pulled the blanket down. "I'm starting to think you only want me for my sexual prowess."

"Well, if the dick fits."

He belted a cheeky grin and wagged his finger.

She smirked and shook her head with a silent laugh. She grabbed her sleep shorts and tank top from the dresser and made a quick change.

"I enjoy this view." An unabashed grin covered his face, as he lay in the bed watching her take off her jewelry.

"Most men prefer me *not* putting clothes on after I take them off," she teased, sliding beneath the blanket with him.

He tucked her into his chest, wrapping his arm loosely around her middle. "You always smell so good. You have this fresh flora scent. Like a field of wildflowers." He nuzzled into her hair, taking a deep breath.

A giggle escaped her. "You're ridiculous."

"I think you like my brand of ridiculous."

She did. She really did.

His bare chest pressed against her back and his long fingers skated under her tank top, running lazy circles along the small swell of her belly. No amount of exercise or healthy eating gave her the flat, toned stomach of a Lucy or a Mae. Perhaps it was genetics, or the chocolate cake and waffles, which she'd never give up. She occasionally fell victim to the insecurity of not having a perfect body, but it was always fleeting. She liked her body. It was strong, but soft. The way August's hands roamed along her belly, and the growing bulge pressed against her ass telegraphed his appreciation for her body. It was the cherry on top of her "I have a little snack pouch but I'm still fucking beautiful" sundae.

"Sir, you said we were napping," she teased, rubbing her backside against his erection.

A chuckled groan came out of him. "Clearly my dick didn't get the memo."

Threading her fingers in his, a thrill crisscrossed through her with the knowledge of the effect she had on him. The lusty unscrupulous part of her wanted to take advantage of this goddess-like power she had over him, gliding her hands across the muscular planes of his body and below his boxers. But he needed to sleep, not be sexed up, despite what the rigid length poking her was saying.

"Tell me about the snowflake," she said, scooting her backside away from him in hopes of alleviating the erection situation.

Pulling her back into him, he continued his lazy circles along her belly. "It represents Diana. She died around Christmas. The funeral home had a tree decorated with snowflakes in the lobby. I remember sneaking away from the calling hours and sitting in front of it. I asked the funeral director why they did snowflakes instead of angels. I guess I thought they'd have angels...you know for those that had left us. They explained that each snowflake is unique, just like our loved ones. When I turned eighteen, I got a snowflake in honor of Diana."

"That's beautiful." Nora ran her fingers up his forearm. "She's always with you."

"Yeah." His hands moved to her wrist. "It's a token to remind me that she's always with me. Kind of like your watch."

The muscles in Nora's throat worked. "It was my mom's. My dad gave it to her. She always wore it." Nora's eyes flicked to the dresser where the simple wristwatch lay. There wasn't anything special about it, except it had been hers and that he'd given it to her.

"It keeps them close to you. I've noticed you wear it most of the time and touch it when you're stressed or thinking. I knew it was special to you and once you told me about your parents, I suspected it was from them."

"She'd been wearing it that night. I was obsessed with timing things. I wanted to use it to time how long it would take us to get home. I was holding it when the accident happened. It got scratched and wasn't working, but grandpa fixed it so I could keep it."

"I bet your mom would love how you use it to keep us on track during filming."

A wistful laugh bubbled out of her. "I wonder what they'd think of me. What grandpa would think of me."

"If my parents, who are already in love with you, are any indication, they'd be so proud of you. From everything I know about Grandpa Scott, he'd be bragging about his hotshot field producer granddaughter."

"I wish I could…" Emotion gathered in her throat.

"I know." He squeezed her middle. "I wonder what Diana would think of Derrick and me. I love what I do. I know it's crazy to so many people. They snicker at me at industry parties calling me the ghost guy."

Guilt churned inside her. She'd never mocked or made fun, but she'd rolled her eyes. She'd made no secret that paranormal shows weren't her passion. After season one wrapped, she'd been applying for field producer positions with non-paranormal shows. Hell, she was waiting for Travis Olson to offer her a spot with *Great Escape*.

"I was one of those people. I am sorry that I—"

"You never made me feel like a joke. You were clear that you didn't believe in ghosts, but you never disrespected what we did. You probably took it more seriously than anyone. You made the show better…you made *me* better."

Nora twisted to face him.

An earnest expression blanketed his face. "When Travis Olson dismissed our show, you defended us. It wasn't the first time I've seen you do that. I know you didn't believe in the paranormal, but I never questioned you not believing in me and in *our* show."

Our show? Did he mean Derrick and he or her and him? How often had he winked at her saying, "This is *our* show" or "This is *our* baby"?

"I love what I do," he went on. "It's just strange to think that if I hadn't lost Diana, I may not be doing this. That I'd be someone else entirely."

"Be some*where* else entirely." Her voice was soft and a little mournful.

Their eyes wove in wordless realization. Both their gazes seeming to say the same thing, "With someone else entirely."

An ache pricked in her chest at the idea of a life in which she'd never met August.

"I love my sister and I wish she could be here with us. I wish she could have sat at that table today, joining in with my parents on the Derrick and August embarrassment train. I would have loved her to meet you because I know she'd adore you."

Her lips tugged up in a soft smile. "I think I would have liked her too."

"Yet, as much as I wish Diana was here, I don't think I would be willing to give up the life that I have for that to happen." His voice cracked. "I've never told that to anyone else, and I know it makes me a monster. What kind of brother wouldn't trade his life for his sister? I feel so guilty."

Raising her hand, she caressed his cheek. "I know."

"I know you do, my sweet Nora."

"The only difference is that you live in spite of that guilt, and I've let it control me. I know you said that I'm not dead inside and that's true—at least, I'm starting to believe that—but I haven't really been living my life. I've played it safe. I've held people at bay. I've not taken chances."

The truth roared within her. At thirty, she'd not yet fully lived. For so long she'd stood on the sidelines of her own life. Since coming to Putman House, she'd slowly broken away from the shackles of her guilt. From that first moment she pulled up and met Gideon on the front porch, she started to change. Long before she'd known the dead lived in this place, she'd started to live. Putman House had a strange power. Like it was giving her a second chance to live her second chance life.

Her gaze linked with his. "But not anymore. I want a life that honors who they were and what they gave me." Hadn't they given her life? Who was she to not cherish that gift, wearing it every day like she did her mother's watch?

Choosing life, she kissed him, their mouths collided in a slow dance of need. With their deepened kisses, wildfire blazed through her. Moving astride him, she ground against his arousal.

"God," he groaned with pleasure, gripping her ass in a tight squeeze.

Head tossed back, she moaned as he moved her against his hardness. The delicious friction surged liquid need in her veins. Every inch of her burned for this man. She yanked off her shirt.

"Fuck, you're so pretty, baby," he rasped, his hands cupping her breasts.

Back bowed, Nora whimpered with his gentle tweak and then roll of her hard peaks. Coiled tension spooled at her core with the caress of his rough hands against her skin and the rock of herself against him.

"Oh, my sweet Nora," he murmured, rising up to suck her right nipple into his mouth. "We're supposed to be napping."

"Do you want to stop?" she panted.

He answered with a playful slap of her ass, followed by a hard suck of her nipple.

"Yes!"

His teeth grazed one hard peek, making her back arch. "You like that, baby?"

In reply, she ground her hips against his length.

His hands moved down to her upper thighs, massaging as he continued his decadent assault of her breasts, her pleading whimpers only coaxing him to maintain his tantalizing pace. He seemed intent on consuming her inch-by-inch as his hands and mouth reverently roamed her body.

Gliding his fingers below the silk of her sleep shorts, he skated them across the lace of her panties. "You're soaked." He nipped below her earlobe. "I love how wet you get for me."

She'd never thought she liked dirty talk during sex, but his praise ignited her like a forest fire.

He slid under the fabric and ran a finger between her folds. "You like that."

"Yes," she hissed with pleasure.

His fingers moved against her, finding that perfect teasing rhythm. The pressure at her core spiraled tighter and tighter. He slipped a finger inside while continuing to work her clit with his thumb. Her hips moved against him, riding his hand with unashamed enthusiasm.

"That's my greedy girl." His low timbre dripped with wicked promise. "I'll give you what you need." He pushed another finger inside her.

The delicious fullness surged pleasure within her as he hit the perfect spot and sent her over the edge.

"August!"

He captured her cries with a hard kiss. If his arms hadn't been folded around her, she'd have floated away in that moment. Not just from the sated contentedness that sighed through her limbs, but with the lightness that came with this man. With the ability to shuck off the chains of her past sorrow and the knowledge that he'd cared for her before she was brave enough to do so.

"You are so fucking beautiful. The little noises you make when you come. The goofy, yet somehow sexy smile you get just as you climax." He withdrew his fingers and lifted them to his lips, licking each one. "How sweet you taste."

Clamping her hands around his face, she took his mouth in a devouring kiss. Their blended taste was the perfect kiss of belonging. Him to her. Her to him. Them.

"I need you inside me. Now." Her demand was breathless.

Moving his hands down her body, he slipped his fingers back beneath her underwear.

"Not your fingers. I want your cock."

"Oh, god, that was about the sexiest thing you could have said," he groaned into her neck. "But I only planned on napping with you. I don't have a condom with me. They're in my room." He raised his head, a pained smile on his face. "I'm sorry, baby. Let me fuck you with my mouth and fingers. Let me take care of you, my sweet girl."

She bit her lower lip. "I have an IUD for birth control. I haven't been with anyone since we met, and I was tested. I'm safe."

August's mouth dropped open. "You haven't been with anyone else since we met?"

"I didn't want anyone else."

He seemed to take in her words. His expression was unreadable.

He slid her off his lap and got up from the bed.

Had she said the wrong thing? "I'm sorry. We don't have to…"

"No…I need to be inside you." The soft chocolate of his eyes smoldered. "I haven't been with anyone else since we met either. There's only been you for me. I only want you, Nora."

With a devilish grin, he dropped his boxers, knelt on the bed and took hold of the waistband of her sleep shorts and underwear, yanking them both off in one swift action and positioning himself between her thighs.

Pleasure hummed through her as he pushed inside. The delicious stretching sensation of her body accommodating his girth washed over her.

"Like fucking silk," he growled. "Nothing has ever felt like this. Your pussy feels so good."

Her pelvic muscles clenched with his dirty words.

"Does my sweet girl like when I praise her?" He eased deeper inside her, making it difficult for her to respond with anything other than a needy whimper. "Let me make you feel as good as I do right now. Trust me?" he asked, gripping her hips.

"Clearly." Her response was a breathless laugh. No other man had been inside her unsheathed before. She'd never wanted that closeness. Not until August.

"Let me know if this is too much."

Raising her hips, he bent her legs in a pretzel-like fashion, giving him deeper access.

"Oh…my…fuck…."

With a wicked grin, August thrust deeper. The slow steady pace of him sliding in and out of her surged a delicious tightening. It spooled and spooled and spooled within her until she thought she may crack apart from the need for release.

"August, please…"

His fingers gripped her hips, angling her just a little higher and thrusting harder into her until finally the tension crested, and waves of pleasure engulfed every inch of her.

"Fuck!" she cried.

He nipped at her lips. "I'm not done with you yet."

Her limbs were jelly. What more could he have for her? What more could she have to give?

"Tell me if this is too much and we'll stop."

"Don't stop." The sensation of him deep within her, with no barriers between them, was too addicting.

Unfolding her legs, he placed them high on his hips. The sweet release of orgasm dripped through her as he extended her pleasure with slow, almost decadent, thrusts. Wrapped around him tightly, she moved her hips in tandem with his.

"Fuck, baby." His breath grew ragged.

The wild look in his eyes mixed with his relentless rhythm tightened a second knot inside her. Each slam of their hips pulled it tighter and tighter as he drove harder and harder.

"Come for me again, baby."

"My…god…August." Her nails bit into his shoulders as her entire body convulsed in ecstasy.

He silenced her cries with a deep kiss. His once precise movements turned frantic. She arched her hips and writhed against him, driving him closer.

"Goddamn." With a final pump, his body shuddered. Hovering above her, their gazes intertwined.

Warmth flooded her. Every muscle relaxed, not just from the sex, but with the sense of rightness.

She ran her fingers through his hair. "Will you hold me while we finally take that nap?"

A playful grin curved his lips. Pulling out of her, he moved beside her and laid on his back. "Of course. Let me clean you up first."

This thoughtful man. She laughed.

After they'd cleaned themselves up, they slipped back into bed. He tucked her into his nook. "Remember to tell me if you need me to let go…or else I'll never let go."

She melted into him, inhaling the fragrance that mingled a little of her, a little of him, and a lot of them. "I don't want you to ever let go."

CHAPTER 21

It's all about Beth

Sunlight tiptoed into the room underneath the closed door. Production had set up their command center in the parlor beside Melody's office in the back of the house. There'd been a few hiccups during their first night of filming. Around midnight, the lights in the house flickered, causing Nora to mutter Beth's name under her breath. The ghosts had promised to keep themselves quiet and away from the house during filming, however, the aroma of lavender waltzed through the room from time-to-time, indicating Beth was poking around.

At three a.m., when Dusty left to use the restroom and Nora was alone in the command center, Beth appeared to give her opinion that Dusty shouldn't wear a white tux for his wedding. "White is never appropriate for a fall wedding," she chided. Clearly, she'd eavesdropped on their conversation about his forthcoming October nuptials.

The former lady of the house leaned into the nosey neighbor archetype. It would be damn near impossible to keep Beth at bay for the remaining six nights of filming. Too bad she couldn't be locked in a room like she had done to several people over the last century. Melody shared that the ghosts of Putman House had a bad habit of locking guests and two former Mrs. Putmans in rooms for rude behavior like criticizing the original wallpaper that Beth chose.

Note to self, don't insult Beth's interior decorating skills. An icy shiver ripped down Nora's spine at the thought of being trapped behind an unopenable door.

"I have fresh tea and coffee," Lucy chirped, strolling into the room.

Nora half-expected tiny woodland creatures to dance along behind her.

"You're a godsend, Lucy!" Dusty yawned, stretching.

Placing the to-go cups on the table, she beamed. "It helps that there's a functional kitchen. I even baked some fresh blueberry muffins. I'll grab them, so everyone can munch before we wrap for the morning."

Of course she bakes. How had Lucy been up most of the night, had time to bake, and rolled in at six a.m. looking fresh as a daisy? Nora frowned, catching a glimpse of herself in the mirror hung on the wall. Wayward tendrils escaped her once-smooth ponytail. Dark circles formed below her eyes. Tiny dribbles of tea dotted her white *Ms. Independent* T-shirt.

"Did someone say muffins?" August appeared at the door. An unbridled smile stretched across his face and his hair mussed from the last few hours curled up on a cot in the library.

For the first night of filming, the brothers slept in separate rooms of the house where ghostly activity had been reported by some of the witnesses that they'd interviewed. They drew straws. Poor Derrick got the basement. August set up an old-fashioned alarm clock in the basement to go off at four a.m. to scare his brother. Each episode featured at least one brother-on-brother prank, generally orchestrated by August.

Pink caressed Lucy's cheeks. "Yeah. I made them this morning. They should be cool, let me go grab them." With a coy smile to August, she glided out of the room.

Dusty let out a long chuckle. "She's got it bad for you, Gus. I wouldn't be surprised if she has a T-shirt with your face on it that she sleeps with at night."

August waved him off. "Nah, it's the typical production assistant thing. They want to impress the bosses. Like how she always remembers Nora's tea."

Standing, Dusty placed his hands on his lower back bending and stretching. "Pretty sure she doesn't blush when she brings Nora her tea."

Nora crossed her arms over her chest. "She sure doesn't."

August's right eyebrow cocked.

Dusty's gaze darted between them. Muttering something under his breath, he stepped to the credenza against the wall where Lucy set the to-go cups. "I'm going to take this and go let your brother out of the basement."

"What?" Nora pivoted to the monitors, where a bewildered Derrick appeared on screen, scratching his head, and staring at the closed door. "How did that get locked?" She turned to August with narrowed eyes. "Did *you* lock him in?"

"That wasn't me." His hands went up in defense.

"Nah, it gets stuck. Melody told Benji and me yesterday. She said a few of the doors around the house stick every now and then. Let me rescue Professor Hottie. Save me a muffin," he paused, nibbling on his lower lip. "Make that two. Benji won't be here until seven for Derrick's interview with that historian, so nobody is here to count my carb intake."

Once Dusty left the room, August shut the door. Wickedness sparked in his eyes. Like a hungry wolf, he stalked toward Nora.

Her sex clenched with want. It had been thirteen hours since she'd last touched him. The entire night had passed with stolen glances in rooms or her fingers grazing his image on the monitor when nobody was looking. August said that he burned for her, but she feared she would be in ashes by the end of this shoot. Every fiber of her was consumed by this man.

"I've missed you," he murmured, folding his arms around her. Nuzzling in her hair, he inhaled deeply.

"We're ridiculous," she laughed.

Coasting his hands to the small of her back, he moved his mouth inches from hers. "I take it that *you* missed me too." His hot breath was a teasing kiss.

She closed the distance, taking his mouth.

"So, that's a yes."

She smirked. "Do you think the door got stuck on Derrick or was it one of the ghosts messing with him?"

"Why would one of the ghosts trap him? If anyone from the crew was going to get locked in, it might be Benji. He made some unfavorable comments about the wall sconces."

"Beth told me that Bill is very protective of Melody. Maybe he's noticed the budding romance."

"Nah." He shook his head. "It's been totally PG-13 between them. Nothing to affront the sensibilities of our Victorian ghost friends. Well, at least Bill. From what you've said of Beth, she may be disappointed. It's less steamy and more sweet Hallmark romance between Derrick and Melody."

"What has he told you?" She hadn't got a chance to talk to Melody since lunch yesterday, but spotted Derrick and her laughing in Melody's office, when she came into the house to set up last night.

"Brothers never divulge secrets."

"Even to girlfriends?"

His lips quirked. "Girlfriend?"

Her mouth went dry. Had she called herself that?

"Nope." He planted a knee-wobbling kiss on her lips. Pulling back, his boyishly charming grin lit his face. "I'm not letting you take that back. Girlfriend." He was almost joyful in his smugness. "I'm holding you to that."

Her brow wrinkled. "Does that mean you'll dish about what Derrick said?"

He gave her a nipping kiss. "Nope."

"Tease!"

"Me? A tease?" His hand gripped her ass, squeezing. "Have you seen you in these jeans?"

"The door won't open," Lucy's muffled voice called through the closed door.

"Did you lock it?" she whispered.

"No." August shook his head. "Maybe this is one of the rooms with doors that stick."

The faint scent of lavender flickered in Nora's nostrils. "Beth," she laughed. "I think you have a ghostly wing-person." Pressing a quick kiss to his lips, she slipped out of his arms and walked to the door.

"Thanks," Lucy said as she walked into the room holding a plate of muffins.

"No, thank *you*." Nora scooped up a muffin. "I'm going to take this and my tea and head out for a walk in the clearing. Let Dusty know he's in charge of Derrick's interview with the historian, then everyone can break until seven."

The cool May air filled Nora's lungs as she made her way to the clearing. It was just after six, and she wanted a little time to herself before day two of ghostly group therapy. Although, part of her suspected August may find an excuse to join her soon. Either way she'd get a chance to unwind before paranormal psychodrama ensued.

The clearing was empty besides a few chirping birds in the canopy above. Sliding down to the base of the tree of ill-repute, she stretched her legs out. It was the perfect spot for a little breakfast picnic. Just Nora, her muffin, and a cup of tea.

"Oh, this is good," she moaned, biting into the still warm muffin.

Yumminess burst in her mouth with the collision of tarty berries and the sweet bready part of the muffin. Forget every snide thought she'd had about Lucy, the live-action Belle was okay in her book as long as she continued to bake for the crew.

"I do miss a good baked good." Bill's deep voice interrupted her carb heaven.

She looked up into his stony face. "Don't you ever smile? You're too serious."

"I believe the saying is the pot calling the kettle black."

"Look at you, making a joke," she sassed between bites of her muffin. "Although, I'm smiling more these days."

"Love does have that effect on us." He slipped his hands into the pockets of his gray trousers.

"I don't know if love is what's happening with August but—"

An almost musical quality filled his husky laughter. "You sound like me when I met Beth. My brother Alexander saw it before I did."

"How did you meet?"

"It was never supposed to be Beth. It was Alexander's wedding. She was the distant cousin of his bride Cassandra. She was a spinster."

Nora scrunched her face in annoyance.

"I know. Even in 1881, I thought that was bollocks. She

was twenty-six and the world had decided her value already. She was so much more than someone's potential wife. Still is. I'd imagine if she lived now, she'd have done a many great things. She's brilliant, stubborn, passionate, witty, and loves fiercely." Admiration shimmered in his blue eyes.

"You loved her instantly, didn't you?"

He let out a long sigh. "I did. Even if I wasn't willing to admit it right away. We met at the wedding. My mother was trying to introduce me to Beth's younger sister Judith." He winced. "Dreadful girl. All she cared about was pretty dresses and marrying a rich man. I escaped the attempted coupling and went to the lakeside where I found Beth reading Mary Shelley's *Frankenstein*. I wanted to know what type of woman left a party to read a scary story." A smile broke across his face. "Turns out the type I would marry. Two months later, I brought her here, proposing and telling her I'd build her our home. A place where we could always be together."

Nora's eyes flicked around the clearing. The lush green trees danced in the gentle breeze. In the distance the soft babble of a brook filtered into the clearing. It was such a lovely place to make promises about forever.

"Forever?" Nora rose to her feet.

Sighing, Bill gestured to himself. "Of course, this isn't what I had meant by a place for us to be forever."

Forever? The word danced inside of her. Nibbling on her lower lip, she tapped her fingers against her watch's face.

He'd promised Beth forever and here they were. Granted it wasn't the forever he'd likely envisioned, but a promise kept.

"Bill, when you found Beth dead why did you apologize?"

"I didn't murder her, if that's what you're playing at." His brow puckered.

"No. I know. I believe you."

Bill gaped. "You do?"

"Melody believes you, which should be enough, but my gut tells me you're innocent. There's no science behind it, but my grandpa always told me to trust my gut."

"I think I like this grandpa of yours." Affection softened his features. "When our son died, I blamed Beth."

"Why? What happened?"

Bill closed his eyes, a painful expression etched on his face. "We had a small cottage on the lake, and we'd go there in the summer. I loved taking Beth out on our rowboat. Then when Willy came along, I'd take both. We were supposed to go out on a picnic on the lake, but I canceled so I could meet with a potential business partner. I told her never to go out without me, but she was stubborn. I don't know what happened, but I came out on the dock to find the boat tipped over. Willy clung to the boat screaming for his mother. My heart stopped. I couldn't see Beth. I dove in, telling Willy to hold on to the boat."

Oh god... Nora placed her hand on her chest, where a dull ache formed.

"I jumped in, looking for her and found her. I was so relieved. She was alive and pulling on her skirts. Those goddamn dresses women used to wear. Her skirts were tangled on something, dragging her down. I could see the panic in her eyes, and she screamed to go to Willy. She was more worried about him. She was such a good mother. It makes what I did all the more cruel." He swallowed hard as emotion welled in his eyes. "I thought he was fine. By the time I pulled her free and we found the surface, Willy was gone. He must have let go. My brother Alexander came out, hearing the commotion. He dove in, and I told him to take Beth. She fought him, wanting to find our boy. I dove in. By the time I found him…it was too late."

"I am so…" She stopped herself from uttering that clichéd statement. Who wouldn't be sorry for such a horrific loss?

But sorry didn't fix it. It would only appease her own sadness for their loss. It wouldn't ease their grief.

"Grief can make you say terrible things. After we recovered the body, Beth broke down. She cried, slamming her fists into my chest and asking why I didn't save him first. That I should have left her. That I should have saved him." His voice quaked. "Instead of telling her the truth, I snarled 'Why did you not listen to me? Our son would be alive if you weren't so goddamn stubborn.' I let my anger over losing my son push my wife away. I wasn't even angry with her. I was angry with myself for failing as a husband and a father—for not saving them both."

Nora stepped close, lifting her hand to his shoulder. The prickling cold tingled as her hand passed through him. "What was the truth you didn't tell her?"

"That I'd always choose her first. That there was no life for me without her."

"Why didn't you tell her that?"

"Because what kind of father would I be? I loved my son. I still do. I thought he was safe, and all I could think about was Beth. How I couldn't lose her. But I did anyway. I pushed her away with my cruel words and killed her spirit as if I had been the one that pushed her down those stairs. Over the months after Willy, I watched her dissolve into a living ghost. She drank more and more. She locked herself in her room. I did that to her. Instead of comforting her, I failed her. I failed her that day on the lake and every day after. I didn't kill my wife, but I stole her life from her." His voice cracked.

The confession sat heavy in the air between them.

"I understand guilt," she said softly.

"It's not the same. I made choices," he growled, starting to walk away.

"We all make choices. It was my birthday, and I chose to have my parents take me out instead of having dinner at home. My mom gave me a choice. She'd make breakfast for dinner, which was my favorite, or we could go to Pizza Palace. If I had chosen breakfast for dinner, they'd be alive." A tiny quake shook her words.

Bill stopped.

"Have you told Beth what you told me?"

He shook his head.

"You should tell her."

"I don't deserve absolution," he gritted.

"Now who's the stubborn one?"

He moved to walk away.

"Fine!" She let out an annoyed breath. "You don't, but she deserves it. By not telling her, she'll continue to carry the guilt of what happened. Is that what you want?"

Bill whirled. His face contorted into a snarl. "No... I love her."

"Then prove it. Tell her how you feel. Tell her that it's not her fault. Tell her that the last thing you thought about before you died was her, and that's why you're here. That you promised her forever, and you're here to keep that promise."

"How do you know that?"

Nora moved beside him. She'd suspected, but this conversation confirmed it. Beth was the reason they were all there. She knew it. "That doesn't matter. I'm right, aren't I?"

"Yes." Bill swallowed thickly. His eyes locked with Nora's.

"And she was who you were thinking of when you died, wasn't she Gideon?"

Bill spun toward where Gideon stood at the edge of the clearing.

"Yes," Gideon confessed.

CHAPTER 22

Bill Makes a Joke

"**W**hy were you thinking of *my* wife?" Hands balled into fists, Bill stalked toward Gideon like a lion ready to strike.

Thrusting her entire body at Bill, Nora reached and grasped for his shoulders to stop his approach, forgetting that she couldn't actually touch them. Her body hurled through Bill and slammed to the ground with a grumbled curse.

"Nora!" August shouted, coming into the clearing at the moment of her less than graceful impact. He dropped to his knees beside her and lifted her into his arms. "Are you okay? What happened?"

A sting throbbed in her elbow from where she'd collided with a stray rock nestled in the grass. "I'm…" she grimaced, rubbing at her arm.

"Mr. Putman, it's not like that." Gideon's calm voice jolted Nora's attention back to what was unfolding.

Bill's long fingers gripped the white collar of Gideon's

shirt. "What was it like then? Is this why you are here? Are you in love with *my* wife?"

It appeared that ghosts could touch each other. She'd file that away for later. Right now, she needed to stop Bill from killing Gideon – or whatever a ghost could do to one another.

Jumping to her feet, she placed her hands on her hips and scolded Bill like an unruly child. He ignored her completely.

August rose. "What is going on?"

"I'd like to know the same thing," Beth said, her tone curt.

Both ghosts and humans turned to look at the phantom matriarch.

"I'm trying to find out why Gideon's last thoughts were of you. Was there something going on between the two of you? Was that why he was the only one that you allowed to visit you in your room after Willy?" Bill seethed.

"It wasn't like that." Gideon yanked himself out of Bill's hold.

"William Putman are you *jealous* of Gideon?" Laughter belted out of Beth. The furrowed creases of her brow melted, and tiny crinkles formed around her eyes.

"Well, it's not *that* funny," Gideon protested, his lips pursed. "I was considered rather handsome for my age. I'm only ten years older than you."

Beth smiled. "Oh, you are still handsome, but we know I wasn't *your* type," she said with a saucy lilt.

"Ooohhhhh," Nora said, drawing out the word as realization hit her.

"*Type*? What does that mean?" Bill's gaze jumped between Gideon and his wife.

"I wasn't who Gideon loved."

"Who was, then?"

Gideon closed his eyes. "Frederic."

"Our coachman?" Bill's brows ticked up.

Gideon nodded.

Beth strolled fully into the clearing and stood beside Gideon. "It's not like today. Gideon and Frederic couldn't be together. Not like us or them." She pointed to Nora and August. "They couldn't marry like that lovely Dusty and Benji."

Remorse softened Bill's features. "I'm sorry old friend." He outstretched his hand to Gideon, who took it.

"It's alright—"

"No, it's not," Bill interrupted. "You've been a loyal friend for a long time."

Gideon cast his eyes to the ground, shuffling his shiny black shoes in the grass.

Bill placed his hand on his shoulder. "I shouldn't have let my anger blind me to that."

"You seem to do that a lot," Nora muttered.

"Hmph," he grunted. She couldn't tell if that was annoyance with her for pointing it out, or with himself for allowing anger to guide his actions.

He turned back to Beth. "How did you know about Frederic and Gideon?"

"I walked in on them kissing in the carriage house," Beth said, flashing a coy smile.

"She has a tendency to do that," August mumbled.

Beth shrugged, biting away a growing smile. It was the expression of someone that was sorry they'd got caught but was unlikely to stop snooping.

"Mrs. Putman kept our secret and found ways for us to be together. She was a loyal friend… She risked her reputation if the truth had been discovered." Affection tugged up at the corners of Gideon's mouth.

"I didn't risk what you did. You should have never had to hide your love for each other. Stupid closed-minded people," Beth harumphed.

Nora stepped closer to the three ghosts, who stood in the center of the clearing. "Why were you thinking about her when you died?"

"Mrs. Putman always smelled like lavender. When I was having my heart attack, I smelled it and thought of her. She must have been in the room when it happened." He gestured at Beth.

"I was. I tried to help you, but I couldn't..." Emotion welled in her eyes. "...I stayed, so you wouldn't be alone. That's why I was there when you came back."

The pieces clicked into place. It wasn't a *thing* that bound the three to Putman House. It was a *someone*. Both men were pulled back by or because of Beth. Bill's return made sense. Guilt and unspoken truth tethered him to her. But what held Gideon here? It had to be more than just the fragrance of an old friend as he lay dying.

Beth tilted her head. "What does this have to do with our therapy session for today?"

"Nora wanted us to remember everything that happened when we died, including our last thoughts. Both Gideon and I thought of you."

Anger flamed in Beth's features. "Are you saying this is *my* fault? That we're all here because of *me*?"

Nora gnawed on the corner of her mouth. "I'm not sure, but I think you're the magnet that pulled Bill and Gideon back here, and why they are still here."

"Wonderful!" Beth tossed up her hands. "Another thing that's *my* fault."

An icy gust of wind whipped across the clearing, nearly knocking Nora over. August wrapped his arms around her, tucking her into him, blocking the brunt of it.

"Calm down, Beth." August raised his voice over the howling wind, his body swaying just a bit.

"Calm down? Just like a man! Heaven forbid a woman

have *any* emotions," Beth sneered. "You're all the same. Blame us and then tell us to calm down."

Tree branches jerked in the intensifying wind. Twigs and loose pebbles shot across the clearing, pelting against trunks and through the ghosts.

"Nobody is blaming you, Beth." Nora took a tentative step, her voice steady. "I'm not saying it's your fault, but that you may be the reason. That they came back *for* you, not because of you."

"That's the same dish, just served in a different way. Don't treat me like a child, Nora. We're friends. At least, I thought."

"We are." The harsh wind beat against Nora. A sting pulsed in her eyes from the windblown dust particles. "If we weren't friends, I wouldn't tell you this. I wouldn't want to help."

"For the love of god, Beth!" Bill yelled. "If you don't calm down, someone will get hurt. Do you want that?"

Beth whirled on him. "Fuck you!"

He stumbled backwards. Pain contorted his face as if her words slapped against him like a fist.

The gusts gained strength. August's grip tightened around Nora. They teetered and battled to remain standing, while dodging the airborne debris that zigzagged around them.

"Bill, leave!" Nora ordered. If they were going to help Beth get a handle on her emotions, they needed to get rid of the biggest trigger of them all. Her husband.

Head shaking, his brow furrowed. Each wrinkle of his face spelled out determination. "No. I'm done leaving. I'm done not doing what I should have done a long time ago."

"It's not the—" A thick branch broke off from a tree and flew toward them. "August!" She shoved him to the ground, falling atop him. The branch whizzed over their heads. "Are you ok?" Her hands traced his face, ensuring he was unharmed.

Nodding, August rolled them over, resting his body over hers and cocooning her between the safety of his chest and the ground.

"Nora!" Beth gasped. "I'm so sorry. I didn't...I didn't mean..."

"I know," Nora assured, tilting her head up to look at Beth.

She tugged at the fabric of her long robe. Her face drawn in an expression of painful remorse. "I am so sorry. It is all my fault." Eyes closed, her voice wobbled. Her features gentled with the stilling wind.

Arms still folded tight around Nora, August cautiously raised up, pulling them to a seated position. "It's alright. We're not hurt."

"They're okay, Beth." Bill's voice was tender.

"Yes, Mrs. Putman, we're all okay. We know you didn't mean it." Gideon moved closer to her, placing his large hand on her shoulder.

Blinking her eyes open, she looked up at him. "I'm so sorry."

"It's okay. We're all okay."

Beth shook her head. "No. Not for this." She motioned around the debris covered clearing. "Well, I am, "she winced. "But I am sorry for..." She seemed to search for what to say.

A tight frown anchored Gideon's face. "It's not your fault that I'm here. It's—"

"It's my fault. It's all my fault." Bill placed his hand on his wife's arm, and she tipped her head up to him. "We're here because of me... because I failed you."

Beth's mouth went slack.

"It was all my fault. Willy. You. Even Gideon." He raked his fingers into his thick auburn waves. "I should have never chosen work over Willy and you. If I hadn't... the accident wouldn't have happened, or I would have been there to save you both."

Beth turned away from him.

With gentle movements, he reached out and guided her back to him. "I allowed my anger at myself to cloud my vision. It was never your fault. You did everything to save Willy. You were willing to sacrifice yourself for *our* son." He swallowed hard. "*I* was the bad parent. I wasn't willing to sacrifice you."

Beth just glared; her stare icy.

"I love you. I wasn't willing to lose you that day… but I lost you, nonetheless. You were so angry with me and instead of accepting that, I made the wrong choice… I failed you. Then, I lashed out." He gripped her shoulders as if clinging to a life raft for salvation. "I didn't push you down the stairs, but I killed you. From the moment I pulled you from the lake, you died a slow death at my hand."

Emotion flickered in her stoney expression, melting the hard edges that lined her face. That flicker seemed to coax him on.

"I love my son, but a life without you…" His gaze turned to the sky. "I don't deserve forgiveness, and I'm not asking for it…" Dropping his stare back to Beth, his hands moved to her upper arms, pulling her a little closer. "Willy didn't die because of you. Gideon isn't here because of you."

"But you are," she snapped, her lips drawn in a firm line.

"Of course. I promised you forever. As long as *you* are here, I will always be here."

The darkness in her eyes faded to a soft green reminiscent of lush grass after a gentle spring rain.

He raised his right hand to her cheek, caressing with both tentative and slow strokes. "I have never stopped loving you, and I never will. I never deserved you. I think our hundred plus years together has shown that. Somehow, I was lucky enough to have you love me— even if it was just for a moment."

"The things you said—"

"They were unforgiveable," he rasped. "I was wrong...so goddamn wrong. I knew it even then. I came to you that night. When you sent me away, I shouldn't have gone. I should have held you and told you how sorry I was. That I loved you. That I still do."

"You should have let me go. You should have saved him," she said, her voice cracking.

"I know! I thought he was safe. He was holding onto the boat. I was wrong." He cried. "All I could think was about you. Willy needed his mother. I couldn't let him lose you. *I* couldn't lose you."

A familiar ache surged in Nora's chest. For just a moment, she felt her dad's large hand wrapped around hers and heard her mother's laughter.

"But *we* lost him." Beth yanked herself out of Bill's hold, slamming her fist against her chest.

He pulled her back into his arms. "I know... and then, I lost you."

"You threw me away."

"I am so sorry. I—"

Beth pushed her hands against his chest and slipped out of his arms. "It's too late."

"For me, but not for you."

The words seemed to steal Beth's ability to speak. Her mouth moved, but nothing came out.

"I need you to know that this isn't *your* doing. None of this is your doing. Please tell me you hear me...that you understand."

"It changes nothing!" She threw her hands up, her stare venomous. "He's still gone because of *us*! You saved me instead of him. I shouldn't have taken him out on that rowboat. If I hadn't let him jump, the boat wouldn't have tipped over," she howled, crumpling to the ground in heaving sobs.

Falling to his knees, Bill enveloped her in his arms. "I know my darling, I know," he soothed, running tender strokes down her back.

The ache in Nora's chest crawled up and up, lodging in her throat. A cluster of the unsaid choked to come out. Not to soothe, but to free. Not just them but her, too.

"Willy wouldn't want this." Nora's words were barely a whisper, but somehow it drew the Putman's attention.

They were two sides of the same coin. They'd lost their child, and she'd lost her parents. Each imprisoned by never ending grief and guilt. Putman House was like a beacon. It not only pulled the ghosts back but brought Nora here. There were too many parallels between their story and hers.

Coincidence is how the unimaginative try to explain fate's path, baby girl. Life has a way of taking us where we need to be. Grandpa Scott's words bolstered her resolve to keep going.

"He wouldn't want you two to blame yourselves. He loved you both." She flicked her gaze between both Beth and Bill.

"How do you know what our son would want?" Bill demanded.

"Because I am Willy."

In so many ways she was. If the coin had been flipped, Willy may have stood on that lakeshore, his clothes dripping and body trembling, waiting for his mother and father to emerge... Or instead of little Nora's eyes popping open and gasping for breath, it was her parents who awoke to find her gone. Just a flip of the coin...

"I've long wondered what it would be like if they had survived, and I had not."

"Oh, Nora...no," Beth whimpered.

Nodding, she lowered to her haunches in front of the

Putmans. "It would break my heart to see them sad. To watch them blame themselves. The last thing any child wants is for their mom and dad to be sad. Willy loved you, and he'd want you to be happy. To be the mom that cared for everyone, even if they didn't invite her to."

The dawn of a shaky smile budded on Beth's face.

"To be the dad that pretends to be all stern and serious but quietly pushes little girls on the swings to make them happy."

Wistfulness softened Bill's features.

"She's right." Gideon's face crinkled in a sad smile. "Willy was the happiest little boy…always smiling. He wouldn't want this. It wasn't either of your faults."

"It was a terrible accident. You thought he was safe, and he was. You couldn't have known. You were just trying to save his mother…save your wife," Nora said.

"They're right," Beth murmured, resting her palm on Bill's cheek, pulling his gaze to hers. "It wasn't your fault. It wasn't my fault. It was just a terrible accident."

Fingers trembling, he took her hand from his cheek and pulled it to his lips, pressing a tender, almost reverent kiss. "I am so sorry, my love."

"I'm so sorry," she croaked.

"It's time to let go of the guilt. Let go of the grief." Nora reached out her hand, allowing it to hover over the now joined hands of the Putmans. "It's not letting go of those that we lost but unshackling ourselves from what doesn't allow us to live our life that honors them."

August's palm rested on her shoulder, acknowledging the significance of this moment. It wasn't just their bindings she was trying to break, but her own. To free them all from the guilt that anchored them to the lives—if you could call it a life—that each lived.

She looked to August, whose eyes shone with encouragement and understanding. "This is our second chance to honor them with how we live."

Beth's head tilted to the right. "But we're dead."

"Sweetheart, technically, I think we're the living dead," Bill corrected, clearing his throat.

Nora arched an eyebrow. "Bill, was that a joke?"

A wry playfulness tugged at the corners of his lips. "Someone told me I was too serious."

CHAPTER 23

A or B?

Nora remained crouched in front of the Putmans for several more minutes. The rainstorm of tears gentled as Beth looked up, eyes beseeching, and asked, "What next?"

Exhausted after wrapping up the session, she and August escaped to the carriage house for a nap. Nora pondered the question as she lay tucked into August's nook. The warmth of his body blanketed her in a sense of safety.

The only answer she'd been able to give Beth in that clearing was, "We live." But what did that mean? Nora was just figuring out what that meant for herself. She had no idea what it meant for a trio of Victorian phantoms.

"Hey," August rasped sleepily, nuzzling into her hair.

"Hey," she breathed.

Despite the uncertainty of what was next, she wasn't nervous. Yes, there were questions about what happened once they left Putman House, but not about how being with August felt like she'd found a missing puzzle piece. Not since

Grandpa Scott had she allowed herself to need anyone. Even as much as she loved Mae, there wasn't a thrumming need for the relationship. Not like this. It was utterly terrifying.

"I like this." He combed his fingers into her hair, brushing away wayward tendrils behind her ear. "I like going to sleep with you. I like waking up with you."

"I like it too," she whispered.

"We wrap filming on Sunday and…" He nibbled on his bottom lip, as if considering his words carefully before proceeding. "I know you head back to L.A. to start postproduction, and I have a weeklong break before heading to the next location. Derrick and I were planning to stay here for a few days with our parents before heading to Virginia. But I had a thought…" He soothed his fingers down her arms. "Option A, you postpone editing for a few days and stay with me. *Or,* option B, I fly back to L.A. with you and, when you're not working, we spend as much time together as possible before I leave for Virginia. I can stay at your place, or you can stay at mine. I do have a *very* big bed but think I'm a fan of these smaller beds if it means I get to snuggle you like this."

"What?" Her mouth went slack. "You can't blow off your parents! They mentioned like eight times at lunch how excited they were to spend next week with you two."

"Option A it is. My parents aren't old-fashioned, but let me talk to Melody about renting a room here next week. The idea of sexing you up in my parents' guest room is a real boner killer."

"We'll address your use of the phrase 'boner killer' later." She sat up and gawked at him. "I didn't choose an option."

"Well, I just assumed." He grinned boyishly.

"I can't."

"Why?"

"I can't postpone editing. We have a schedule." She gestured wildly.

"First, I'm technically the boss."

She rolled her eyes. He *never* played that card…well, unless he really wanted something. She'd try to ignore the little zing of happiness that ripped up her spine at the thought that what he really wanted was her.

"Second, you are always a week ahead of schedule, so I'm not worried."

"I can't crash your time with your parents."

Waving his hands, he chuckled, "It's *not* crashing. Who do you think suggested option A?"

"Oh my god, they are shipping us hard." She pointed at him. "You really are a carbon copy of them."

The smirk on his face was identical to the one Gemma wore when she'd gleefully pointed out that their backyard would be perfect for a wedding. Part of her knew she should be running for the hills. This was all too much and too soon!

But was it? The last two years had been a slow dance of getting to know each other.

"I can't." She gnawed on her lip, casting her eyes down. Even to her ears the protest lacked any conviction.

Tucking his hand beneath her chin, he lifted her gaze to meet his. "Trust me, I'll have the counter argument to any excuses you have for why you can't. If it's a matter of you not *wanting* to do this, then I won't push. I'll respect that, but if it's just you feeling like you can't…isn't it time to let yourself live?"

It was almost the same words she'd spoke to Beth and Bill.

"I am so used to living with the can'ts." She sighed.

Nobody ever imposed them on her. They'd just found their way into her life. At first, each can't was just a safety rail ensuring she'd never get hurt again. But like any safety rail, eventually it became less protective and more about hiding.

"I know." His fingers trailed down her upper arms. "If you don't want this—"

"I want this." The declaration sprinted out of her. Clamping her hands on his face, she locked their gazes. "I want you. I'm just…I'm scared."

"It's okay to be scared. It means that this is important to you." He leaned in, claiming her mouth in a slow kiss. "Forget the can'ts, let's just focus on what we want, and I want you. I want you to call me a moron when I say something stupid. I want to hold your hand when you're scared, when I'm scared, or just because. I want to explore the places you've read about and find new ones for us to discover together. I want to take you for waffles. I want to hold you when we sleep. I want to make sure you have your five cups of tea every day…"

Her eyes widened with realization. The tea that magically appeared in the hands of Derrick or one of the production assistants was August's doing all along.

You, she mouthed.

"If you look in my wallet, you'll find two packets of English Breakfast tea. Some men keep condoms in their wallets, I keep tea."

She laughed. "You carry tea bags?"

"After they didn't have your favorite in Prescott, I put some in my wallet just in case."

Happy fireworks erupted within her. Over the last two years, this sweet man had burrowed into her heart. She'd not noticed it, but since their first meeting she'd ever so slowly been falling for him.

"Option A," she said, the brightness of her smile reaching her eyes.

"Option A." He grinned. "Now, that we've settled *that*… new option A, you sit on my face, or B, you sit on my face."

Laughter burst from her.

His hands moved to her thighs, inching up her sleep shorts. "This is not a laughing matter, Nora. I'm *not* kidding. Take off your bottoms and get on my face." It was almost a growled command.

She bit her lip, tamping down the "can't" that wanted to sneak out. Rising to her knees, she pulled off her T-shirt and tossed it off the bed. Then, she shimmied out of her shorts. Pushing him to his back, she licked her way up the ridges of his taut torso, allowing her sex to brush against him.

"Good girl," he purred when she straddled his face. His grip tightened on her hips, holding her in place.

"August." She bit back her moan with the first slow lick down her center.

"Mmmhmmm," he groaned before gently sucking on her needy bundle of nerves.

Gripping the headboard, she moved her hips against his working mouth. Tension built with each hardening suck, playful flick, and taunting lick of her clit.

"Yes..." she whined with the slow slide of his finger inside her.

Akin to the slow crank of a jack-in-the-box his taunting ministrations coiled pleasure at her core. He knew exactly what her body craved and just how to give it to her. He'd tease and play with feather-light licks amping up her need, keeping her on the edge. Then just as she thought she'd burst with frustration, he'd devour her, giving them what they both wanted. The almost feral noises he made, as if she was his last meal and he'd never have anything so good again melded with her strangled moans. It all colluded in spooling that delicious pressure tighter within her.

"Fuck!" she cried and then shot her hands to her mouth to stifle her moans. She had no idea if Melody was in the carriage house and didn't want to call attention to what was happening in the guest room. While Melody may not mind,

Nora felt a little bad about turning her lovely guest room into a pleasure palace. Though, not bad enough to *not* do exactly that.

Legs shaky, she moved off him. A self-satisfied grin stretched across his glistening face.

"You look very smug," she said, skating her fingers down the hard planes of his body.

"I'm just getting started." He sat up and pulled her onto his lap. The bulge in his boxers rubbed against her still sensitive core, causing pleasurable aftershocks.

"Yeah," she hummed, grinding herself against him like a cat in heat.

He had this uncanny ability to wring orgasm after orgasm from her and somehow still find more. It was like she had a secret O-town stash that only he had the combination to unlock.

Taking his mouth in a consuming kiss, their blended tastes made her heart race. "Make love to me."

It was as close as she'd ever came to saying those three words to anyone.

"Nora." The muscles of his throat worked. "I lo—"

She stole his words with a ravenous kiss. The can'ts rioted within her. *You can't say this. I can't say it. You can't possibly feel this. I can't say I love you, but I do.* She'd lived with them for so long it would be foolish to think she could let go of all of them at once. The can't didn't allow the words to be verbalized, but she could express it in action. She could allow their bodies to speak those words.

Guiding them up to their knees, her hands tugged at the waistband of his boxers. After her frustrated whine, he broke away and ungracefully pulled them off and almost fell over in the process.

Her palms slid down the ridges of his stomach. "Someone's excited," she crooned, wrapping her hands around his cock.

"Nora," he groaned with pleasure.

That wicked smile of hers got bigger.

Sitting back on his haunches, he guided her to settle onto his lap. "Much better," he murmured, as the tip of his erection brushed against her clit.

"I can make it even better." Taking him in hand, she ushered him inside her.

His eyes darkened. "I don't know if I'll ever get used to this." He moved her in a slow rhythmic rock against him.

"Having sex?" Her lips lifted.

His hands skimmed up her body, weaving into her sleep-mussed tresses, and cupping the back of her head. "Having you."

The cadence of her heartbeat stuttered. His words claimed and his stare seemed to gather her up and hold her close. Like that wild horse that Mae teased her that she was, part of her wanted to run away from this. With each soothing stroke of his fingers against her scalp, gentle rock of his hips, and seemingly endless gaze locked on her, the resolve to run faded.

Her hands cradled his face. "You have me."

"And you have me."

Tethered together, their bodies moved as one. His lips trailed down the column of her throat past her collarbone to her breasts. Back bowed, she served herself up to his savoring sucks, quick nips, and soothing kisses. He gripped her backside, guiding her hips to meet his intensifying thrusts. The pressure bloomed.

"Kiss me," she whimpered, wanting to fuse to him in every possible way at that moment.

His mouth slanted over hers, drinking in her muffled

moans. Her release extended with his continued pumps until his orgasm vibrated through both of them.

As they circled back to reality, their woven gazes remained fixed. The ravenous darkness in his eyes softened. A contented expression etched on his face. The pads of his fingers skated down her spine, calming her trembling body. The mixture of the physical reaction from orgasm and the intensity of the feelings swirling inside her made her limbs shaky.

"August..." she breathed, unable to form words beyond his name.

She hoped in those two syllables she could convey everything she was feeling at this moment. Never had she felt so right, yet so wrong at the same time. She wasn't the same Nora that stepped through Putman House's front door just a few days ago, but yet she'd never felt more herself, and that scared her.

He wrapped his arms around her, tucking her into his embrace. "I feel it too, baby."

She rested her head against his shoulder, her limbs draped around him. Their intertwined bodies offered safety. He had her, and she had him. As terrifying as it was to want —to *need*—someone as much as she did August, it felt right. With him came a wholeness that hadn't been there for a long time.

What if he leaves me behind, too? The fear hissed inside her. Eyes shut tight, she clung to him and said a silent prayer to whoever was listening to not lose this.

"Option A, I tell my parents you are my girlfriend, or option B, I continue to call you 'My Nora,'" he murmured.

She lifted her head and took in the boyish grin lighting his face. "Can't I be both?" It was the one *can't* she was pretty sure he'd *not* have a counter argument for.

CHAPTER 24

Double Date?

The pitter patter of rain tapped against the window. A series of thunderstorms with interludes of drizzle consumed much of the night. The intermittent claps of thunder and flash of lightning were the perfect backdrop for filming at a haunted Victorian mansion. It was as if Nora had conjured it straight out of central casting.

The only downside was that August wasn't a fan of thunderstorms. The normally unflappable six-foot-four muscley man jumped with each boom of thunder while investigating the attic. Several times over the night, Nora walkied him with comforting words, causing Dusty to raise an eyebrow and snark, "Maybe just join him in the attic." After a few death glares from Nora, Dusty called it a night and headed to the hotel.

Note to self, Dusty totally suspects. Nora sighed and reached for her tea but found nothing. Looking around, she spotted it sitting on the credenza. "Beth," she muttered.

The phantom menace had been pranking Nora most of

the night by moving her teacup around the room. Other Beth tricks had occurred during shooting. Closed doors opened. Chairs were moved. Once she relocated August's Sabres cap from the nightstand to the floor.

She retrieved her tea and sat down to watch the monitors. August sat cross-legged on the floor in the attic, surrounded by boxes labeled with *Christmas Decorations*, *Winter Clothes*, and *Dad's Shit*. The last one made her chuckle.

They were still running the planned experiments for this investigation. For the remainder of the night, August would be in the attic with the music box device, a tool to detect changes in electrical fields that would indicate the presence of ghosts. Derrick was doing Electronic Voice Phenomenon sessions in the library. They had made a deal with Bill, Beth and Gideon to not overexpose them, although Beth pushed the limits of that agreement.

Nora's gaze flicked between the two screens. As field producer, she spent much of the time watching the footage captured by the tripod cameras and handhelds that fed directly to the monitors in the command center. It allowed her to make notes about what things to pull into the episode, making editing the show far easier. Dusty was typically side-by-side with her, but he'd spend tomorrow overseeing interviews with subject matter experts that would be cut into the episode, so he left at midnight to sleep.

"Anyone here?" August's deep voice pulled Nora's attention to his screen.

Even in the grainy black and white hue of the night vision camera, he was beautiful. While handsome was a more typical word to describe the dusting of dark stubble along his strong jawline, the tiny dimple that popped in the left cheek of that boyish smile, his creamy hot chocolate eyes, and thick dark strands, to Nora he was beautiful. Like her own living breathing masterpiece come to life just for her. But his true beauty radiated from that big heart of his.

"You are in *so* much trouble," she groaned, laying her head on the table's cool surface. She was a goner for this man. The only consolation was that she knew he was just as gone for her. Their lingering kisses and the reverent way he held her after they'd made love this afternoon soothed away any fear that he'd not felt as strongly for her as she did for him.

Made love? She tapped her head against the table. Was this really happening? Was she falling? Yikes, was she in love with August Chandler?

The slow, creepy ice cream truck melody of the music box yanked Nora away from her thoughts. Blinking she gazed at the monitor, where August sat gaping at the music box.

"Is someone here?" he repeated. His nose scrunched and nostrils flared.

"Beth," she sighed, realizing what he was smelling. Yep, someone was there.

"I think I got him." Giddiness coated Beth's words as she poofed into the room.

"You promised you'd make yourself scarce."

She shrugged, an unrepentant expression covered her face. "I didn't manifest myself. I remained invisible."

Nora leaned back in the chair, shaking her head. "You and I have *very* different definitions of being scarce."

"Whatever, I'm compelling TV," she clucked, moving to the empty sofa in front of the window and taking a seat. Her silk robe draped on and hung through the sofa.

In so many ways Beth, Bill, and Gideon appeared as real as Nora or August, but it was moments like this that reinforced that they were a different kind of real. They existed. They had emotions. They could interact with the people and world around them.

Gideon had explained to Nora that he and Bill had some ability to touch things and people, but Beth had much greater skill in that regard.

"Whatever?" Nora shook her head. "You really do watch *too* much TV."

"Well, I have nothing but time to fill." With a long sigh, she frowned.

"How are you doing?" Nora sat up. "I know this morning was a lot."

She flung her head back. "I saw Bill in the garden earlier and did not feel like strangling him."

"That's progress." Her right eyebrow quirked. "So, what did you feel instead?"

At that moment she was channeling her inner Dr. Unaka. He'd be so proud of her. Perhaps she was better at this therapy thing than she'd thought.

"I...I..." Beth's brow furrowed in thought.

"It's just us girls," she coaxed.

"I've been angry with him for so long..." Her green eyes flicked around the room as if looking for a way out of this conversation, or perhaps out of her truth. "...but I've loved him longer. I never stopped loving him. Even at the end. Even when I thought he'd killed me. How messed up is that?" She flung her hands into the air.

Nora shifted in her seat. "Did you *truly* believe he killed you?"

Jumping up, she paced the room. Then she stopped and stared at Nora. "No. I don't think I really did. I was just so angry...so hurt...so disappointed about how he reacted after Willy. But I think I always knew that Bill didn't do it...that he'd never hurt me like that."

"What do you think happened to you?"

"I don't know. I wonder if Bill was right and maybe it had just been a horrible accident. I had been drinking a lot. Every night Agnes, Gideon's niece, brought me a glass of sherry. Well, it started as *a glass, but...*"

Nora nodded.

"It was easier to numb myself to everything." She placed her hands on the bridge of her nose and pinched. "I think the blind anger at him was just another way for me to numb myself. Ghosts can't drink. We can't get drunk, but we can lose ourselves in our emotions. The anger kept everything else at bay."

"I get it. I use distance to do the same thing. Keep everybody away and I don't have to feel the fear."

Beth's head tilted. "The fear of what?"

"Being left behind."

Beth glided to Nora, placing her hand against her cheek. A prickling cold caressed her face.

"You don't seem to be holding others at a distance. At least, not since I've known you."

"I'm not. At least, I'm trying." She fiddled with her T-shirt's hem. "Something has changed in me since I first came to Putman House. I don't know how to explain it, but it's like I'm coming alive here."

"A house of the dead is bringing you to life. Interesting."

A tiny laugh snorted out. "You sound like my therapist."

"Well, I do watch a lot of Kelly Clarkson, and my home-girl has lots of sage advice. Lay on the couch and tell mama *all* about it!"

"You are *not* at all what I expected a Victorian ghost lady to be like."

"Met a lot of Victorian ghost ladies in your travels?" she teased.

"Ha!" Nora grabbed her cup of tea from the table. "By the way, stop moving my tea, or I'll get an exorcist."

Beth's sheepish smile was unconvincing.

Sipping her tea, Nora grinned with the memory of

August pulling that tea packet out of his wallet and placing it into her hand when he came into the control room to get a spare battery for his handheld and noticed her empty mug. Maybe it was the desire to help Beth after her confession that she'd never stopped loving Bill, or perhaps her own swoony heart wanting everyone to feel what she was feeling, but there was a calling to second chance ship the Putmans.

"We should go on a double date."

CHAPTER 25

Swooning for the Chandler Brothers

"**D**o you think this is a sound plan? I mean, they just stopped hating each other," Derrick said, tapping his fingers against the kitchen island's smooth surface.

"Of course," Nora assured, slicing some strawberries for a small fruit salad.

After they wrapped filming that morning, Nora gave the ghosts a break from group and took a long nap with August. The crew was shooting interviews with some of the experts at the county's historical center and wouldn't be back until around seven. Between now and then, Nora and August would be going on a picnic with Bill and Beth.

"Plus, they didn't *hate* each other; they were just hurt," Melody offered.

Derrick rubbed the back of his head. "Didn't she throw all of the good china at him?"

"In Aunt Elizabeth's defense, none of that actually could have hurt him." Melody pointed a carrot stick at him.

His face pinched.

"It will be fine." August patted him on the back.

"I just don't want to see anyone get hurt."

August placed a palm on Derrick's shoulder and nodded. "Nobody is going to get hurt. I promise."

Nora's heart swelled. As strong and capable as her August was, he was still a little brother. It was sweet how Derrick worried for him and the Putmans. The starry look in Melody's eyes demonstrated that Nora wasn't the only one swooning for a Chandler brother. There'd been a moment of considering bringing Melody and Derrick on the ghostly date, but Beth nixed it. They were still a little cautious about how Bill may react to the handsome professor turned paranormal TV heartthrob wooing his beloved niece.

"That's a lot of food." Derrick gestured to the basket on the counter.

"It's for four people. Not to mention August often eats for two." Melody closed the basket, clasping it shut.

"Yes, but two of the people are ghosts that do not eat."

"We shouldn't treat them any different. That would be discriminatory." Melody pursed her lips.

Derrick's mouth dropped open. "No…I didn't…I would never…. I didn't mean it like that…I swear I'm not ghost prejudiced," he sputtered, his face turning red.

Melody leaned over the counter, pinching his cheeks. "You're *too* adorable sometimes. I'm just messing with you."

The red in his cheeks turned scarlet.

August stood behind him, smirking and shaking his head.

"I know you're kidding, but I do want to apologize for implying anything negative about your aunt and uncle." He plucked a napkin off the small stack beside the basket and began rolling it with his hands. "Perhaps to make it up to you I can take you to lunch."

"I'd like that." She smiled.

"Great." Derrick stood up, pulling the keys out of his pocket. "Maybe we can check out that little café my parents told us about at lunch."

Melody began to untie her apron. "Let me just go change."

"If you want, but you look pretty just as you are." Derrick's soft gaze drifted down Melody's figure.

Melody did look pretty. Her dark curls were pulled up in a high ponytail. A simple off-the-shoulder white tunic was paired with a pair of black leggings and flip flops. Nora imagined it was hard for her to not be pretty in anything.

Pink rouged her cheeks. "Okay." She hung the apron on the hook in the kitchen. "Let's go." Grabbing her cane, she moved to the door.

Happiness fluttered inside Nora. It was *too* adorable. Like puppies kissing each other.

Derrick turned to August, who thumbs-upped and mouthed *smooth*.

Rubbing his hand at the nape of his neck, Derrick shrugged and pivoted, heading to the door. As he reached the door, Derrick held it open and then planted his palm on the small of her back as he guided her out.

"Touchdown!" August made goalposts with his hands once the door shut behind them.

"They're like the Hallmark version of us."

"What does that mean?" August asked, rounding the counter, and coming up behind her.

"I'm pretty sure Derrick isn't the 'sit on my face' type," she quipped, leaning into his firm chest, his summery woodsy scent cocooned her.

Every one of her nerve endings sparked to life when he dipped his head close to her ear and whispered, "Who do you think taught me everything I know?"

"What?" she guffawed.

"Oh, my parents gave me the *talk*, but Derrick was the one that gave me the real advice."

"Like what?"

"Like…" His hands moved up her torso to her breasts, palming softly. The pads of his fingers rubbed against her hardening tips through the thin fabric of her dress. "…always taking care of your partner's needs and wants first." His hands slipped under the top of her dress, massaging over her lace bra.

"August." Her breath hitched with the first nipping kiss of her earlobe.

"We have thirty minutes." He pushed down the cups of her bra, freeing her aching breasts. "And we're *all* alone."

"What if they come back?" she gasped with his tweak of her nipple.

"It's a risk I'm willing to take." He nipped at her earlobe.

She bit back the "can't" that tried to come out.

He rolled and pinched her taut peaks, eliciting a small whimper from her. "I can't wait until we don't have to worry about time or anyone hearing us… For when I don't have to hold back with you."

"You've been…"

His right hand lowered to the hem of her dress, lifting and bunching the fabric at her waist to massage her core through the silk of her underwear.

"…holding back?" she moaned, her head lulled back against him.

"I told you I've had two years of imagining the things I wanted to do to have you screaming my name and digging your nails into my back." He moved her panties aside and drew a finger through her folds.

"All the ways I want to have you." His fingers stroked against her clit in slow, taunting caresses.

The delicious click of his belt unbuckling shallowed her breath. "This will just be a teaser for what will come, when I have no time constraints and can properly take care of you. Bend over." His palm rested on her back, gently guiding her to the counter.

Pressed against the cool surface, she felt his hands drag down her panties. Already slick with arousal, her body vibrated with need. His hands held her hips as he slowly entered her. A delightful ache burned as he pushed deeper inside.

"My sweet, sweet Nora," he rasped, sheathing himself completely in her. He pulled himself almost fully out and then quickly thrust back deeper.

"August!" she moaned.

"I love when you say my name like that."

The relentless teasing pace of his thrusts caused a collision of pleasure and need within her. The bite of his fingers into her hips holding her in place as each pump drove her closer to the edge. His right hand moved to the apex of her sex, massaging her throbbing clit.

"Oh…god. Don't stop," she whimpered, bucking against his working fingers.

"I won't, baby. I'll take care of you."

"I know… You always will." It was a breathy cry. Her entire body…her entire self was coming undone. Her breath panted in cadence with her racing heart. "August?" She blinked as he stopped and pulled her up. "Is something wrong?"

He turned her and lifted her to the edge of the counter. "No, everything is right…" He pushed back into her. "So fucking right…" His hands held her face. "I love you, Nora."

The air *whooshed* out of her reminiscent of being punched in the stomach. Only there was no pain. She just couldn't breathe.

"I have been in love with you since you called me a moron after I bought a case of Pellegrino when I confused it with prosecco for the crew to toast our first season." His fingers threaded in her hair. "I know this may scare you, but I can't hold it back anymore. I can't hold anything back with you."

"August… I…" The words wouldn't' come. No matter how much they swirled inside her, she couldn't say them. To make them real. To make how she felt about him a real living thing.

"It's okay. You don't need to say it." He pressed his forehead to hers. "Just let me love you."

Unable to speak, she nodded.

Their stares tethered. His hips moved in a languid rhythm. There'd be no coming back from this. No coming back from him.

As the orgasm drowned her, she clung to him, terrified to let go. A quake shook across her body, not from the aftershocks of her release but from the emotions within her, demanding to come out in three words.

"I love you," he murmured into her hair.

She just squeezed tighter.

CHAPTER 26

A Perfect Place for Lovers

Sated, changed, and knees still a little wobbly, they walked with hands clasped, to the small brook on the other side of the clearing. August was in love with her. In true August fashion, he didn't hold back. Despite his claim that he had been holding back. His entire body expressed how deeply he felt for her.

A flip through the memory album of the last two years provided clue after clue of his love. The tea. How his palm found its way to the small of her back when they walked across crowded rooms. His insistence to always ensure she had french fries. The way his chocolate eyes drank her up.

Just let me love you. His plea sang in her as they reached the grassy shoreline along the brook.

A rainbow of wildflowers lined the stream. Lush willow and birch trees waltzed in the gentle spring breeze. Beth said the clearing was the perfect place for lovers, but with her hand blanketed by August's warm palm, she'd contend this was the definition of perfect. Even if she hadn't verbalized it, yet. Even if her limbs itched to run away. It was perfect. This place. This man. Despite the fear that stalked inside her waiting to pounce with its can'ts, she'd keep going.

"Bill?" August steps halted, tipping his head to the far end of the streambed where Bill crouched. "What are you doing?"

Deep in concentration, his fingers in the shape of a claw, he reached for a pink flower. "Damn it!" he grunted as his hand passed through it.

"Are you trying to pick that flower?"

Rising, he blew a frustrated breath. "When courting a lady, you bring flowers."

Nora's heart squeezed with how adorable this gesture was.

"I can touch things from time to time, but it's in spurts. I never seem to be able to hold on to it for long. Pushing things is one thing but holding them always seems to be out of my grasp." He shook his head. "Maybe this is a sign."

August squeezed Nora's hand before dropping it and striding to Bill. "I got you." He plucked the flower. "I can give it to Beth on your behalf."

"It's not the same." His forehead creased and arms crossed over his broad chest.

It was sweet how he wanted to bring Beth flowers. The child-like pout over not being able to do so was not so sweet. Nora chose to give him some slack. It had been a long time since he'd *courted* anyone, especially the wife he'd been in an over century long spat with.

"It's not the same if *you* give it to her."

"Suit yourself." August shrugged, walking back to Nora and slipping the flower behind her ear. "Beautiful."

"Thank you."

Bill motioned to them. "My point exactly."

"For two years, August orchestrated everyone on set bringing me tea. When I found out, it just made me fall for him more." She turned to Bill. "So, sometimes it means more than you think."

Face scrunched, he looked down to the flowers and then back to Nora. "I did it so wrong before…I just want to do it right this time."

"Second chances don't require perfection," she offered.

Nodding, he seemed to consider her words.

"Grandpa Scott?" August's question was punctuated with a knowing glint in his eyes.

"Grandpa Scott."

"I think I like this grandfather of yours," Bill said.

"I'm here," Beth announced, appearing in front of them. "On a date…in my robe and nightgown."

"Well, if the date goes well, you're in the appropriate attire for the after-date portion," Nora quipped.

"The nightgown would only get in the way," Bill said, and everyone turned to look at him. The widening of his eyes communicated that he'd not meant to say that out loud. "Ah…picnic." He gestured to the basket in Nora's hands.

To say it was an awkward start to the double date may be an understatement. How does one double date with ghosts? Perhaps a romantic picnic beside a babbling brook wasn't ideal. The four of them sat on the red checkered blanket, food strewn between them, in clumsy silence. A stiff Bill sat, long legs stretched out, on the opposite side of the blanket from Beth, who sat on her knees. August and Nora sat across from them, his arm looped around her waist.

A double date may have been a bad idea. First, Nora had never actually been on a double date. Her knowledge of the practice came from watching movies or TV. She knew small talk was expected. How does one small talk with ghosts? *How was work? Oh, I spent eight hours haunting my former home.* The less than stellar conversation played out in her head.

How does one help two people fall back in love? Hell,

how was she supposed to know? She'd barely understood how she'd fallen in love with August. One moment he was the man driving her nuts with his insistent positivity, and then he was the man that didn't just make her believe in magic but feel it each time he looked at her.

Fingers tapping against her knee, Beth let out a long sigh.

Yup. This was a bad idea. What to do? Nora peered up to the above white wisps of clouds painted across the blue sky beseeching them for answers.

"How did you two meet?" August asked. The casualness to his tone was in sharp contrast to the whirlwind of anxiety within Nora.

Her gaze shot to him. *Why didn't I think of that?*

He squeezed her middle as if saying, *I got you.*

The sensation of belonging surged in her. He said he had her and he did. Pushing past the fear pulsing in her, she nuzzled into the idea of being with someone…of being a team again.

You and me against the world, baby girl. It had been so long since she'd been the other half of a team.

"At my brother's wedding," Bill said.

Beth arched an eyebrow. "You make it sound so benign."

"Oh, nothing about you or that night was benign," he said with a devilish grin.

"Not *benign*? Why, Beth, did you have *your* own cries of passion that night?" Nora teased, grabbing a grape from the bowl in front of her.

"Not *that* night," Bill offered, wickedness gleamed in his expression.

"William Putman!" She wagged her finger at him.

His long arms reached out, taking her hand, and weaving their fingers together. "Don't worry my dear, I won't share *that* memory. That's just for us."

Something sparked in Beth's eyes as she looked back at her husband.

"The night we met, my mother had introduced me to Beth's younger sister Judith. My mother thought Judith would make a perfect match for me…" A grimace covered his face. "…she did not. When I escaped her endless prattling about lavender dresses, I came upon a woman in a tree. The most beautiful woman I had ever…I *have* ever seen."

Beth lowered their still intertwined hands and scooted a few inches closer to him.

"She sat reading Mary Shelley's *Frankenstein* on the lowest branch. Her pink dress and legs dangled. It was rather scandalous."

"There was nothing scandalous about it," she protested with a slight pout.

"I could see your ankles!"

"You loved it." A flirty smile erupted on her face. "You always enjoyed my ankles."

"My dear, there was *very* little I didn't enjoy about you. Above all, I loved your spirit. How you tossed off convention, fleeing the most dreadfully boring party to climb a tree. I think I fell in love with you when you called me a scoundrel for intruding on your quiet reading spot."

Beth bit her lower lip.

"Very smooth Bill," August praised.

That single question from August seemed to break open the dam. The four of them wove between stories from their lives and some rather interesting tales from the Putman's afterlives, including how Beth used to hide Melody's grandma's keys and purse.

"She was a terrible woman and always smelled like cabbage," Beth groaned.

Nora tilted her head. "Why would you hide her keys, then? Wouldn't you want her out of the house?"

"Exactly." Bill's stern face had melted to an open softness. Happy crinkles kissed the edges of his eyes as he laughed.

"Well, I'm not the only one that got up to some questionable behavior. Remember how you tormented Melody's boyfriends?" Beth pointed at her husband.

"None of them were worthy of *our* girl."

Nora and August's eyes met in silent conversation, seeming to agree not to let Bill know about the budding romance with Melody and Derrick.

"Ummm…" August cleared his throat. "What did you do to them?"

"Well, there was Jacob, who tried to take her to the prom. When he arrived, Bill tripped him, and the poor boy fell off the porch and broke his arm," Beth offered.

"I heard him tell one of his friends that he thought Melody would be a *sure thing*. That the blind band girl wouldn't turn down the quarterback," Bill protested, his face pinched.

"Jacob Morrison?" August asked.

He nodded.

"He was a jerk. Good call, Bill."

"Then there was Logan, who you terrified at night by opening and closing the closet door when he came home with her for the holidays." Beth arched one brow.

"I believe you had a hand in that too, my dear." He crooned. "Didn't you keep turning his lights on and off?"

Realization lit her face. "Oh, I did… What was it about him we didn't like?" She tapped her fingers on her chin.

"I believe you didn't care for his comment on the wallpaper in the parlor."

"Oh yes, awful boy."

"We should warn Derrick about commenting on the décor," Nora whispered in August's ear.

"Agreed." He squeezed her middle.

As the stories flowed, Beth inched closer and closer. Now she sat, tucked into Bill's side, his arm draped around her. There was a sweet comfortability between the two of them as she occasionally leaned into him or tilted her face to him as he spoke. His large hands caressed along her upper arm.

"This was such a lovely idea," Beth cooed. "Thank you for organizing this, Nora and August."

"Of course," Nora said, packing up the basket.

The crew would start arriving in two hours. Nora wanted to get things cleaned up and slip back into work mode. She'd spent most of the day in a girlfriend role. The memory of August's hands roaming her body and earnest gaze as he said he loved her was a new continent to explore. For so long she stuck to the safe path, never straying. Today, she'd strayed so far that she wasn't sure how to find her way back—or if she wanted to.

"Would you like me to help?" Beth asked, interrupting Nora's wandering thoughts.

"We've got this." August's palm rested on Nora's shoulder.

We. She inhaled deep, allowing the sensation to drip through her.

Bill stood up and reached his hand down to his wife. "Would you care to join me for a stroll in the garden?"

With a tentative smile, Beth took his hand. "Okay."

As the Putmans disappeared down the grassy path, August clasped Nora's hand and helped her to her feet. "I think that was a success."

She watched them disappear down the path. "I hope so."

Placing his hand on her chin, he ushered her stare back to him. "No matter what happens with Beth and Bill, you've made a difference. Even if they don't come back together as a couple or figure out their unfinished business, I think you've helped them find some peace."

Nora shook her head. "I don't know about this unfinished business thing. I think you're wrong there."

"I was right about the ghosts."

"Smug much?"

He banded his arms around her. "Can you blame me? I have you."

She snorted. "Now who's the *smooth* one?"

His hands went to her cheeks and tilted her gaze up to him. "Seriously, why don't you believe in unfinished business?"

The words clustered in her throat. *Just tell him.* Unlocking the vault inside her, she exhaled. "My parents."

His mouth opened and then closed.

"If ghosts are here because of unfinished business…" Her voice shook. "…why wasn't I enough for them to stay?"

"Oh, baby." He kissed the center of her forehead.

She melted into his chest. "You don't need to say anything. You don't need to fix it. Just hold me. Just…" She swallowed thickly. "…love me."

That's what he did. She wasn't sure how long they stood there, his arms around her, chin resting on top of her head. With every layer of herself she offered him, he just held her tighter. Loved her more.

Tipping her head up, she broke the companionable silence. "Let's go back to the carriage house. We have almost two hours until the crew arrives. I'd like to have you snuggle me on the couch while we watch *Is It Cake?*."

"Why, my sweet Nora, have I converted you to a snuggler?" His mouth quirked.

August scooped up the basket and Nora folded the blanket. Looping her arm in his, they walked back to the carriage house. In the distance, they could see Beth sitting on the small wooden swing set on the far side of the backyard, a smiling Bill pushing her. Their quiet laughter drifted across the yard. Nudging each other in the ribs, Nora and August beamed.

"You did that," he said, tipping his head toward the ghostly couple.

Nora looked at the smiling pair and then to August. "No. *We* did that."

Taking her hand in his, they strolled to the carriage house. God, she loved this man. The three little words crawled up her throat with each step upstairs.

Tell him! Tell him! Her pulse quickened.

He pushed the kitchen door open and they stopped dead in their tracks.

"Oh my god!" Melody shrieked.

Melody's naked body lay draped over that same kitchen island that Nora had had to thoroughly clean two hours ago, her legs bent and Derrick's head between her thighs.

"That's right, baby," Derrick almost growled between her legs.

"Not oh my god, but *oh my god your brother and Nora!*" Melody patted Derrick's head.

"What?" He looked up, his wide eyes peering between Nora and August. "Fuck!" he shouted, leaping up and gathering Melody's naked body in his arms and covering her with his own.

"I told you...taught me everything I know," August quipped, elbowing Nora's side.

"I guess he's more sit on my face and less Hallmark than I thought." Nora cooed.

CHAPTER 27

A Pair of Brontë Heroines

Nora: I think I'm in love with August.
Mae: Think???
Nora: Well...not think. I know.
Mae: First, oh my god! Second, OH MY GOD! Third, have you told him?
Nora: No.
Mae: Well, that's not surprising.

Lines creased Nora's forehead as she stared at the phone. Protest danced at the tips of her fingers waiting to be typed. But Mae had a point. She'd never been in love. Hell, there'd never been even the inkling of a strong like with anyone. The phone pinged, dragging her attention back.

Mae: Are you scared he doesn't love you in return?
Nora: I know he loves me. He told me.

He told her a lot. In the twenty-four hours since he said "I love you, Nora," he'd repeated that declaration in so many ways. His fingers traced the words on her shoulder when he bent over the monitor in the command center during last night's filming. His lips pressed those words into her after pulling her into the kitchen while the crew did post morning interviews with Derrick in the library. His deep voice murmured it into her hair as they lay naked, limbs tangled, after this morning's post-nap sex.

Mae: Then why haven't you told him?

Why, indeed? She let out a long breath. She could almost see the soft concern in Mae's eyes in the words on the screen. It was the same question Nora asked herself. She'd been so close to saying it before they walked in on Melody and Derrick.

After escaping the apartment to give the mortified couple that kept saying "We thought you wouldn't be back for another hour" some privacy, they headed to the entertainment room on the first floor.

That didn't seem like an appropriate moment. At least, that's what she told herself. Oh, the lies she told herself at the many, many more moments after that one that were perfect for her to tell him how she felt. When he appeared on set holding a mug of tea for her. When he was listing to Lucy all the *very* wrong reasons that Kevin Arnold from *Home Alone* was the superior Christmas hero to *Die Hard's* Jack McClane. When he pressed her close in the shower this morning, murmuring that she was lovely.

Nora placed her hand on her fluttering heart. There'd been so many untaken opportunities to say it. She could almost hear Dr. Unaka ask, in his thick Bronx accent, "Why are you scared to claim your feelings?"

Claiming something makes it real and once something is real, it can be taken away. The imaginary conversation with Dr. Unaka played out. It may be time for a real discussion with him.

Nora: Maybe I'm too broken to love.

Mae: That's some bullshit. You love. You love deeply. I

know that, because you love me, and I love you. You're just scared. This is textbook romcom angst.

Nora: This seems like too heavy of a convo for text.

Mae: Agreed! But the director is giving me the side-eye. It's our last day of filming. Once we're done, I'll call, and we'll process. I'll be the Judy Greer to your Katherine Heigl.

Nora: I love you, Mae. Thank you. *Purple Heart Emoji.*

Mae: Progress! See, you can say it! I love you too. *Purple heart emoji.*

Sighing, she slipped her phone into her pocket. She'd talk it out with Mae later, but she knew the answer already. Saying the words out loud made this real...*and real things can be lost.*

She headed downstairs, where Melody and Derrick's hushed voices filtered from the entertainment room. There'd been a brief chat after the two put their clothes back on and slinked downstairs like two people that got caught doing—well, doing what they'd been doing. Ever the younger brother, August folded his arms across his chest and asked Melody what her intentions were with his brother. "To make sure we remember to lock the doors," she said, flashing a devilish smile. Derrick wholeheartedly agreed. After that everyone shrugged and moved on. Well, outside of the random high-fives and suggestive comments he tossed his brother's way when they interacted during filming.

Nora walked into the room, hands over her eyes. "I'm not looking. Just grabbing a cup of tea."

"Hilarious," Derrick deadpanned, drawing out the word.

Melody threw a tea towel at Nora, who easily caught it. "This morning you two said you weren't going to mess with him anymore!"

Lifting the tea towel to her chest, Nora feigned innocence. "What? I was just making sure I wasn't interrupting anything. Just being a *good* house guest."

"Oh, yes I could hear what a *good* house guest you were being this morning." She held up two fingers. "Twice."

So, she and August hadn't been *that* quiet. "Point made."

Derrick smiled proudly. "My lady is very smart."

"Which is why you should listen to me." She poked his ribs with her manicured finger.

"You're right, of course."

Nora arched a brow.

"I should head over. I need to meet August for a video conference with the field producer for our next episode." With a quick kiss to Melody's temple, he left.

Nora tilted her head to the door that Derrick just walked out of. "What was that about?"

Melody exhaled a long breath, gathering up her dark curls into a messy bun. "Derrick wants to stay here next week. Since you and August are staying here, he thinks it would be fun. We can do couple things."

"Couple things?"

"You know, board game nights, picnics, going to the movies, and making dinner together."

Nora's brow creased. "*Wait,* that doesn't sound appealing to you?"

"It does," Melody sighed, leaning on the counter and placing her hands under her chin. "It really does."

"Then what's the problem?" As the question left her lips, she thought of her text exchange with Mae. Pot, meet kettle.

"Uncle William."

"Ohhh."

The chat during their double date reinforced that Bill hadn't been open to any of Melody's past young men. *Young men? God, you are hanging with Beth too much!*

"This week was one thing. It was easy to hide our..." She

motioned with her hands as if it filled in for the word relationship. "…But there wouldn't be an entire crew here to help hide whatever is happening with us."

"What if you tell Bill? Like, what if Derrick does the whole ask for permission to court you thing?"

"Court me?" she scoffed.

"Your aunt and uncle are rubbing off on me." Nora leaned her head on the counter, laughing.

"First, the only person's permission he needs to date me is mine. Second, Derrick suggested that and…"

Nora raised her head. "And?"

"I *really* like him. I've had a crush on him since I was thirteen. Even as adults, it never went away. If I ran into him in town while we were both visiting our parents, something always fluttered in my belly."

Nora reached, placing her palm atop Melody's hand. "Telling your aunt and uncle makes it real."

"Yeah." Melody took Nora's hand, intertwining their fingers.

Fear was such a powerful bond to break. Nora understood that better than anyone. She wanted to give words of encouragement, but they'd feel like lies coming from the same lips that the words "I Love you, August" hid behind.

"Mae is right, we *are* a pair of Brontë heroines, complete with all the emotional baggage and angst." Nora scrunched her nose.

"I'd rather be a Denise Williams heroine. Lots of great sex with hot men."

Nora waggled her brows. "We're kind of that, too.

Nora said goodbye to Melody, grabbed her tea, and headed to Putman House. She strolled into the command center to find Lucy leaned over August, her lips inches away from his ear as she spoke.

"It would be perfect, don't you agree?" she cooed, batting her long eyelashes.

"What would be perfect?"

August looked up from the laptop. "It's a possible location for next season that Lucy found."

"It's a manor house in rural Ireland. It's near the village my mom's parents are from. Super haunted." She wiggled just a bit as she spoke.

Nora arched a brow. "Ireland?"

"Yeah, I've been recently inspired to add a few international locations to next season."

She smiled. That inspiration was her. Just this morning they snuggled, talking about some of the places on her list to visit, and Ireland was on the top of that list. It had been Grandpa Scott's dream to visit the small village in County Cork where his grandfather came from.

"When I asked Gus about future plans for the show and he mentioned Ireland, I instantly thought of this place." Lucy twirled a dark tendril around her finger. "I only hope I'm still with the show to be part of it."

Oh, she's good. Nora smirked. She'd seen this game before.

"Gus," Benji called from the doorway. "Someone's fucking with the tape for X-camera placement. They are gone. I have *no* idea where you want them for tonight."

"Gone?"

"Phantom Menace," Nora clucked. That was the nickname they gave Beth because of her countless pranks.

He chuckled.

"Phantom Menace? What does *Star Wars* have to do with this?" Benji blinked.

"Just an inside joke." He winked at Nora and then moved to the door. "I'll help you with the cameras."

"Gus," Lucy said, her voice dripping with honey. "Do you want me to email that info I mentioned?" Her hands played with the pendant of her necklace, calling attention to the hint of cleavage in her V-neck.

Nora fought the eye roll but not *that* hard.

"Sure. I'll look at it in the morning. Thanks for the suggestion, Lucy." He nodded and then followed Benji out of the room.

Nora picked up her tea and eyed Lucy. She wasn't jealous of Lucy but cautious. After Nora returned to L.A., Lucy would remain with the rest of the crew for the next episode. While Lucy was lovely and sweet, there was an undercurrent of calculation there. It wasn't a new game. Many within the industry flirted, flattered, and used relationships of all varieties to get ahead. Even if Lucy's flirtation with August was real—which she doubted—Nora didn't worry. August loved her. Plus, the beauty of a boyfriend with golden retriever vibes was loyalty.

As much as Nora recognized what Lucy was doing, she felt protective of her. Ten years ago, she'd been Lucy. A bright-eyed production assistant eager to get her big break. Some directors, producers, and executive producers would take advantage of that. August definitely wasn't one of them, but there were so many.

"You're good at your job, Lucy," Nora offered.

Lucy closed the laptop, peering up with her innocent doe eyes.

"Let your work speak for itself."

"Excuse me?" Her glossy lips pursed. "What does that mean?"

Nora placed her mug down and walked toward Lucy. "Just that you're very talented and smart. You have good instincts and you're hardworking. Focus on that and you'll get where you want to go. Trust me." She rested her palm on Lucy's shoulder, hoping she got it.

Her forehead creased. "Okay." A short beat was punctuated by their assessing gazes until Lucy broke the quiet. "I'm going to go to the kitchen to refresh the snacks for the crew. Any requests?"

She shook her head.

"Nora! Raj's boom mics are missing," Dusty grumbled, stomping into the room. "He's freaking out and so am I. First the X-cameras, now this. What the hell?"

Beth. Nora groaned, pinching the brim of her nose.

"On that note, I'm going to go get snacks," Lucy giggled, strolling across the room.

"Carbs! I need carbs to get through this day!" Dusty called.

Nora placed her hands on Dusty's upper arms. "No, carbs. You have a tux to fit into, remember?"

"You're *no* fun," he pouted.

"They have to be around here somewhere. Grab Raj and we'll split up to look."

I'm going to kill the Victorian ghost lady, she thought as she dug through boxes in the attic. Each member of the crew took a different floor of the house and the carriage house, minus August and Derrick who were on a video conference with the network. Most of Beth's pranks were harmless and hadn't messed with their production like this. Her lavender aroma hadn't graced the house during the day. In a very un-Beth-like fashion, she'd been scarce since this morning's group therapy session, which was less therapeutic and more Gideon and Nora arching eyebrows at the flirty exchanges between the Putmans.

"You think helping someone tackle their unresolved grief and reunite with their husband would stop them from pranking you," she muttered, swiping away cobwebs in front of her.

Her phone vibrated from her back pocket. It was likely Mae. This was no time for emotional processing. Although, Mae may have suggestions of how to get back at a prankster ghost.

"You would *not* believe what I am doing right now," she groaned.

"Was it waiting with bated breath for my call?" The deep voice did *not* belong to Mae.

A glance at the screen showed an unknown L.A. phone number. "Umm?"

"And here I was hoping I'd left such an impression that you'd recognize my voice. It's Travis Olson."

Nora gaped. "Travis Olson." She'd almost forgot about him. Why was he calling? Executive producers never called unless… Her pulse ticked up.

"I'll admit I was skeptical, but your reel made me a believer. Well, not in ghosts, but in Nora Scott. I'd like you to join *The Great Escape* as one of our field producers."

"What?" She leaned against a stack of boxes. The flimsy JENGA-like structure was unable to support her, and she tumbled backwards. "Fuck."

"Fuck? That's not the normal reaction I get when offering someone a job."

"Sorry." She winced. "I just fell over some boxes." She stood up and rubbed at her backside.

A deep laugh filled the other end of the line. "Sounds like we'll need to upgrade our insurance with you."

Was this happening? Had she finally got a chance to produce a travel show? A lump formed in her throat. If she took this job, she'd be saying goodbye to *Haunted Hideaway*.

To… She shook her head. No. Leaving the show wouldn't mean leaving August. Although, how many times had she seen these on-set relationships fade to black after filming ended?

"I'd like to set up a formal meeting for next week to discuss details," he went on. "Will you be back in L.A., or should we do a video conference?"

"Uh." She dragged her teeth over her lower lip. "I've not accepted the job, yet."

"I just assumed."

So had she. A week ago…hell, four days ago, it would have been an automatic yes. No hesitation. This was what she'd been working the last ten years for. Her childhood dream was right in front of her. All she had to do was reach out and grab it.

"It's Wednesday. I'll give you 'til Friday. Call me at this number, and give me your answer. If I don't hear from you by Friday at five L.A. time, then I'll assume it's a no. Don't pass up this chance. I think you could be a great travel show producer. I think we could do great things together."

She blinked. "Friday. You'll have my answer then."

"Until then," he said, ending the call.

CHAPTER 28

Doors

Nora paced the length of the attic. This should be a happy moment. She should be jumping for joy. She should be planning celebratory waffles with August.

August. His name halted her steps. He'd been so supportive. He'd told Travis that he'd be a fool not to hire her. He'd said he'd let her out of her contract to take this job…to leave their show. *Our show.*

With an unsteady breath she lowered to the dusty floor. Her stare locked on her phone. In two days, she'd need to tell Travis her decision. What would it be?

Nora: I'm freaking out! I got the job, and I don't know how I feel about it.

No answer came. Mae was likely filming. She kept her phone on silent when she was actually shooting, so there wouldn't be a response until after she'd wrapped.

The only notification on Nora's phone was the little low

battery warning. A downside of a house full of ghosts was drained batteries. The common paranormal theory was that ghosts used batteries and electrical devices to power themselves. Like their version of a protein bar. It had been one of the theories proven right by the ghosts of Putman House.

With a long sigh, Nora rose and slipped her phone into her pocket. She'd head back to the command center to charge it and see if anyone found the missing mics. After that she may hunt down her Victorian prankster and perform a verbal exorcism. Then there'd be some serious thinking about what should be the easiest decision of her life but now felt like the hardest.

Each wrung in her career ladder over the last decade in television production had been about getting her here. For Nora to produce a *real* travel show like the ones she'd gotten lost in with Grandpa Scott as a little girl. It was now within her grasp, but something twisted inside causing a queasy uneasiness to engulf her.

If only Grandpa Scott was here with his farm-spun sage advice. His tried and true "Trust your gut, baby girl" wasn't working. Nora's gut was a mess of knots.

She closed the attic door, fixed her eyes on the open door at the bottom, and started down the narrow staircase to the third floor. As she reached the middle step, the door slammed shut.

Let it be the wind. Her pulse raced.

The click of the lock confirmed it wasn't the wind.

Nora ran down the remainder of the stairs and seized the doorknob. "I'm in here! Let me out!" She twisted and pulled with no luck. It was locked. She was locked in. Someone had locked her in.

"Beth!" She slammed her fists against the door. "This isn't funny. Unlock the door. Please!"

Nothing happened. No soft scent of lavender lingered nor a musical voice cooed, "Did I get you?" Beth didn't manifest with her unapologetic wry smile. It was just enclosing walls and snatches of light from the last flickers of the dying lightbulb.

"Breathe," she commanded herself, placing her hands at her abdomen. "In for one…" She inhaled deeply. "…Out for two." She let out the breath and repeated the action to calm the frantic pace of her breathing.

As her breath steadied, she pulled her phone out of her pocket and called August.

"Crisis adverted!" His cheerful voice filled her ears. "We found the mics. Well, actually Lucy did. Somehow they ended up in the basement. Raj's meltdown is over. We're getting things set up for the shoot."

"Great," she said, her voice shaky.

"Are you okay? Where are you?" Concern laced his question.

"Trapped." The rapid beat of her heart thrummed fear through her.

"What?! Baby, where are you? I'm coming. Where are you?"

Sucking in a deep breath she pushed out the words. "I'm in—"

The phone went dead.

"Fu—fu—fucking ghosts," she stammered. "Air…air…I need air."

She turned and ran back up the stairs, only to find the attic door stuck. Twisting the doorknob and slamming her entire body against it did nothing.

"No! No! Beth, please," she shouted, tears stinging her eyes.

She ran back down the stairs and flung herself against the

door. Pounding and screaming, she begged for someone to come. To help. But no one came. She was alone. Trapped.

"You're...o...kay..." Breath unsteady, she flicked the rubber band at her wrist, hoping the sting would sooth.

The lightbulb gave one last flicker and went out. Each tug of the rubber band proved useless against the darkness. A painful sob escaped from her.

Limbs shaky, Nora leaned against the wall. Its rough wood morphed into the cool metal of a car door. Unmovable. She squeezed her eyes closed, hot tears rolling down her cheeks. Her breath came in hiccupping gulps. Every muscle in her body tightened.

"No," she whimpered, lowering to the stairs.

The muffled echoes of that night whirled within her.

"Go back, baby!"

"It's not your time, little one. I said go!"

"No! Mommy! Daddy!"

Then it's dark and quiet. Until she's in her bed, a scratchy blanket draped over her. No, it's not her bed. There's a faint beep-beep sound and the smell of antiseptic. An icy tingle pressing against her small shoulder and a cool whisper of air upon her forehead like the shadow of a kiss accompanied the words "We'll always be watching."

"Nora!"

Sandalwood and Bergamot filled her nostrils, coaxing her eyes open. A sting pricked her eyes from the light streaming into the once dark stairway.

"Oh, baby, I've got you," August murmured, folding her trembling body into his embrace. "I've got you."

"Air," she croaked.

Lifting her into his arms, he held her close and carried her down the remaining steps.

"Oh, my word, Ms. Nora." Gideon's concerned voice met them at the second-floor landing. "What happened?"

"I think the door got stuck and she got trapped," August offered.

"No." Her voice shook. "Someone...someone...locked me in."

"What?" Gideon and August said in unison.

"Beth," she gasped.

"No, Mrs. Putman wouldn't—"

"Oh my god!" Lucy exclaimed, appearing in the hallway. "Is Nora...okay?" She pointed at Gideon. "Who is he?"

"She'll be alright. We're leaving Putman House. Tell the crew to pack up." August snarled his command.

"It wasn't Mrs. Putman," Gideon protested.

"Who else has a history of locking people into rooms and playing little pranks?"

Nora tipped her head up. She'd never heard him so angry.

"After everything Nora has done for her..." He let out a seething breath. "We're done. Tell them to stay away from us. We'll leave tonight. This experiment is over."

"Gus...wait," Lucy pleaded.

"Not now, Lucy. Find Dusty and have him get everyone packed up and out of here. We'll regroup at your motel to discuss."

"But—"

"Lucy!" He barked.

Nora placed her hand on his bicep, squeezing. "August."

Pressing a kiss against her forehead, he nodded. "Sorry, Lucy. Please go do your job. Let me take care of my Nora."

"Your Nora?" Lucy's eyes widened, and her lips trembled.

With that, he moved to the last set of stairs. Nora melted into his strength. She closed her eyes as they took step after step until the early evening's cool, fresh air washed over them. The air filled her lungs and eased her rigid muscles.

Soon she found herself, still cradled in August's arms, in

the clearing. The evening's orchestra played around them with the grasshopper's soft song, the nearby brook's murmur, and the breeze's gentle whistle. Her ponytail had come undone, allowing his fingers to comb into the loose tendrils. Her heartbeat and breath steadied.

"We can't leave," she cleared her throat, her voice scratchy. "We have a schedule."

His mouth pulled into a tender smile. "Only you'd be concerned about our filming schedule."

"The schedule aside, we made a promise to Melody."

"She swore they weren't dangerous, but Beth locked you in that stairway. You could have been hurt…really hurt."

But *had* she? In the moment, blurred with the gripping panic, Beth seemed the most likely of suspects. But none of it really fit Beth's MO. Her pranks were always harmless and silly.

What would have driven Beth to lock Nora in? This morning Beth radiated with happiness as she flirted with Bill during group. Beth showed no inclination of anger at anyone, let alone Nora. It didn't make sense.

"I don't know what I would do if anything happened to you." August swallowed thickly.

"I'm okay." She stroked his cheek. "You found me."

The pads of his fingers traced her lips. "I'll always find you."

"August…I—"

"Nora, are you okay?" Beth's panicked voice filled the clearing.

"I told Gideon to tell you to stay away," August growled, his arms tightening around Nora.

"It wasn't me." She stopped in front of them. "I would never do anything to hurt Nora. We're friends."

Nora placed a hand on August's cheek. "I believe her."

His face wrinkled. "But you said—"

"I was wrong. I was scared and not thinking clearly." She rose to her feet.

August quickly followed. His chest pressed against her back, bolstering her shaky legs.

"I'm sorry, Beth. I shouldn't have accused you." She reached out her hand.

Beth took it and the cold tingles zinged across Nora's skin from her ghostly touch.

"Who was it, then? It wasn't the door getting stuck. It was locked when I arrived. I had to break it down," August added.

"You broke *my* door?" Beth's lips pursed.

"To save the woman I love."

"Forgiven." She winked at Nora. "Such a dashing young man you have."

"I know," Nora sighed, leaning into his warmth.

"But he does bring up a good point. Who locked you in?"

"It was me." A quiet voice caused them to turn to the clearing's entrance. Lucy stood, wringing her hands, flanked by two stern-faced male ghosts.

"Proceed Ms. Lucy," Gideon ordered.

"I am so sorry. I didn't know you didn't like small spaces. I just thought…"

"What did you think?" Nora asked, her eyes narrowed.

"She wasn't thinking." Bill crossed his hands over his chest.

"I just wanted to impress Gus." She looked down at her feet and then back up. "When I heard you talking to someone in the attic about taking a new job, I thought this was my chance. I didn't think. I just acted. If you went missing for just a bit, then they'd have Dusty replace you and…"

"And you thought you'd replace him." Nora frowned.

"I know it's unheard of for a production assistant to jump in as an associate producer, but I wasn't thinking. I knew it would only be for tonight but hoped it would lead to a chance for next season."

"So, you locked me in." Her nose wrinkled. "How did you lock the second door? Both doors wouldn't open."

"That's one of the doors that gets stuck," Gideon offered, an apologetic expression etched on his face.

Nora nodded, her gaze narrowed at Lucy. "It was also *you* that hid the mics, wasn't it?"

Like a child caught stealing money from their mom's purse, her eyes turned down and she nodded.

Disappointment and pity filled Nora's chest. This industry was tough, especially for women. There were few opportunities for them, which sometimes bred a competitive cutthroat climate. Some women—but not all—saw each other as competition to take out instead of allies to support one another. If it hadn't been for women like Mae and few others, Nora may have fell victim to the same mindset.

"After you two left, she confessed everything to me," Gideon explained. "I told her she needed to tell you what she'd done. I could see the remorse in her face. Sometimes emotions cloud our judgement, and we make mistakes we regret forever."

"And I regret this," Lucy sniffled.

"You should." August seethed. "You're fired."

Lucy blanched.

The hard edge of his voice jarred Nora. She'd never seen him so angry or curt. He was right, of course. Lucy was so fired. Locking her in her own personal hell aside, she'd messed with the shooting schedule. Her actions jeopardized the entire production. Assistants had been fired for *far* less.

"I understand. I'll go." Lucy turned but then pivoted back. "Nora, I am truly sorry. I know my actions are unforgivable. I never wanted anyone to get hurt."

We all deserve second chances, baby girl.

Grandpa Scott's words never rang so true. This clearing was full of those that had needed or got their second chance. Including herself.

"Lucy, wait," Nora called after her. "I meant what I said earlier, you're too talented and hardworking to not succeed. I have your number. When I get back to L.A., let's meet up. You can either let this define you, or you can move forward. If you want to move forward, I'd like to help you."

A creased dipped Lucy's brow. "I did something horrible, and you want to help me?"

"I can't explain it myself, but yes. If you'll take me up on it."

August squeezed her middle, drawing her attention to him. A small smile lifted the corners of his lips. *You're amazing,* he mouthed.

"Okay," Lucy said. "Thank you, Nora."

"You have a good heart Ms. Nora," Gideon said, as they all watched Lucy disappear down the path.

"Wait, does she know you're all ghosts?"

"Yes. She had a little freak out as you call it when Beth ran through the wall hysterical and looking for you. Bill was in the room when Mr. August received your call and enlisted us to search the property for you."

She looked around at the tiny, weird family she'd formed since coming to Putman House. "Thank you all."

"Thank Gideon. He was the one that figured out it was Lucy." Bill smiled, placing a hand on Gideon's shoulder. "I came upon them. Her confession wasn't as spontaneous as he made it sound. He confronted her and she broke."

"Why did you suspect Lucy?" Nora asked.

"It was Agnes," he said, sorrow sketched across his face.

"What does your niece have to do with it?"

He turned to Beth. "I am so sorry. The night you died, I saw Agnes in the shadows on the third-floor landing. The look in her eyes…" He shook his head. "…at first, I thought it was shock. Then…I knew. She was the one that pushed you."

"Oh my god," Beth gasped, her hands coming up to her mouth.

"What?" Bill gritted through clenched teeth.

"I suspected but wasn't sure until after they arrested Mr. Putman. Agnes was a sweet girl but sometimes got lost in her own daydreams. She believed that if Mrs. Putman was gone, then Mr. Putman would marry her."

"I barely spoke to the girl. Why would she think that?" Bill snapped.

Beth glided across the clearing, taking Bill's hand. "I know." She turned to Gideon. "Go on."

"I confronted her, and she admitted that she'd pushed you. Then she cried and kept saying she didn't want to be hung. She begged me to protect her." His dark eyes seemed to bore into them. "She was my only family. She was like my daughter. I should have said something. But I didn't…and then I died…and still said nothing." He looked at Beth." Then you greeted me in my afterlife. You've been a good friend to me, and I did nothing but lie to you…lie to you both."

"To protect Agnes," Beth offered in a soft voice.

"To protect your child," Bill added.

"I am…words fail to express how deeply I regret not saying anything."

"I don't," Bill said. "My Beth was gone either way. Your silence brought me to her sooner."

"But after…I should have said something…"

Bill took Gideon's hand in a tight clench. "There are far too many things we all should have done or said. I'm tired of thinking about what I should have done. It's time we turn our eyes to the here and now."

Beth laid her palm atop both men's joined hands. "The past is over. Let's let go of it and just hold on to what we have

—each other. We love you, Gideon. And if you need it, we forgive you. But there is nothing to forgive. You did what any parent would do to protect their child."

A dull ache radiated in Nora's chest as she took in the sight of the three ghosts embracing each other. The ache both painful and a little sweet. To think how far they'd all come.

"Thank you," Gideon said, stepping back. A strange glow illuminated his features. His gaze lifted to the sky and then back to them.

"What's happening?" Nora asked, slipping out of August's hold, and moving toward the trio of spirits.

"I think I'm being called home." A smile curved his lips. "I can hear Frederic calling me."

"What does that mean?"

"That was your unfinished business…the reason you were here," August said.

"No." She shook her head. "There's no such thing. If so, why are they still here?" She gestured to Beth and Bill.

"She's right. Why are we still here?" Beth turned to Bill.

His face creased. "I don't know… But I did promise you forever. Maybe this is our unfinished business—to live our forever."

She nodded and leaned in to his side. "Perhaps."

"Old friend, before you go—"

"I'll find Willy and keep him close with me and Frederic until you can join us. I promise."

"Thank you." Gratitude shone in Bill's eyes.

Gideon looked up. "Goodbye."

The light around him grew brighter and spread like bursting sunbeams. Nora squinted and shielded her eyes. The light engulfed the entire clearing and then disappeared in a flash.

Nora scanned the clearing. "Gideon?"

August placed a hand on her shoulder. "He's gone."

"No! No!"

"It was his time…his unfinished business was…" His hands stroked her arms. "…Baby, I'm sorry."

Ghosts were real. They were here because of unfinished business. Then why were her parents not here?

CHAPTER 29

Run

Like the rapid flap of a hummingbird's wings, Nora's heart stuttered in her chest. Out of everything that she'd learned since coming to Putman House, this was the one thing that stole her breath. Watching Gideon disappear in that flash of light was like being drop-kicked in the stomach.

He's gone. She shook her head over and over again willing it to not be true.

"Baby," August said, his hands tightening around her upper arms. "Look at me, please."

"No." She yanked out of his hold. "I need…I need…"

What *did* she need? Everything was upside down. Everything she had thought was wrong.

"Nora." He reached for her, halting her steps.

Hot tears dripped down her cheeks. "I can't…I can't…"

"You can." Concern lined his face. "I know what you're thinking and it's wrong."

"Nora, what is it?" Beth moved closer. Her soft lavender

scent folded around Nora like a hug, trying to soothe away what was wrong.

Nora's mouth remained drawn in a firm line.

August went on, "I know what you're thinking and you're wrong. You *are* a reason. You're *my* reason."

"What reason? What are you talking about?" Bill demanded.

Beth looked to the empty space in the clearing once occupied by Gideon and then back to Nora. "Your parents."

"They…didn't…come…back…" She stammered, dashing away her tears. "I…wasn't enough of a reason."

The voices…*their* voices flooded her. That tunnel with its endless darkness that she'd wandered into in the world between the living and wherever Gideon had ended up. Where her parents ended up. Them telling her to go back.

"They didn't want me…they yelled at me to go back," she whimpered.

"Of course, they told you to go back." Beth stepped closer, placing her phantom hand on Nora's chin, and guiding her gaze to hers. "They wanted you to live."

"But—"

"No buts," Bill interjected. "As parents, all we want is our children to be safe. They wanted you safe, so they sent you back. They did what they thought was best."

"Then why didn't they come back? I needed them! Why wasn't I their unfinished business?"

"Because their business *was* finished. You were alive. That's all they wanted. Their sweet little girl to have a life… to have a future. One where she grew up to be a beautiful and amazing woman." Beth attempted to brush away Nora's messy strands, but her fingers merely passed through.

"Your parents would have wanted nothing more than to see you become who you are, but unfinished business isn't about what *we* want. Sometimes it's about something more.

That more may have been just knowing you were alive. That you were safe." A softness lightened Bill's expression.

"How do you know?" she sniffled.

"Because we're parents," Beth said. "I was willing to give my life for Willy. I know your parents were willing to give theirs for you."

Bill's voice cracked. "We make choices as parents. Whether the wrong or right ones, it's always out of love. I thought Willy was safe and that he needed his mother, so I dove in for Beth. Your parents thought you were safe, so they left you behind…so you could live."

"They knew Grandpa Scott had you. They knew if they couldn't be there, that he was." August's warm eyes bore into her.

Their words filled her, but didn't seem to fill the painful hollowness inside her. They may be right. They may be wrong. She didn't know. What she did know is that her parents were gone. That she'd been left behind.

"You're right." She swiped at the tears. "It's just been a lot today. I think I'm just a little emotional." It was a half-truth to cover her lie.

"Let me take you back to the carriage house. We can lay down."

"What about filming?" she asked.

He smirked. "Oh, my Nora."

Hours later, Nora lay in August's arms, the gentle rhythm of his breath as he slept was her lullaby. He'd given the bewildered crew the night off. There were so many questions. What happened to Nora? Why had Lucy left? Who is the woman in the bathrobe and man in the undershirt sitting in the garden? His response was, "We'll talk in the morning."

The only thing the crew didn't ask about was why her hand was in August's. The only response was a "You owe me a foot rub," uttered by Dusty to his smirking fiancé, and high-fives between Raj and the rest of the crew.

After a long hot shower, they fell fast asleep. Nora must have conked out for a few hours, but it was still dark when she woke. Moonbeams from the open window bathed the room in dim light, allowing her to make out the shape of her mom's watch on the dresser.

Were the Putmans right? Nora wanted to trust her gut, but her skeptical heart wouldn't allow her to rest in the idea that her parents' unfinished business was simply her being alive.

Sneaking out of August's arms, she tiptoed out of bed. For a moment, she took in his sleeping form illuminated in the moonlight. So much of her wanted to crawl back into that bed and wake him up with kisses. To let herself get lost in their lovemaking. To revel in the idea of this sweet man telling her she was his reason. To tell him that she loved him.

She swallowed hard. She'd been running her entire life. From the truth. From the guilt. From the grief. From love. She could keep running away from something or start running *to* something.

With quiet movements, she grabbed some clothes and tossed them in a weekender bag on the chair in the corner as she was dressing. Staring at August, she whispered "I love you" and then snuck out of the room. In the kitchen, she scrawled a note, folded it, and scribbled his name on it. She placed the note on the island beside his cellphone, slung the bag over her shoulder, and left.

CHAPTER 30

Time to Live, Baby Girl

The tire swing dangling from the maple tree hung motionless. It had been two years since she sat in front of this house and ten since she'd stepped inside. She pulled out the keys from her bag and strode to the brick walkway leading to the front porch.

The house had been in the Scott family since great-grandpa Scott bought it in 1946, after returning from the Pacific. It had passed to Nora after Grandpa Scott's death and had remained vacant-ish since then. She rented it out to traveling nurses or Airbnb'd it to folks coming into town to enjoy Missouri's little-known wine country. Some of the folks from Grandpa Scott's church helped out with taking care of the property. As painful as it had been to come back, the idea of selling it sliced across her heart, so she kept it. Currently it was between guests.

She sucked in a deep breath, slipped the key into the lock, and pushed the door open. The soft scent of vanilla from one of the plugins that Nora asked Mrs. Thompson, the housekeeper, to replace monthly filled her nostrils. Grandpa loved the smell of vanilla. He said it always reminded him of her grandma Jean, who always made fresh muffins in the morning.

Shutting the door, she slipped her bag off her shoulder and placed it on the hardwood floor. She wandered through the house as if it were a museum, each room evoking a different memory. Waffles drizzled with fresh berries and hot syrup at the kitchen table. Garland draped down the banister and twinkling lights of the Christmas tree in the front room's window. Blanket forts in the living room for watching old black and white movies.

With a wistful smile, she stood in the living room. That same cushy blue recliner still sat tucked in the corner. She'd paid for some of the furniture to be replaced over the last few years, but not that chair. It had been his chair. He'd sit, legs propped up and a warm smile on his face, laughing as they watched their travel shows together.

"I wondered when you'd come, baby girl." His gruff voice filled the room.

She threw her hands to her heart. A little jolt of fear thrummed in her. Not at his voice, but that if she turned around that he wouldn't really be there.

"I'm here, baby girl. I've always been here."

Tears welled in her eyes as she spun to face him. "Grandpa."

He looked just as he had the day she'd said goodbye. His warm blue eyes, the same as her dad's, sparkled as he took her in. A cheeky smile stretched across his weathered face. His thick silver hair was slicked back, as he always had it. He wore his favorite red flannel pajamas, blue robe, and brown slippers. He'd worn it the day he'd passed, and Nora had asked for him to be buried in it.

"I've missed you so much." The tears ran down her face.

"Baby girl, don't cry." He eliminated the distance between them.

"You can talk. You can walk!" The last few years of his life, the ALS stole his ability to speak and confined him to a wheelchair.

"I know!" He did a little jig, eliciting a watery laugh from her. "I've missed your laugh."

"I've missed everything about you." The tears fell in earnest.

He folded his arms around her. Somehow the icy wisp of air spread warmth across her body. It was impossible. She was in Grandpa Scott's arms again. He'd been here all along.

"I'm so sorry that I didn't come back."

Something cold pressed against the top of her head, which she suspected was his lips.

"I knew you'd be back when you were good and ready. My baby girl never does anything until she's ready."

She tilted her head up. "If I had known."

"None of that. You're here now and, if I know my girl, you're here for a reason. Let's go make a cuppa and talk." He winked.

They sat opposite each other at the small round kitchen table, Great-grandma Scott's gold rimmed tea set between them. Steam rose from the cup of English Breakfast in front of Nora. It was both surreal and comfortable to sit across from again.

"My Hollywood girl. I'm so proud of you. Mrs. Thompson and I watch your show." He beamed.

Her forehead scrunched. "She knows about you?"

"Yes. She has the gift and can sense me even when I go invisible."

"Ah…when you go quiet." She nodded.

"Quiet?"

"I have a ghost friend. She's a murdered Victorian lady, and she calls it going quiet," she explained, picking up her teacup.

"I guess Hollywood really does take all types," he huffed a husky laugh.

"I didn't meet her in Hollywood."

He leaned back in the chair. "Tell me all about it."

And she did. She filled him in, as best she could, about the last ten years. About meeting Mae. About her job. About the Putmans. About the job offer from Travis Olson. About Melody and Derrick. About August. So much about August. Well, not the things that would make grandpa go poltergeist on her young man.

"Sounds like you're in love." He let out a long whistle.

"I am." Her cheeks heated. "I really am."

"Isn't it great?" He smirked. "It's also the scariest goddamn thing ever." He cast his eyes to the sky. "Sorry, Lord, for the curse."

"It is. I haven't told him how I feel yet."

He shook his head. "You're so much like your dad. He was head over heels for your mom, but it took him three years to ask her out on their first date. Did you know *she* proposed to *him*?"

"You never told me that."

"They'd known each other since high school, but your dad didn't ask her out 'til his first year of college. They were both at UMKC. Two years later, she said in her plucky way, 'I think you're in love with me and want to marry me and are terrified to ask, so I'm going to do us the favor and say yes.' Then she started planning the wedding. He was so happy the day they got married. I never saw him as happy as that day until you were born." A wistful smile kicked across his face.

"I've been thinking and talking about them a lot."

"Is that why you're here instead of with your August?" he asked.

She gripped her teacup. "Yeah."

"The last time I saw your parents was in your hospital room."

"What?" Her eyes went wide. "After the accident?"

"I about fell out of the chair. I had fallen asleep by your bed and when I woke, they were there watching over you."

"How were they there?"

"From what Mrs. Thompson explained to me some ghosts are tethered to places and others to people. I was drawn back here because this was where I was happiest. It was where I was with your grandma, your father, and you, baby girl."

A prickle of guilt pulsed in her chest. He'd come back here for her, and she'd not been brave enough to come back. All this time she could have been with him.

"None of that." He wagged his finger. "Don't be getting all guilty on me. I've been happy here. There's been lots of life in and out of this house to keep me entertained. I get to walk out and watch the sunsets in my fields. I get to visit with Mrs. Thompson and watch your travel show." Pride lit his face.

"Travel show? Most people call it a ghost show." She sipped her tea.

"People lack imagination. They travel, so it's a travel show. The ghosts just give it some spice."

God, she loved him. He had a way of smoothing over any of life's wrinkles. It didn't matter if it was something tiny or large, he knew just the right things to say.

"Back to your parents. So, they were there. After my heart fell back down into my chest from where it had jumped up into my throat, they explained they wanted to make sure that you were safe. That you were with me. I told them that I'd always be there for you."

A lump clustered in her throat.

"Your dad hugged me. I'd never been so cold and yet so warm at the same time. Your mama kissed me. Then they said their goodbyes to you. This big flash of light filled the room, and then they were gone. Part of me thought maybe I'd dreamt it, but then when I came back, I knew it was no dream."

"They'd come back for me," she breathed.

"I think they wanted to stay, but when it's your time…it's your time." His hand reached across the table. "They loved you so much and I imagine they're still watching over you."

They came back for her. Beth and Bill were right all along. She *had* been their unfinished business, just not in the way that she thought. Once they knew she was safe and cared for, they were at peace. And she had been loved. He'd been everything to her. Mother. Father. Best Friend. As much as there was always an ache in her chest for them, he'd filled her up with so much love.

She reached her hand across the table. Her hand passed through his, but the tingly sensation strangely mimicked the feel of his once warm paw against hers. "Thank you for always being there for me. Then, and now…and all the times in between."

He'd never left her. The grandpaisms she held on to ensured that. He was with her every step of the way. Somehow the magic in the world that August spoke of had wrapped her up in the loving embrace of those she'd thought she'd lost. They had been there with her all along.

"I love you so much." She moved her fingers through his hands as if squeezing it. "But I don't want to be your unfinished business…your reason for not being with them…being with grandma."

"I'm not sure why I'm here, but I'm happy. I've had a good afterlife, and it just got better."

She smiled. As much as she didn't want to be the reason he was stuck, she was so grateful to be sitting across from him.

"Now, let's talk about this job offer. What are you going to do, baby girl?"

CHAPTER 31

Grandpaisms

Crimson, amethyst, and burnt orange painted the sky in a brilliant sunset. Nora sat in the tire swing, her long legs dangling as Grandpa Scott pushed her.

They'd spent the afternoon discussing Nora's life and the decision she needed to make over tea until grandpa shot from the table announcing, "Nothing a good swing won't cure" and then led her outside. As a kid, she'd spent so much time on this tire swing, either by herself with a book or with grandpa pushing her. Sometimes they'd talk, and sometimes they'd just allow the companionable silence to envelop them.

Tonight was one of those sweetly silent evenings. Nora's bare feet periodically dragged against the cool grass below. Her long hair hung loose.

"Are you expecting someone?" Grandpa asked, tipping his head to the road.

The farmhouse sat on ten acres several miles outside of the town of Lakeside. Blacktop faded into a dirt road that led to grandpa's farm. Any vehicle coming down the road would be someone who was *very* lost or someone coming to the house.

A black SUV eased down the road and turned onto the gravel driveway. Nora slid from the swing.

"August."

"Your August?" he said, one silver eyebrow quirked.

She nodded, watching as he turned off the vehicle.

"Well, at least I don't have to worry about him being scared of your ghost grandpa." His lips puckered. "Although, I do want him *a little* scared of me. I have to put the fear of God in him so he never hurts my baby girl."

"Behave, or I'll rent the house to polka musicians." She *tsked*.

"Devil child," he chided with a chuckle.

August got out of the car and strode across the yard.

"What are you doing here?" Nora asked.

He pulled a folded piece of notebook paper out of his pocket and held it up. It was her note. She didn't need to read. She knew exactly what it said.

August,

I'm not running away from you, but I am running. I'm doing this for me. For us. I'll always be a little bit of a skeptic, so I need to see things with my own eyes, and that's what I'm doing. Know that there's one thing I'm not a skeptic about anymore, and that's how I feel about you. I don't want to write it. You deserve to hear me say it, and I will. I'll be back, I promise.

~Your Nora (Always)

"I know you said you'd be back, but I also said I'd always find you, and something told me to come," he said.

"Plus, you're madly in love with my granddaughter," Grandpa interjected with an almost smug tone.

The dimple on August's left cheek popped with the brightness of his smile. "Plus, I'm *madly* in love with you." He tipped the brim of his Sabres hat to grandpa. "You must be the famous Grandpa Scott."

"You must be the famous August Chandler."

"Pleasure to meet you, sir." August reached out his hand.

Grandpa Scott's hand passed through August's in an almost-handshake. Both men wore large grins.

Two of the most important men in her life were meeting each other. It fizzed happiness within her.

"How did you know I'd be here?" She nibbled on her lower lip.

"You were so quiet last night after everything about your parents. I knew you were spinning a bit. Then I woke up and you were gone. I had a hunch that you came here. I drove to the airport and took a flight to Kansas City. Derrick found the address and sent it to me. So, when I landed, I rented a car, and here I am."

"He's a resourceful one, isn't he?" Grandpa chuckled.

"That he is."

"I'm going inside to give you two time to chat." He pointed at August. "No funny business young man. She may be an adult, but she'll always be my baby girl."

"Yes, sir."

With an icy kiss to her temple, grandpa shuffled into the house.

"Did you find what you were looking for?"

"And then some." She stepped closer to him.

"Yeah?" He smiled. "You want to talk about it?"

"Yes, but not now." She circled her arms around his neck.

"What do you want to do?" His lips were a breath away from hers. "Remember no funny business, Ms. Scott."

"Call me your Nora."

"My Nora." He nuzzled his nose with hers. "My sweet Nora."

"I love you, August…my August."

Her entire body melted into his kiss. She was where she was meant to be. With the man she was meant to be with. More importantly she was choosing to live the life she was always meant to live but had been too scared to do.

"Travis Olson offered me the field producer job," she said as they broke their kiss.

"He would've been a fool to not offer you the job." His hands threaded through her hair. "I'll miss working with you."

"What would taking the job mean for us?"

"Nothing. It changes nothing. I still love you and still plan on being with you. It just means lots of sexy video chats in our future when we're not in the same location, but we'll make it work." His fingers traced down her hairline.

"What if I don't want to make it work?"

His brow dipped. "What does that mean?"

"My dream has always been to produce a travel show, and that's what I've been doing. I've already been living my dream…with you. I don't want to give that up. I want to stay with *Haunted Hideaway*. I want to stay with you."

He cradled her face, locking eyes with hers. "You have me. You always have. You always will." He took her mouth in a deep kiss. "Are you sure? What about producing a *real* travel show?" He used air quotes.

She swatted him. "August Chandler, do not disparage *our* show."

"Noted," he chuckled.

She looped her arms around his nape. "Plus, I have a plan. I'll continue to field produce *Haunted Hideaway,* and in the off season you'll serve as key grip for me and Mae while we film *Girls on the Run* together."

"I do like when you tell me what to do," he cooed with a flirty lilt.

"I'd also like to spend some time with grandpa."

Like the Putmans, she wasn't sure why he was still here. Was it for her? Or something else? Instead of trying to find the reason, she decided to just enjoy the magic and luck that she'd so long denied the existence of. The magic that brought him back to her. The magic that started with an elevator stuck between the twelfth and thirteenth floor with the man that brought her back to life.

"We may have to throw in visits with my parents or else my mother will murder me." He banded his arms around the small of her back.

"We wouldn't want that. I plan on a *very* long life with you."

EPILOGUE

\- After Putman House
One Year Later

"**I**s white appropriate? I mean I've heard the things going on in the carriage house," Beth teased, waggling her blonde eyebrows.

"Says the woman whose cries of passion can be heard by the inn's guests every evening," Nora *tsked*.

It had been an amazing year. They'd just arrived back from shooting in Ireland before the show took a few weeks off for nuptial and honeymoon activities. Nora finally signed on with Mae, making *Girl on the Run* now *Girls on the Run*. The running Nora was doing now was all *toward* things, not away. Between her three episodes producing *Haunted Hideaway* this season, she bounced between filming around the world with Mae, visits with grandpa, and time with August.

Bill and Beth had still not figured out their unfinished business, although they didn't seem to be trying too hard. They were ensconced in their own afterlife honeymoon. Thanks to walking in on them in the clearing, library, parlor, kitchen, and once in the foyer during visits to Putman House, she'd learned ghosts could have sex. Who knew? They were still learning so much about the afterlife. Thanks to having the Putmans and Grandpa Scott as their spirit consultants, they collected an arsenal of information about ghosts, all of which upped their game for *Haunted Hideaway's* upcoming fifth season.

"Aunt Elizabeth, you behave." Melody wagged her finger.

"You listen to the bride," Nora warned.

Melody was the quintessential bride in a mermaid-style wedding dress that hugged her curves, with a starfish headpiece woven into her dark curls. When Nora and August had returned to Putman House after the impromptu trip to the farm, they had found Melody pacing in front of the library. Like something out of an Austen novel, Derrick was inside asking for Bill's blessing to court her. Within six months, he proposed.

They planned a small wedding. Just Melody's parents, the Chandlers, August, Nora, the Putmans, and Mae, who was ordained to be the officiant. It ensured a day of not having to explain to wedding guests why there was a woman in a silk robe and a man that walked through the tables. Gemma and Fred were introduced to Bill and Beth in the fall. After the initial shock, they leaned into it. They even joined Nora and August for Thanksgiving in Missouri with Grandpa Scott.

"Oh, sweetheart," Melody's mom beamed, walking into the room. "You're the picture of perfection."

"My girl." Her dad swiped at his eyes.

Nora's heart swelled at the image of father and mother embracing their daughter. Part of her would always miss her parents at moments like this, but she knew they were there. Even if they couldn't be there in the way she wanted, they were always present. Plus, she liked to believe they'd sent her lots and lots of stand-in parents. Grandpa Scott, Gemma and Fred Chandler, even the Putmans.

"We should head down. We want to stick to Nora's schedule, or she'll get all frowny-face on us," Beth chirped, motioning for everyone to leave.

Nora rolled her eyes but flashed a large grin.

Derrick and Melody exchanged vows under a rose covered arbor in the back garden. Mae's mix of humor and heartfelt officiating had guests both laugh and dab their eyes. Both sets of proud parents sat beside Beth and Bill in white folding chairs along the grassy aisle. August stood up for Derrick and Nora for Melody. As the happy couple recited their vows, her gaze locked with August's, that dimple in his left cheek punctuated his large grin.

After the ceremony and pictures, there was dinner and dancing in the garden. The inn was closed for the family-only event. It was a simple, elegant affair. As the sun set, the fairy light bedecked trees illuminated the garden. With the first note of *Breakaway* by Kelly Clarkson, August took Nora's hand and twirled her. Happiness fizzed inside her as he spun her across the grassy dance floor.

"I can't wait to dance at our wedding," he murmured, pulling her in close.

"Good thing I asked you to marry me in Ireland."

Instead of August's traditional prank on his older brother, Nora enlisted Derrick's help for a little surprise at the Irish countryside manor they investigated. During an EVP session, the brothers went back and forth about something on the digital recorder. August said there was nothing. Derrick insisted there was something. There was nothing.

The fifth time August said, "Dude, it's not saying anything," Nora crossed the room and said, "I know what it's saying." Then she got on one knee and proposed. August gaped and then scooped her up in his arms laughing. When he put her down, he pulled a ring box from his pocket. He'd been planning on proposing as well.

"Good thing I said yes." He beamed.

"Good thing." She rose to her tiptoes, pressing a soft kiss.

As they danced, Nora's gaze roamed around the garden. So much love waltzed around her. Couples kissed. Friends embraced. Parents beamed. Siblings laughed. Love was alive and well and living in a house full of second chances.

The End

**Thank you for reading *Happy Ever Afterlife*. If you'd like to explore more of my books, turn the page for a sneak peek at the first chapter of
At First Smile**

SNEAK PEEK- AT FIRST SMILE

Cane Austen and Me
Pen

"Mommy, what's she doing?" The small chirp of a child's voice draws my attention.

I am not the aforementioned "mommy," but my head tilts toward the tiny human anyway. There's something in the shock and awe in their voice telling me there is a small finger pointing at me.

"It's her stick—"

It's a cane. I don't correct the wrong terminology. Instead, my smile tight and white cane ahead of me, I stroll down the not-yet-fully awake Buffalo-Niagara Airport terminal.

"It helps her see."

Ah, if only it were that magical. It's barely seven a.m. After spending a week with my mother, I lack the temperamental bandwidth to explain to this woman and her child the intricacies of being legally blind. It's a cane. It doesn't help me see, but rather it's a tool to allow me to use nonvisual cues to get from point A to point T. Right now, the point T I'm destined for is the Tim Hortons tucked into the airport's food court.

Aunt Bea always said I was a shining light illuminating the darkness in the world's understanding of what it means to be blind. It's why I've dedicated so much of the last ten years to educate people through my social media page, Cane Austen and Me. To my thirty-thousand followers, I'm the "It" blind girl, documenting my every day and big adventures with Cane Austen, my white cane, helping the non-visually impaired world's knowledge be just a little less obscured about vision loss.

The knowledge that I'm no longer Aunt Bea's little light aches deep in my heart. I can almost feel her soft arms folded around me as she cooed, "Pen, you'll help them understand." No matter how tired I was, she'd have expected me to stop. Explain how the cane works. Tell the child that not all blind people can't see. Set his mommy dearest straight on the blind people facts, helping their little human grow up without misinformation and ensuring that other little humans – ones like me with failing vision – don't repeat the storyline I'd faced as I grew up.

Clear their vision, Aunt Bea's sing-song words dance in my heart.

Sighing, I pivot on my strappy, wedge sandals and head toward the sound of the mother and child. A little boy sits, feet kicking, beside a woman, her long hair gathered into a messy bun, at a half-full gate.

"Hi. I'm Pen." My free hand gathers my long auburn hair, brushing it onto my right shoulder. The action soothes the pulse of anxiety. No matter how many times I do this, it's still awkward as fuck. *Good thing I love you, Aunt Bea.*

The little boy tips his head to his mom, whose forehead puckers in confusion.

Yep, I'm weirding them out. Frankly, I don't blame them.

Most people don't have a lot of interactions with the legally blind. Let alone one who walks up to them and introduces themselves. Thanks to Aunt Bea, that is exactly who I am. Even if there are days – like today – where I wish I wasn't. Where I'd rather fade into the crowd, unseen and forgotten.

"I heard you ask about my cane," I lace just enough sweetness into my words to not send anyone into a sugar-rush. "This is Cane Austen. I'm legally blind, and she helps me stay safe. See how I sweep the cane? It's called constant contact and helps me trail things to guide my path or find things, so I don't trip and fall." With a tight upward curl of my mouth, I demonstrate how I use the cane.

"Are all canes girls?" The little boy's face twists into a pout.

A genuine smile kicks across my face. "Not all, but this one is."

"Why did you name it Cane Austen?" The woman's eyebrows knit.

"So she'll help me find my Mr. Darcy," I quip, making the woman snort with laughter.

It was the same reaction Aunt Bea had. This is my tenth Cane Austen. I've had a new one every year since I was sixteen. While everyone else was getting their first car, I was getting my first cane. The eye condition I have, retinitis pigmentosa, progressed to the point that a cane is necessary to keep me safe. I'd been diagnosed at age six, so I knew my vision was fading to black at a glacial pace…slow but unstoppable. The gradual progression of vision loss didn't lessen the painful realization that, while classmates were getting their licenses and cars, I was facing just another way in which I wasn't like them.

Not allowing me to wallow, Aunt Bea presented me with my first white cane. Blindfolding me – which she found hilarious – she dragged me into the driveway where she gifted me a white cane tied up with a giant red bow. She'd even put a Porsche sticker on it, winking as she affirmed that her niece would travel in style. "You gotta name this bad bitch," she'd crooned, explaining that the cane was my car, and everyone named their vehicles.

The little boy worries his lower lip, as if considering his words. "What does 'legally blind' mean?"

What, indeed? To the world blind means you can't see, but unsuspecting civilians didn't realize that blindness is served on a spectrum. The majority of legally blind people are like me, with some usable vision. There's a whole medical explanation that Trina, my ophthalmologist bestie, would bore people with at parties. I keep it simple, saying I have enough vision to get myself in trouble but not enough to always get myself out of it. Which is why I avoid trouble. As adventurous as Aunt Bea raised me to be, I don't take uncalculated risks.

After finishing my impromptu blindness in-service, I leave the smiling mother/son pair and redirect myself toward Tim Hortons. My flight to LAX doesn't board for another hour, so I have ample time to secure my sought after breakfast sandwich and make it to the gate to lose myself in my steamy romance audiobook. There's something delightful about listening to the swoony and sometimes illicit words of a favorite male narrator, with his hot guy voice, in public places. The idea of exposure makes the risk so much more rewarding. Whoever ends up sitting next to me on my flight home would, no doubt, turn a violent shade of red if they only knew what I was listening to.

Grinning, I stroll toward Tim Hortons. *Bless the airport gods!* I fight the urge to wiggle my hips, spotting only one other person in front of me. The sweet ecstasy of a multi-grain breakfast sandwich and apple cinnamon tea is within my grasp. Besides seeing Trina, Tim Hortons was the only thing bringing me joy on this trip back to Buffalo. After moving to Seal Beach, California with Aunt Bea at seventeen, this Western New York staple was the only thing I missed. That includes my mother, who was already on husband number three at that time, and had *no* problem letting her teenaged daughter move cross country without her.

Whenever Aunt Bea and I went home, the first thing we'd do was hit Tim Hortons. Each Christmas, Mom sent us an assortment of teas, coffee, and hot chocolate from the retailer. Even this last Christmas. Though there's no longer a coffee drinker in the house.

I swallow the growing lump in my throat. Adjusting the large weekender bag on my shoulder, I force my focus to the back of the head in front of me. Only, in order for my gaze to actually land on the back of the man's head requires craning my neck. *How tall is he?* I'm five eight, but he's a giant.

"The card machine isn't working," the peppy cashier says to the tall man.

"Oh." His large hand slips to his pocket.

No doubt the action is to grab the wallet bulging from his back pocket and not to call attention to the way the faded jeans hug his firm backside. One that Trina would joke that she could bounce a quarter off. Although, I could think of far more pleasurable things to do with that ass.

Stop checking out his behind! Pushing my red-frame glasses atop my head, I twist my now extra foggy vision away from the tall man's cute butt. I mean, how would I feel if he was ogling me like I'm the last cupcake?

That might be a nice change. It's been a minute since someone looked at me with the same kind of covetous gaze that I'd used when looking at baked goods after that ill-begotten month I tried to give up carbs. Life's too short to not eat a cookie or ten.

"Shit!" he grumbles, closing his wallet. "Is there an ATM around?"

Second-hand embarrassment on his behalf flushes my cheeks. Few people carry cash on them. My always prepared motto means I'm not one of them. No matter what country I'm in, my wallet remains stocked.

The cashier taps the counter. "I think there's one down by gate twelve."

"Thanks. I'll run down and come back," he says, slipping his wallet into his back pocket.

Poor guy. My lips drag into a frown. Traveling is frustrating enough but to toss in an unnecessary trip across the airport terminal is obnoxious.

"No need, I got this," I offer, pulling my glasses back down. "I have cash."

"No, it's–" His words halt as he spins to face me. Beneath the brim of a blue cap, a smile curves at his lips. Its brightness is accentuated by his tidy dark beard.

A sudden swoop seizes my stomach, causing an explosion of butterflies. *That's new. Am I into men with beards?*

A navy Henley molds to his muscular frame. A fresh woodsy scent wafts from him, eliciting scenes of a pre-dawn walk through a dew-kissed forest. His entire aesthetic screams sexy lumberjack. Like someone who would press you against a tree, its rough bark biting into your bare ass, while even rougher hands held you in place.

Good lord, perhaps I need to cut down on my dirty audiobooks.

"That's kind of you, but I have cash. It's just in the bank." A gentle, barely noticeable Irish lilt mingles with his low gruff timbre.

I love the way unique voices tingle along my nerves. Perhaps my dulled vision heightens the way I hear the world, but I revel in the musicality of voices, picking out the unique notes that make each one distinct.

"Those pesky banks holding our cash hostage." My smile lifts, just a little bit more, with his soft chuckle. "It's really no big deal."

"Are you sure?"

"This will give me at least five karma points for the day." Stepping up, I join him at the counter.

"Are you in need of karma points?"

"Well, I did send my mother to voicemail this morning." *Twice.* But he doesn't need to know that.

This trip I lasted three of the five days I'd planned to stay at my mother's house, a new record, before I sought refuge. On day four, I retreated to Trina's, feigning that she had more reliable Wi-Fi for me to work from than the farmhouse my mother lives in with Charlie, her latest husband.

He grins. "I wouldn't want to get in the way of you reaching Nirvana."

"Thanks." I brush my long hair behind my ear, facing the cashier. "Can I get a large apple cinnamon tea and bacon, egg, and cheese breakfast sandwich on a multigrain bagel."

The cashier shakes their head, a big laugh bursting. "That's two apple cinnamon teas and bacon, egg, and cheese breakfast sandwiches on a multigrain bagel."

Twisted toward the man, my eyebrow arches. "Tea?"

He wags a finger. "That judgy eyebrow may cost you some of your karma points."

I gesture at him. "You just don't seem the *tea* type."

"What type do I seem?"

I frown and cock one hip. "Like 'drinks gasoline while eating a burger made out of the grizzly bear he just killed with his bare hands' type."

"That's preposterous," he scoffs. "Everyone knows moose make better burgers."

"I stand corrected." I laugh, pulling out my wallet.

After paying for our food, we slide down the counter.

Drinks in hand, we stand waiting for our breakfast sandwiches. Other customers file up to the counter, while we remain in silence. Not uncomfortable or awkward silence, just companionable. Sipping my sweet, spicy tea, my eyes flick between the staff preparing our food and the sexy lumberjack beside me.

I play the game we all play when meeting someone: using the little external clues to put together a picture of who he is. His clothes are comfortable and well-worn, but clean. One hand grips the to-go cup, while the other brushes the back of his head as if he's nervous.

Do I make him nervous? *No, that can't be.* Men like him make people nervous, not the other way around.

Gnawing on my lower lip, I try to think of the last man I made nervous. Besides Cael, Trina's fiancé who was terrified that her oldest and closest friend wouldn't give him the stamp of approval, the last man with a wisp of nerves around me may have been Alex. *Ugh, Alex.*

"Pen," I blurt.

His head tips to the right. "Pencil?"

Laughter bubbles out of me. "My name is Pen. Well, it's actually Penelope Meadows, but my friends call me Pen."

He grins. "Rowan."

Of course, his name is Rowan. That name radiates big D hot guy energy. Not a Herman or Stanley vibe about him.

"Nice to meet you, Pen." His hand envelops mine, sending a jolt of something zipping along my nerves.

I try not to fixate on that little tingle but have to admit failure. When was the last time my body reacted to someone like this?

"So, are you coming or going?"

Seriously? Coming or going? Who am I? I school my features into a pleasant smile stamping out the blooming wince at my non-stellar verbal skills.

"Excuse me?"

"Are you coming into town or leaving?"

"Both."

"Overachiever," I tease, pivoting towards him, and my arm brushes against his. My senses hum with the quick caress of his muscular body against mine.

He clears his throat. "I drove down from Hamilton, Ontario to catch my flight."

"So, where you heading to?"

"L.A."

"Me too!" I say with far too much pep.

What is wrong with me? I'm like an overexcited puppy. I should be cool and indifferent, not exclaim with the fevered devotion of two ten-year-olds exchanging friendship bracelets on the first day of camp.

"Well, *not* L.A. I live in Seal Beach, but LAX is a direct flight getting me the hell out of here sooner."

Why am I sputtering? *Awkward, party of one.*

"Not a fan of Buffalo?" He shifts, turning to face me.

"I have nothing against Buffalo as a city. People are nice. Love the wings. It's just…"

Stop talking, Pen! Do not emotionally vomit on this poor man. All he wanted was breakfast, not to have you overshare.

"…just prefer being home." I tighten my hold on Cane Austen's handle.

"Buffalo's not home?"

"Not anymore." I shake my head.

Rowan's hat brim shadows the upper half of his face, making it hard to read his expression. Reading facial expressions isn't my forte. Even with the limited vision I do have, it's often difficult to make out the tiny cues that can be found in someone's face. Aunt Bea always talked about the stories in the eyes. Those are stories I'm unable to read. If I'm close enough and the light is just right, I can make out some of the little eyebrow ticks, lip quirks, or forehead wrinkles.

My stories come from the voice and energy. Everyone has a kind of energy they exude. It may make me sound like the lady with a different crystal for each day of the week, but it's something I've learned to trust.

Right now, the energy coming off Rowan telegraphs annoyance, but I don't think it's directed at me. Despite my oversharing, his broad frame remains mere inches away. His obscured gaze fixed on me.

He nods. "I get it. I've only lived in L.A. for three years and it feels more like home than Hamilton where I grew up."

"Canadian boy, eh?"

He snorts at the terrible joke laced in my even worse Canadian accent.

Smirking, I raise my tea to my lips. "So, how did a nice Canadian lad end up in L.A.?"

His hand rubs his neck. "Work."

"What do you do for wo—"

"Christ," he groans, yanking out his cell from his back pocket. "Sorry, this is the fourth call in a row that I've ignored. I need to take this."

"Sure." I smile.

Holding the phone up, he grumbles, "This best be important." Pivoting, he strides away from the counter.

"Ma'am." The cashier holds up two bags with what I suspect are our breakfast sandwiches.

With a nodded "thank you," I take them. In literally five seconds, I've lost Rowan. Scanning the now bustling food court, he's disappeared into the crowd. Do I wait? Do I try to track him down? Do I just take his sandwich in hopes that I run into him again? What if he comes back and thinks I stole his sandwich? Although, I paid for it, so it's not stealing.

"Excuse me, do you see that man I was with?" I ask the cashier.

"He went over there." She points.

"Where? Can you verbally explain?" I hold up Cane Austen in a nonverbal reminder that pointing is not the best way to give direction to the visually impaired.

"Oh, sorry." The blush can be heard in her voice. "Far right corner… My right, not yours."

"Thanks."

Turning, I set off listening for his voice. Moving through the crowd, I make my way toward the far-right corner. Voice recognition is the best way for me to find people in large gatherings. Although, it's not ideal with someone I just met, there's something about Rowan's voice that has imprinted on me, both distinct yet familiar. Like nothing I've heard before but somehow something as well-known to me as my own.

"Damnit, I told you I don't want to do that," Rowan growls.

I halt. Not because I've found him, but due to the frustration underscoring his words. He's pissed.

"This is fucking bullshit."

Really pissed.

With his back to me, he carries on in an annoyed mutter with no idea I'm standing behind him, eavesdropping. It's not intentional, but I'm listening, nonetheless. Granted, my relationship with Rowan is five minutes old, but this anger reads wrong on him. Like an ill-fitting Halloween costume. Also, I'm not going to overthink my use of the word relationship.

Raking my teeth against my lower lip, I clutch the sandwich bag. I should turn, run away, and give the sandwich back to the cashier. Let them give it to the angry man. Not because I'm scared. There's no nip of fear telling me to stay away. Rather, it's more like witnessing someone do something they don't want to do.

"You're being a real motherfucker," he snarls, causing a few onlookers to clear their throats.

Ouch. I don't blame them. His tone is harsh.

Dropping his duffle by his feet, Rowan's rigid stance slumps. His free hand grips the back of his neck. The movement communicates regret.

"I'm sorry. That was uncalled for." Scuffing his sneakers along the floor, he lets out a beleaguered sigh. "I know. You're *my* motherfucker."

Aw. It's almost sweet the way it rolls off his tongue.

"We can discuss this when I get back. My flight gets in..." Pivoting, he comes face-to-face with me, mouth slack. "Pen." It comes out almost pained.

Crap! "I wasn't listening... Well, I was, but not intentionally. I—" I hoist up the Tim Hortons bag. "Breakfast!"

"Thanks," he says, drawing out the word and taking the offered bag.

"Sorry."

The muffled voice of whoever is on the other end of the call crackles between us.

"I should go." Frowning, I turn and hurry away.

So fricking embarrassing. Rowan is clearly having a day and I'm all like "Here I am holding your breakfast sandwich hostage while eavesdropping on your conversation with someone you fondly refer to as motherfucker."

Finding my gate, I fold myself into an uncomfortable plastic chair to devour my breakfast sandwich and fall into my latest audiobook. The sultry timbre of Wesley Williamson – my favorite narrator – helps me escape into the world of thousand-year-old hot vampires with Mr. Darcy vibes. The story being woven in my earbuds helps me leave the last week behind. Leave why I came back to Buffalo, the tension with my mother, and the awkward meetcute with Rowan.

Rowan. My stomach flip-flops between a sigh and a flutter at the thought of him. I hope everything turns out okay with he and motherfucker. It seemed to have turned the corner before he'd caught me listening in. I scan the boarding area, wondering if he's here. He's not. At least, I don't see him which doesn't mean he's not here. He's bound for L.A. Are we on the same flight? The Buffalo-Niagara Airport is small, but not *that* small. There are several airlines flying direct to Los Angeles in this time window.

"Penelope Meadows, please see the agent at gate eleven's counter." A voice booms over the sound system, interrupting the vampire/awkward girl meet-cute.

Hitting pause, I sling my bag over my shoulder and shuffle with Cane Austen to the counter. "I'm Penelope," I say, reaching the agent.

"Ms. Meadows." The agent beams. "Your seat has been upgraded. I have a new boarding pass for you."

"Upgraded?" I blink.

"You're still in a window seat, but you've been moved to first class. Seat one-A. We'll start pre-boarding in a few minutes for our passengers with disabilities. Would you like assistance going down the jetway?"

First class from Buffalo to Los Angeles? Perhaps I had earned some karma points after all. Thanking the agent and telling them I wouldn't need assistance, I head back to my seat.

Pulling my phone from my pocket, I check my messages. Despite the frown, guilt swirls in my stomach at the four unread messages from my mother. Sighing, I open them and respond.

Me: I'm at my gate.

Mom: Good! Did you click on the links I sent you to those clinical trials?

Eyes closed, I release a hard breath. If it isn't messages about my love life, it's ones about studies to cure my eye condition. *She means well,* Aunt Bea's cautious warning plays on repeat inside me. Opening my eyes, I reply.

Me: I'll look at them when I get home, so I can see them on the larger screen. I'll message when I'm home.

It's a lie, but my energy for this familiar conversation is nonexistent.

I swipe to my message with JoJo, my West Coast bestie. Trina is insistent that I'm allowed two best friends if I designate them by coasts. Trina Lyons, who is two years older than me, was my first bestie due to close proximity. She lived next door until I moved with Aunt Bea to California. I met JoJo Rivers a year later as freshmen in undergrad.

Me: Flight is on time. You still picking me up at the airport?

JoJo: Does a hobby horse have a hickory dick?

Me: A simple yes would do.

JoJo: Then I wouldn't be me. Tongue out emoji.

I snort just a bit. Even with the magnification program on my cell, I have the worst time with GIFs and emojis, so JoJo spells them out for me. It's both sweet and totally self-serving because I'm a hundred percent positive that a majority of the GIFs and emojis that she spells out do not exist.

JoJo: How are you doing, BTW?

God, that's a loaded question. My heart aches just thinking about the many, many responses rattling around in me. How does one respond when their entire world as they know it has been ripped away in a single moment?

Me: Okay.

JoJo: Acceptance smiley face when your friend is pretending they are okay when they're not emoji.

Me: Middle finger emoji.

JoJo: Gasp emoji.

Me: These aren't real emojis emoji.

JoJo: I love you emoji.

Me: I love you too emoji. We'll have all the LAX to Orange County traffic to dig into how I'm doing. I promise.

JoJo: Excited social worker friend emoji.

Hearing them announce pre-boarding, I text goodbye to JoJo and slip my phone into the pocket of my denim jacket. The late June weather is warm, allowing me to sport my favorite pale pink cotton sundress, but the jacket will keep me warm on the plane.

I won't pretend that excitement doesn't crisscross inside me at turning left while boarding the plane. The first-class lifestyle isn't something I've indulged in. Outside of that all-inclusive resort Aunt Bea took me to in celebration of my master's degree. As first-class as I typically get is getting to skip the wait at Bread, my favorite breakfast spot in down-town Seal Beach, because Aunt Bea and I've gone there every Saturday for the last nine years. *Almost every Saturday.*

Ignoring the twinge in my heart, I follow the flight atten-dant to my seat in the front row, which means more leg room. It also means all my things have to go up top. Pulling out the things I'll want quick access to – bottled water, bag of trail mix, phone, and earbuds – I toss my bag into the over-head bin and plop into my seat.

Head pressed against the window, I lose myself in my audiobook which drowns out the flight's boarding sound-track – murmured apologies, cleared throats, and muttered, "I think that's my seat," and the repeated chastising of a passenger for blocking the aisle.

Someone takes the seat beside me. The furnace of their body laps against my skin. A fresh woodsy scent makes my eyelids flutter open. Straightening, I turn my face toward my seatmate.

"Pen," Rowan drawls.

ALSO BY MELISSA WHITNEY

Available wherever you get e-book, paperback, and audiobooks

All books are available in e-book, paperback, and audio. You can get books at Amazon.com: Melissa Whitney: books, biography, latest update or by requesting at your local library or indie bookstore. Signed copies can be purchased through Heartbound Book Shop: Where Every Page is a Love Story.

The Home Series

Finding Home - Book One

Coming Home - Book Two

Making Home - Book Three (Coming Soon)

The At First Series

At First Smile

Stand Alone Titles

In the Hello and in the Goodbye

Happy Ever Afterlife,

ACKNOWLEDGMENTS

It truly takes a village to write any book. This truth is burned deep in me with every book I pen (technically type, but pen sounds fancier). None of my books would make it to you the reader without the loving support of so many people.

Happy Ever Afterlife is here because of Dustin Thompson, who gave me the push I needed to write this story. Sadly, I lost him in the middle of writing this story. I will always be grateful for his belief in me.

Thank you to Meghan Fischer, the alpha reader, PA, and BESTEST friend any author/girl could have. I'm so glad I am finally able to share this story with the world. I know you've been waiting for everyone to meet Nora and August.

Thank you to my editor for this book, Brenda from Notes to Myself Editing Services. https://www.notestomyselfediting.com/

A huge thank you to my literary mama bear Gemma Brocato. Your guidance and support helps me soar.

Thank you to Su from Earthly Charms for this gorgeous cover!

Thank you to the amazing Estelle Grant, who provided consultation and guidance for my characterization of Mae. Check out Estelle's beautiful love stories on KU and paperback!

Thank you to Michael (aka Philadelphia) for providing consultation and guidance on the world of TV production.

Above all thank you to my husband Liam for snuggling every night with me as we fall asleep to paranormal investigation shows like Kindred Spirits, Ghost Adventures, and Destination Fear.

Lastly, and most sincerely, thank you to you, the reader. You have so many options for reading and I am deeply honored that you read my book. Thank you!

ABOUT THE AUTHOR

Melissa Whitney, who hails from Western New York, is a contemporary romance author. As a legally blind woman much of Melissa's work focuses on the exploration of disability, mental health, and trauma through a heartfelt, sexy, and comedic lens.

Melissa's debut novel *In the Hello and in the Goodbye* released in April 2024, with a warm reception from readers for its thoughtful autism and mental health portrayal. Since then, she's released *Finding Home*, a Jane Austen inspired small town romance, *At First Smile*, an own voice hockey romance with blindness rep, and *Coming Home*, a *Little Women* inspired small town romance. Her work has been featured in several publications and on podcasts for its thoughtful, sensitive, and accurate representation of disability and mental health.

Ms. Whitney lives in Southern California with her husband and their rescue pug Milo. When not crafting her swoony stories, she's on the hunt for a pastry, brewing a cup of tea, and diving into her latest swoony romance.

To learn more about Melissa Whitney, you can visit www.melissawhitneywrites.com. Sign up for her newsletter to stay in the know with all things Melissa Whitney. Connect with her on social media (IG: @melissa_whitneyatuhor, Threads @melissa_whitneyauthor or Facebook: Melissa Whitney Author).